"Two Sentinels o_ ____ ____ out fro_

somewhere above him. "Camouflaged units!"

Fantomex spun and dropped into a crouch, already firing, simultaneously issuing a silent call to E.V.A.'s weapons systems. Energy blasts, three-second bursts, waiting for visual confirmation – there.

They had been standing against the tallest limestone formation about a hundred yards away, their outer shells perfectly camouflaged to look like the stone.

Except for the two faintly glowing points of their soulless eyes.

Sentinels, the giant mutant-hunting robots that had been part of the foundation of his own creation.

"Target locked," E.V.A. informed him, a hint of excitement inflecting her voice.

"Fire," Fantomex growled.

ALSO AVAILABLE

MARVEL XAVIER'S INSTITUTE

# TRIPTYCH

JALEIGH JOHNSON

ACONYTE

FOR MARVEL PUBLISHING

VP Production & Special Projects: Jeff Youngquist
Associate Editor, Special Projects: Caitlin O'Connell
Manager, Licensed Publishing: Jeremy West
VP, Licensed Publishing: Sven Larsen
SVP Print, Sales & Marketing: David Gabriel
Editor in Chief: C B Cebulski

Special Thanks to Jordan D. White

First published by Aconyte Books in 2021

ISBN 978 1 83908 084 5

Ebook ISBN 978 1 83908 085 2

Cover art by Anastasia Bulgakova

Distributed in North America by Simon & Schuster Inc, New York, USA
Printed in the United States of America
9 8 7 6 5 4 3 2 1

**ACONYTE BOOKS**

*An imprint of Asmodee Entertainment Ltd*

Mercury House, Shipstones Business Centre

North Gate, Nottingham NG7 7FN, UK

*aconytebooks.com // twitter.com/aconytebooks*

*For Tim, who has never left my side.*
*You are the best kind of super hero.*

# CHAPTER ONE

It started with his death, so it was not an auspicious beginning.

But if this was the great beyond or some other version of an afterlife, it was remarkably boring. He floated in a warm, empty void, colorless and without sound. There was nothing to entertain him, nothing to do but think. He tried to reach for memories of the life he'd led before his death, but the effort left him strangely exhausted. Why should a dead man be weary, if his troubles were over? It didn't seem fair.

This brought him slowly to the realization that perhaps he was not dead after all but only being… remade.

He'd had the ability to heal himself once. At least, he'd thought that was him, but maybe he was remembering a different life or someone else's powers. The memories were like tiny fractals of light drifting before him. Some of them he couldn't quite grasp, and then they disappeared. Lost.

Almost more disconcerting than losing his life, he'd also lost his *name* somewhere along the way. To be fair, he knew he'd collected several names over the course of his strange existence, so he would probably recollect one of them sooner or later. Even floating in this formless void. He was bound to find himself out here somewhere.

Most of his names had been given to him by others. Wasn't that always the way? People lining up to tell you who they think you are. It made them feel more secure when they could fit a name and a role to everyone. Put them in the right box, make them *understood*, and they ceased being a threat. The problem was that people were so very often wrong. Not only that, but they also tended to be unbearably certain and smug in their wrongness.

Certain and smug. Those words described him too, possibly. But they weren't names.

The void around him shifted, turning red, an invasive shade that didn't match his serene mood. Was someone knocking at his door? No matter. He wasn't going to answer.

A presence settled around him like a heavy cloak. Oh yes, there was definitely someone nearby. He was sure of it now. How long had they been there? Time was inconsequential in the void. It could have been a minute or a decade.

Whoever the person was, they were trying to align their energy with his. He felt a second heartbeat thumping steadily alongside his own. It was a bit creepy, if he was being honest. The question was, did they intend to aid him or attack? In his experience, it was almost always the latter. Well then, what if he just flicked their power back at them?

*"I'm losing him!"*

"*Triage, what's happening?*"

"*He shredded the connection, pushed me out! He's never done that before. I don't know if I can–*"

Rude to be interrupted in the middle of a personal revelation. Now, where was he?

Ah, yes, death and names.

Jean-Phillipe Charles.

Now they were getting somewhere. That was a name that had once belonged to him. Charlie-Cluster 7 was another. Had he always been so fond of hyphens? He shuddered to think what pretentious horrors lay beyond the hyphen phase.

Weapon XIII.

Ah, Roman numerals. Of course. Well, they did carry a certain gravitas, he supposed, and that particular designation had meaning for many more individuals than just himself. It opened the floodgates to yet more memories, this time of the group – the deity, if you will – that had created him. The Weapon Plus program had fashioned him into the perfect being to hunt down mutants. He was something new, a mutant-Sentinel hybrid that was nearly unkillable.

Emphasis on the nearly.

The program had created others too, but this was a story about *him*, and so he latched onto the last name that floated into his mind.

"*Fantomex.*"

Yes, precisely.

"*Fantomex!*"

The call was rather insistent. Perhaps it was the universe addressing him. If so, he'd better attempt to answer.

Fantomex. Present. Alive. Resurrection man, at your service. What else have you got for me, universe?

He almost hated to leave that comfortable, introspective void, but the walls were already wobbling and shredding around him, and he was being carried back into the light. It seemed death was done with him.

At least for now.

"What happened?"

"I'm not entirely sure, but he seems to be coming out of his healing trance."

"You mean coma? Catatonic state? Is there even a word for what that was?"

"We thought you'd want to be informed."

The voices blended together as everyone tried to talk at once, but Fantomex finally sorted out that there were three people somewhere nearby, though he only recognized two of their voices. He dragged his eyes open to see where he was, but there wasn't much to entice him to keep them that way. The medical facility was a smallish room with cinder block walls painted in a wretched shade of gunmetal. Machines beeped incessantly, and the air reeked of mildew and hospital – two smells that should never go together.

The individuals discussing him were at first only discernible as blurs of color and motion, but his vision gradually brought them into focus, grouped near the door.

The door. One exit from this room. No windows. He made a note of the layout out of habit, even though he suspected he wouldn't be going anywhere today. Or tomorrow. His body felt heavy and strange, his skin crawling as if he'd been pricked with a thousand needles. And his insides were hollow, like he'd been scraped out with a shovel. How long had he been floating in that void?

He forced himself to concentrate on the people in the room. They would obviously have some answers, but right now they were speaking about him as if he wasn't present. How irritating.

"He will need to be informed at once about his change in circumstances," said the lone woman among the three. When Fantomex saw her face, the turmoil and strangeness inside him eased just a little.

He knew her. He would know her in whatever form she took, and her face was the most welcome sight he'd seen since… well, since he'd died.

She was tall, dressed comfortably in a pair of checked slacks and an olive cashmere turtleneck. Her skin was pale and white, her eyes pupil-less, shining a warm amber color. Her short red hair was trimmed into a bob around her impassive face, but despite the lack of an emotional display, he could feel she was agitated.

She was a part of him, after all.

E.V.A.

Like him, she was something entirely new.

She'd been created to function as his secondary central nervous system, but that was a crude oversimplification. E.V.A. had become much more than that during their time together, evolving from an artificial intelligence to a complex, techno-organic being, sentient and independent, who could take on multiple forms, one of them being the humanoid appearance she displayed now as she spoke to the two men.

Reluctantly, he turned his attention to them. The younger one he didn't recognize, but he already liked the man's sense of style. Warm brown skin, a spill of locs framing a tailored suit with matching tie – he and E.V.A. were the only bright spots in the room – topped off by a pair of copper goggles that proclaimed, *Yes, I'm from the X-Men, but I refuse to be pigeon-holed into spandex nightmare costumes. I have* taste.

Wait, how did he know he was among the X-Men? Ah, yes, the second man – Cyclops. The stoic Scott Summers, with the jaw so chiseled it made sculptors weep. He'd changed since Fantomex had seen him last, acquiring considerable gray in his hair and impressive scars on his body. There was nothing terribly exciting about his jeans and T-shirt, but that hardly mattered. The ruby quartz lenses he wore over his eyes would always be his defining feature. Unlike the young man's copper goggles, these were a permanent fixture that were less about saying, *Look at my unique style*, and more about keeping him from accidentally melting someone's face off.

So, he was among the X-Men again. That kept happening. But where was he now? This didn't seem like one of their usual haunts. To put it kindly, this was much more rustic and... something about the place tugged at his memory. It felt... familiar.

"He's awake. He's listening to us now."

E.V.A.'s voice stirred him from his thoughts. She and the others quickly crossed the room to his bedside, but it was Cyclops who addressed him first.

"Do you know who you are?" he asked. "Can you tell me your name?"

Well, at least all that introspection time hadn't been wasted. He licked his dry lips and said in a croaking voice, "They call me the Wolverine."

A muscle in Cyclops' granite jaw ticked. E.V.A. gave a quiet sigh that carried equal parts relief and exasperation. "I think he'll live," she said.

"He should be dead after what he went through–"

"Christopher," Cyclops said, cutting the other man off, "let's take this slow."

"Too slow and I'll grow bored," Fantomex said amiably. "My apologies for the humor. Let's start over with the name: Fantomex." He eased himself into a sitting position. The heaviness and needle-pain sensation were starting to fade, thankfully, and he was pleased to discover that there was minimal disorientation and muscle atrophy. He felt like he'd been in a healing state for quite some time, which was disconcerting, but his body was still quick to recover, even after death.

Only the hollowed-out feeling persisted.

He determined to ignore it. No doubt it too would pass with time.

"Do you know where you are?" Cyclops crossed his arms, glancing around the spartan accommodations.

"Judging by the décor, I'm tempted to call it a postmodern fallout shelter, but we'll go with the next most appealing option: is it one of your schools?" he guessed. "Not sure which one. The names change so often, it's hard to keep them straight."

"It's the New Charles Xavier School." Cyclops seemed pleased, though it was difficult to tell behind the glasses.

"Well, it's certainly a fixer-upper," Fantomex said, "and abominably cold."

"It suits our needs," Cyclops said defensively. "What we lack in comfort, we more than make up for in security and secrecy."

Security and secrecy. And cold. So cold. Fantomex felt a prickle at the back of his neck. He gazed at the room with new eyes, and an unpleasant awareness washed over him. He knew why the place felt familiar. He'd been here before. The facility they so cheerfully called a school had once been a testing ground for the Weapon Plus program. He should have known he would never fail to recognize a place imprinted with such… memorable experiences. Did the students here realize how many ghosts of traumas past walked these halls? For their sake, he hoped not.

Dismissing Cyclops for the moment, he turned to E.V.A., his voice softening as an unexpected swell of emotion overtook him. "You're a sight for sore eyes, old friend."

She inclined her head. "I'm pleased to see you're still functioning." Her voice held an affection born of their longtime bond. Some things even death couldn't sever.

"My memories have been shaken, stirred, and shattered," he said, with a rueful smile. "What happened to me? How long have I been recovering?"

"Three months," she said, stepping closer and settling herself in an uncomfortable-looking metal chair near the bed. She was so serious. Fantomex experienced a trickle of unease he wasn't used to feeling. "Before that, I was forced to resort to drastic measures to ensure your resurrection."

"Drastic, eh? You make it sound like I was a lost cause."

He tried for a light tone, but he was reassessing himself as he spoke, exploring the parts of his body that had been most damaged... his heart, obviously, but there were other things wrong as well, things he hadn't noticed at first, being so glad that he was alive. His thoughts were different somehow. They felt sluggish and tight, and his powers when he reached for them were slow to answer.

And some didn't respond at all.

Cyclops and the other man – Christopher, Scott had called him – exchanged glances, and Fantomex definitely didn't like what he saw reflected in the young man's eyes.

Pity.

"What happened to me?" he repeated, his tone sharpening.

Cyclops started to answer, but E.V.A. held up a hand. "This is my responsibility."

Gazing down at him, she bit her lip, a very human gesture. It shouldn't have rattled him, that expression of uncertainty, but it did. "You were dead," she said, not mincing words. "I'm unclear how much you remember from what came before, but the Brotherhood had you cornered – you and Psylocke. You sacrificed yourself to save her."

Oh yes, he remembered it. Her words were like a key turning in a lock. He was suddenly back there, caught in the moment when the Brotherhood of Evil Mutants had taken him, when the one called the Skinless Man cut his heart from his chest. How amusing that he'd probably made that same threat to dozens of his enemies over the course of his life: I'll rip your still-beating heart from your chest. But he'd always thought of it as more of a metaphor than a legitimate outcome. Very Shakespearean.

He'd never expected it to actually happen to him.

At least it had been for a noble cause. "Psylocke is safe, then?"

"Yes."

Good. He remembered he'd cared about her, though the feelings were less immediate than they had once been. There'd been others with him too, members of the now defunct X-Force team: Wolverine, Deadpool. The names were coming back, but they carried the same distance that Psylocke's did. Maybe because they were part of a life that was over. He pushed them aside to focus on the now. He needed to know the rest of the story.

"We were able to recover your remains and return to the White Sky Facility," E.V.A. continued, "where an appropriate cloned body could be grown and integrated with your three brains, which were still functioning at limited capacity."

At this, Christopher twitched. "Hang on, did you say *three* brains?"

"It's complicated," Cyclops said. He nodded to E.V.A. "Go on."

"I should have realized the facility was not properly equipped to handle a Sentinel-mutant cyborg," E.V.A. said. "Again, I accept full responsibility."

"For. What?" Fantomex said, grinding his teeth as he sat up straighter on the hard bed.

"The facility made a mistake," E.V.A. said softly. "The A.I. interpreted the presence of three brains to mean that three separate clones would be needed. So three clones were grown, and a brain was placed in each one."

After that, it grew so quiet in the room Fantomex could

hear distant voices coming from down the hall, the sounds of students laughing and talking as they moved between classes. Because, of course, this *was* a school. Students came here to learn, things like how to be a team player probably, how to use their powers to fight holograms in the Danger Room. Maybe basic arithmetic too: one plus one plus one makes three.

"Fantomex." Cyclops was speaking, but Fantomex wasn't registering any of the words.

Empty. Scraped out. That's why everything seemed so slow, why he was reaching for things that weren't there. It wasn't just a facet of his recovery or his lost memories. Some vital parts of himself were simply... gone.

More than his heart had been cut from his body. He'd been completely torn to pieces.

Christopher was speaking.

"How is that possible? Three brains in one body? Look, I'm a healer and I'll admit I thought I could do some pretty cool stuff, but how does he even work?"

"Fantomex was created by the Weapon Plus program using a combination of mutant DNA and Sentinel nanotechnology," E.V.A. explained. "He was raised in the World, a research facility designed as an experimental micro reality, a place meant to mimic parts of this Earth, but where time is fluid and controllable. He was intended to be the perfect mutant-killing cyborg, an unstoppable force."

"Wait, you brought a mutant-killing cyborg into a *sanctuary* for mutants?" Christopher said, his voice a bit strangled.

Well, put like that, it was a bit much to take in. Fantomex

wondered if Christopher realized his mouth was hanging open like a fish.

"Don't worry," he said. "I'm not allied with the Weapon Plus program or its goals, though I do appreciate the unique gifts they have given me."

"I guess that's one way of putting it." Christopher fiddled with the goggles atop his head. "It sounds like the weirdest science project of all time."

So, he was to be cast as Frankenstein's monster now? A hot curl of anger spread through Fantomex, but with an effort he held onto his temper. "France," he said curtly, drawing all their attention back to him. "The 'science project' I was raised in was an artificial reality that was made to look like France. It was imperfect but quite a nice environment, aside from the whole, 'programmed to be a cold-blooded killer' aspect."

Christopher's brow furrowed. "Huh. You know, I thought I detected a bit of an accent."

"Just a bit?" Fantomex rubbed his hands over his face to keep from punching something. Or someone. "Ah, well. One third of a brain. One third of an accent. Easy come, easy go, I suppose."

"That's inaccurate," E.V.A. said, as if sensing his budding fury. "You are a fully functioning, independent being. It's true we don't yet know to what extent your abilities and personality may have been affected by this change, but–"

"For now, at least, we'll say I'm two cards shy of a full deck." He leveled a cold stare at Christopher. "It's time for you to leave, young man. Nothing personal. Nice suit, by the way."

"Triage is still exploring his healing capabilities," Cyclops put in. "He was instrumental in helping guide your healing processes over these last few months."

"Speaking of which," Fantomex said, aiming a finger at the ruby-eyed man, "how did I end up here in the frozen wilds, and where are my other halves, so to speak? Are they down the hall? Is Logan comforting one or both of them?"

"Neither of them accompanied us to the Institute," E.V.A. said. "They left us immediately after the cloning process was complete, and before I could evaluate their conditions. When I initially examined you, it seemed you were fine and ready to travel. But after we left the facility, something happened. You fell into what could only be described as a catatonic state and couldn't be revived. Possibly it was part of your natural healing ability and the recovery process, but you resisted all my attempts to communicate with you, and your vital signs became dangerously unstable. I conferred with Logan, who agreed the situation was dire and put me in contact with Kitty Pryde. After discussing it with the other instructors, she revealed the Institute's location and allowed me to bring you here to seek help. Upon arrival, I'd hoped that Emma Frost might be able to reach your mind, give us some indication as to how badly you were hurt."

"But as it turned out, Christopher was the one who was able to give us the most information on your condition," Cyclops said. "Why do you want him to go?"

"Privacy," Fantomex said. "A man can't be expected to talk about his lost brains with strangers."

He didn't know this healer, and the fewer people who were aware of the extent of his vulnerabilities right now, the better. He wasn't going to give anyone the chance to exploit his weaknesses.

He nodded to the door. "Go," he said, his tone leaving no room for argument.

Cyclops sighed and gestured to Christopher. "Thank you for all your help," he said. "It's entirely possible you saved his life." This with a pointed look that Fantomex ignored. "We'll call you if we need you."

"Sure thing. Good luck, I guess." Christopher was still looking at him with an infuriating mix of confusion and pity as he left the room.

"Now, since my memories are hazy on this topic, tell me about my new… companions," Fantomex said when he'd gone. No, that didn't feel right. What did one call these extensions of himself? Copies? Enemies? Rivals?

*Imposters.* That was more like it. For they could be nothing more than pale imitations, after all. They had to be.

E.V.A. glanced at Cyclops, and by her hesitation Fantomex had the impression this was something she hadn't shared with him yet. "I have no intelligence on their activities since leaving the White Sky facility and separating from us," she said, "but I can give you names and brief descriptions of their current identities. The first, and the one most closely matching your physical description, identifies as male and wears a costume similar to yours but inverting the color scheme, meaning he wears predominantly black with white accents. He goes by the alias Weapon XIII."

"Embracing the dark side, is he?" Fantomex drawled. "Fine, so I have a goth brother. What about the other one?"

"The other identifies as female and goes by the alias of

Cluster," E.V.A. said. "Her costume closely matches your own white outfit with black accents."

Fantomex waited, but she didn't elaborate on those scant details. "That's it?" He'd hoped there'd be more. Not that he particularly cared what they were like, but he needed some idea of their capabilities. He needed to know what powers they possessed that he no longer did.

She spread her hands. "As I said, my information is limited. I can only speculate as to why your counterparts chose to separate from us. It was likely a combination of shock and disorientation at their altered state that motivated them. I had hoped there might be resources here we could utilize to find out more information about the two of them and their recent activities. It could be important to know where they are and what they've been up to."

"Agreed," Cyclops said. "We don't know their current conditions or intentions, and there are too few mutants remaining in the world to leave them unmonitored, especially after what's happened to all three of you."

"Ah, so now we come to it." Fantomex leaned back on the bed, clasping his hands behind his head. "I'm glad to see that your altruism has its limits. So, I'm to be kept here and *monitored* to make sure I behave in my new incarnation? To make sure I'm not unstable?"

His mouth curved in a lazy smile, but he was studying Cyclops intently, once again cursing the man's exceptional poker face.

What did Cyclops actually want from him? He'd forged uneasy alliances with the XMen and its subsidiary teams in the past, when the arrangement was of mutual benefit, but he was hardly in a condition to offer them anything at the moment. And they'd taken some pains to preserve his life over the last few months. Was it really because there were so few mutants remaining that they needed him?

A scraped-out shell was better than nothing, perhaps.

Cyclops shook his head. "I won't waste time trying to convince you that we want to help," he said. "For now, all I can offer is my assurances that you aren't a prisoner here. You can leave whenever you want, but I encourage you to stay at least long enough to ensure you're fully recovered."

"So you're not afraid I might betray the location of your school to certain interested parties for my own benefit?" Fantomex said it lightly, knowing it was a risk to put the suggestion out there, but he wanted to see if he could get that granite façade to crack so that Scott might reveal more.

But Cyclops stayed steady as ever. "No more than you should fear that we'll tell those same interested parties about your current condition," he said. "We both have our vulnerabilities, but we also have strengths we can benefit from. Of course, it goes without saying that if you attempt to take advantage of or harm any of the students here, we'll be having a very different conversation." His tone left no room for misunderstanding. "As you said, my altruism only extends so far."

Fantomex dipped his head in acknowledgment. Thrust and parry. "I can assure you, E.V.A. and I will be on our best behavior while we remain your guests." He added, "And we'll be gone as soon as possible."

E.V.A. shifted in her chair. She looked as if she were about to speak but instead lapsed into silence.

"Get some rest, then," Cyclops said, preparing to take his leave as well. "You've been through a lot."

A more breathtaking understatement Fantomex had never heard.

# CHAPTER TWO

It started with a breakup, so it wasn't an auspicious beginning.

All right, wait, this was no time to be dramatic. Avery Torres shivered, her breath making thick clouds in the frigid air. There hadn't been an actual breakup yet. But there were signs. Symptoms. It definitely felt like there was a breakup impending.

She adjusted her stocking cap over her cornrows and buried her nose in the puffy depths of her winter coat, wishing she'd remembered her scarf as she stomped through the frozen wilderness. When Scott Summers had told her this school was an underground fortress in the middle of an icy nowhere, she'd thought he must be exaggerating, but no, he was not overstating things.

She trailed behind the other students, who were all following Emma Frost on their daily constitutional, as their teachers liked to call it. Avery enjoyed a good long walk as much as the next person. The silence and stillness were peaceful, inviting reflection and contemplation, but today she didn't want to be inside her own head. She needed noise and distraction. Something to take her mind off breakups, impending or otherwise.

"Watch your footing around here," Emma called back to them. Her face was partially obscured by a black fur-lined hood and scarf. "There are thick ice patches hidden under the fresh snowfall from this morning."

Terrific. Just a relaxing morning walk in subzero temperatures on treacherous ice.

"Seriously, I don't want anyone falling and cracking their head open – like last time," Emma added.

"Sorry," mumbled one of the students in an Australian accent. Eva Bell, if Avery remembered correctly. The others chuckled and clapped her good-naturedly on the shoulder.

"Don't worry, you know I'll fix you up if anything happens," Christopher Muse said, grinning.

Right, he was the healer. Avery knew that much. She'd met him on her first day here a couple of months ago. Everyone else already knew each other and had made their own friend groups. She suppressed a sigh. It had been like being in high school all over again, the new girl in class, standing at the front of the room trying not to look like the mayor of Awkward Town.

Not that she didn't have friends. What she had was better, actually, because she had her art, and she had Jane. For now, at least. And this morning walk was exactly the kind of absurd thing she would normally text Jane about. If things were normal.

Had they ever really been normal, though? Avery stomped

off the thick snow caking her boots. When was the last time she had truly felt settled and normal?

See, this was dangerous. Too many directions for her thoughts to go, not enough distractions. Glancing around to make sure no one was paying attention to her, Avery slipped her cell phone from her coat pocket and surreptitiously scrolled through the text message thread she'd started with her girlfriend. The cell reception in this place was nothing, but at least she could look back through this archive of her relationship with Jane, maybe search for clues, evidence of the moment things started to go wrong.

If she was being honest with herself, she didn't need to scroll back very far.

Exhibit A: the last text exchange, sent approximately two weeks ago, when she'd managed to wrangle a day trip to Edmonton for some alone time and cell reception.

*Jane: You're at that museum again, aren't you? I know it's Edmonton, but does the frozen north really have that fascinating of an art scene?*

*Avery: You know what they say: life finds a way, and so does art.*

*Jane: Wow, OK,* Jurassic Park, *there aren't enough poop emojis in the world to express how bad that joke was.*

*Avery: You're proud of me. I can tell.*

*Jane: Guilty. You staring at that painting? The Woman and the Tower?*

*Avery: No.*

*Avery: Maybe. It just speaks to me, you know?*

*Jane: Reminds me, when are we going to speak again? You haven't told me how art school is going up there or*

*sent me any drawings lately. I need details. What have you
been working on?*

Details. Oh, she had details. Like how this so-called art
school was truly a repurposed military facility that sheltered
some of the few mutants remaining in the world. Like how
Avery had been lying when she'd told Jane that she'd dropped
out of the San Diego School of Art and Design to participate
in a special program up here in Canada.

That she was being quite literal when she said her favorite
painting at the Edmonton Art Museum spoke to her. It was
just in a way that no one else could hear.

She hadn't known much about psychometry, the ability to
touch objects and know intimate details about their history,
when she'd first discovered her powers, and there was still
a lot she had to learn, but that's why she'd come here. She
knew she was one of the lucky ones. From the bits and
pieces of stories she'd picked up from the other students, her
journey to get to the school had been much less traumatic
than it might have been had she come to the attention of
organizations like S.H.I.E.L.D.

But she hadn't shared any of those details, which meant
she was lying to her girlfriend by omission. And Jane was
smart, much smarter than her. She was beginning to catch on
that Avery was holding things back, that something wasn't
right between them.

They should have had an honest conversation long before
she'd come up here. It wasn't like Avery was forbidden from
telling anyone that she was a mutant. Cyclops had simply
cautioned her and the rest of the students to be selective with
the people they trusted. He said even if they thought they

knew how their loved ones would react, there was always the chance that those same people would disappoint them in the ugliest possible way.

Avery had never forgotten the expression on his face when he'd told them that. He was usually hard to read wearing those ruby quartz glasses, but not that time. Haunted, that's what he'd looked like. He didn't want any of the students to get hurt.

Avery wanted to trust Jane, she really did, but she hadn't trusted anyone in a very long time.

Her mom had passed away when she was too young to remember. Her dad had gotten sick not long after her powers had first manifested, and she hadn't wanted to worry him, but if he'd recovered Avery would have told him the truth. She knew he would have accepted her, no questions asked, no doubts raised, the same way he'd accepted everything else about Avery, her whole life.

If her dad were still here… what a world that would be.

The sun was making a valiant attempt to pierce the clouds above their heads, transforming the unbroken sheet of snow and ice stretching to the horizon into a brilliant, blinding canvas that stung her eyes. That's all it was, just the brightness making the moisture gather there.

Feeling miserable, and wishing she'd brought sunglasses, Avery almost didn't notice when the student walking a few feet in front of her brought his foot down squarely on a patch of that hidden ice Emma Frost had warned them about. He lost his balance, feet scrambling for purchase on the unforgiving ground.

Without thinking, Avery rushed forward, snagging the

student by his upper arms, locking him in place while he regained his footing. Adrenaline surged through her, her heart going like a hammer in her chest. By the time she'd recovered her equilibrium, the student had turned around and was looking at her in surprise, his cheeks flushed.

"You OK?" Avery asked, trying to place him. The one with the goatee – David Bond, or Hijack, as he was also known. She couldn't keep up with all the codenames.

"Stable now," he said, finding his voice. "Thanks, that was almost a disaster."

He was dressed in jeans and a thick winter coat like her, but *he'd* remembered a scarf and sunglasses. They fell into step together, going slower on the uncertain ground. At first, there was only awkward silence between them. Avery hated small talk, but she was trying to dredge some up when he nodded at her cell phone, which she still had clutched in her hand. Thankfully, she hadn't dropped it when she'd come to his rescue.

"You won't get any reception, even out here," he said. "Believe me, all of us have tried. We aren't technically supposed to have cell phones because they can be tracked and traced, but... well, you have to try to have some connection to the outside world, right?"

"No, I was just–" Trying to figure out a way to save her failing relationship. She mentally shook herself. This wasn't a conversation she wanted to have with anyone, let alone a guy she barely knew. "Yeah, you're right. I was just hoping to get lucky."

"Feeling homesick?"

"Something like that."

To Avery, homesick implied that there was a place she was missing, but even art school in California hadn't felt like home. She hadn't been there long enough. Only when she was with Jane had she started to feel that elusive sensation, that sense of belonging.

Now she was thousands of miles away from that.

"I've been curious about something," David said hesitantly, as if he didn't want to pry into her personal affairs. Still, he plunged ahead. "Well, we've all been curious, really, so I'm just going to ask. Are you in training to join the X-Men or not? Because you go to all the classes, and you participate and everything, even in the self-defense classes, but I've never seen you in any of the Danger Room simulations. And nobody has seen you use your powers, so..." he trailed off, inviting her to fill in the blanks.

He was going to be disappointed. "Look, I understand the curiosity," she said, "but my powers are a blip compared to the things some of the people here can do." She gestured at the students walking ahead of them. "From what I've seen, you all are amazing, and you're going to do great things for the world." She was amused when David puffed out his chest at her words. "I'm here to figure some things out about my abilities, and then I plan to go back to my life. This is temporary."

That had always been the plan.

He nodded, accepting the explanation, though she thought his eyes looked slightly disappointed behind the sunglasses. "Well, are you interested in making some friends while you're here? Temporary ones, anyway?"

He was smiling at her now, so she tried to smile back, but

she thought it came out shaky and uncertain. She wasn't used to people walking up to her and going straight for the friendship thing. Not their fault, necessarily. She went out of her way to avoid people most of the time. It was easier that way.

No, David was probably reaching out because she was a mutant. Safety in numbers, and all that. He wasn't really interested in getting to know *her*. Even if he was, she wouldn't be here long enough to get to know any of them in return.

But glancing over at him, she found she couldn't bring herself to disappoint him again, so she said, "Sure, maybe I can do that."

"Excellent." His smile widened, and then Christopher called to him from up ahead. "Gotta go," he said, "thanks again for the save."

When she was alone, Avery stuffed her cell phone back in her pocket and snuggled deeper into her coat. *Just keep your eyes on your goal.* All she wanted was to understand her abilities and to be able to control them. And to spend some more time with the painting. That was where everything had started, after all.

Which reminded her, she needed to make another trip into Edmonton soon. She hoped she would be allowed. Maybe if she waited a few more weeks. She could tell the instructors didn't like it when she asked. They wanted to keep the school's location a secret, and coming and going was a risk. But Avery was discreet, and she kept to herself, so she'd quickly earned the trust of Cyclops. She wasn't sure about Emma Frost, but it didn't matter. She didn't need to earn everyone's trust.

All of this is temporary, she told herself again as she lifted her eyes to the horizon. It had to be. This was a fortress thinly disguised as a school. It wasn't the kind of place where anyone should look for a family or a home.

# CHAPTER THREE

"Prepare yourselves," E.V.A. intoned. "Simulation commencing in three... two... one."

Oh, Fantomex was prepared. Muscles tensed in readiness, he reveled in the blood pounding in his ears. He could barely stand still while the Danger Room shuddered to life around them.

Three mind-numbing weeks he'd been prowling that moldy medical facility, eating red gelatin cubes and slurping watery broth while his body finished healing itself with excruciating slowness. By the end, he'd been ready to throw himself out into the snow and wait for the wolves to come for him. Were there wolves in Alberta? He made a mental note to ask someone in case he ever ended up in that position again.

Cyclops must have sensed Fantomex was nearing his breaking point because he was the one who'd arranged this little training session, ostensibly as a way to gauge his current power levels. All Fantomex cared about was that he was free, free and back in uniform.

E.V.A., bless her, had recreated it down to the last detail, his white and black costume with its duster jacket tucked around him, guns at his sides and multiple glittering knives up his sleeves. His ceramic-plated mask fit comfortably against his face like a second skin, shielding his mind from telepathic intrusion. Everything about the ensemble made him feel like his old self again.

He was here. He was whole. And he was ready to punch something through a wall.

Fantomex drew a slow breath in and released it, as the blank walls of the massive Danger Room glowed briefly before a series of objects materialized out of thin air. In seconds, they filled the space with color and life, as if a painter's hands moved rapidly over a blank canvas. When the simulation had fully manifested, they were standing on a narrow plateau at dusk, the ground turned to sand that billowed in clouds in a hot wind. Jagged rock formations rose in strange shapes all around them, cast in red and gold by the setting sun. Some of the giant rocks even floated in midair.

He'd requested a holographic battlefield that was similar to the training grounds of the artificial reality he'd grown up in. The Danger Room's technology was highly advanced, but even it had its limits when it came to recreating the wonders and terrors of The World. No matter what his senses told him, he knew he was just looking at a simulation of a simulation. A knockoff.

Now there was a hot, steaming plate of irony.

"Focus," E.V.A. said, as if sensing his thoughts were drifting off track. "Commencing link-up of neuroweapons systems. Targeting function active."

Now that was more like it.

Next to him, E.V.A.'s humanoid form shifted, her body drawing in on itself until she had assumed a small spherical shape floating in the air. It was no larger than a softball, but cast in silver and surrounded by amber bands that called to mind the rings of Saturn. Normally, this was the form she assumed to provide transportation when he needed it, but in this case she had chosen something much smaller so as to make herself less of a target.

They were linked now, and a brief mental scan showed he had access to her full offensive capabilities. Good. He was going to need them.

The ground shook beneath his feet. Taking cover behind one of the larger rock formations, Fantomex directed E.V.A. to fly higher. "I need eyes on what's coming," he said. "How many and how big?"

"Um, don't forget that I'm out here too. I can scout as well."

The voice came over a private comm link, which he'd forgotten was active. Fantomex stifled a sigh. Cyclops had insisted he have teammates for this exercise. How quaint. The one on the comm link was the healer with the good fashion sense – Christopher Muse, or Triage, as they called him. Who was the other one?

A shadow passed over his head, and Fantomex looked up to see a flash of scaly wings as a purple dragon-like creature flew past, snorting a short gout of flame as if to draw his attention. Ah yes, Lockheed. His presence lent the scene more than a bit of an 80s fantasy movie vibe. No matter. He didn't need allies.

"You want to scout, feel free." He ran to one of the rock

formations and scaled it smoothly, his muscles feeling the pleasant burn of exertion as he came to the top. He drew his pistol.

This is what he'd been missing. A fight. A target. Purpose.

"Two Sentinels on your six!" E.V.A. called out from somewhere above him. "Camouflaged units!"

Fantomex spun and dropped into a crouch, already firing, simultaneously issuing a silent call to E.V.A.'s weapons systems. Energy blasts, three-second bursts, waiting for visual confirmation – *there*.

They had been standing against the tallest limestone formation about a hundred yards away, their outer shells perfectly camouflaged to look like the stone.

Except for the two faintly glowing points of their soulless eyes.

Sentinels, the giant mutant-hunting robots that had been part of the foundation of his own creation.

"Target locked," E.V.A. informed him, a hint of excitement inflecting her voice.

"Fire," Fantomex growled.

The landscape was suddenly aglow with amber fire raining down as E.V.A. pelted the robots with energy bursts. They ripped into the Sentinels' outer plating, leaving gaping, scorched tears behind.

Turning, he dove off the formation he'd been standing on and went into a freefall. Over the comm link, Triage gave a startled yelp, but he couldn't see what Fantomex was aiming for – one of the floating rocks was just passing by underneath him. He landed on it and went into a roll. He came up firing again, filling the Sentinels' exposed innards with bullets.

The robots were too torn up from E.V.A.'s energy blasts to retaliate.

Too easy. But so satisfying.

Fantomex surveyed the ground below. Triage was about thirty feet away, clinging like a burr to the side of one of the formations. Lockheed was nowhere to be seen.

The ground shuddered again, throwing him to his knees.

"Behind you!" Triage shouted.

Fantomex rolled, firing blindly. Bullets pinged off a metallic surface – another Sentinel had appeared behind him and grabbed his floating rock perch, holding it in place with one hand while it reached for him with the other.

Too close for E.V.A.'s neuroweapons. Energy blasts would hit him, too. Misdirection. That's what he needed. It would work in seconds.

He focused, sending out a wave of manipulating energy, planting an image in the thing's processors, making it believe that he'd jumped off the rock and started running in the other direction. Any second now the illusion would take hold, and he'd be in the clear.

Any second now...

Then he felt it. Or, rather, realized what he *wasn't* feeling. The power, his misdirection ability. It wasn't there. He reached for it, just as he always had, but it was gone.

Scraped out. Hollow. A knockoff.

"Fantomex!"

E.V.A.'s frantic shout reached him the same instant as the Sentinel's fist. It slammed into his chest, launching him backward off the floating stone platform. Wind rushed in his ears. He fell for ages. Was he really that high off the–

The air whooshed out of his lungs as he slammed into the ground.

Well.

"End simulation."

He wasn't sure who gave the command – he was too busy trying to force air into his lungs – but the barren landscape melted away to reveal the cool metal walls of the Danger Room. Running footsteps approached, and then Triage was kneeling next to him, eyes wide, his skin covered in a sheen of sweat.

"Hang on," he said. "Let me see how bad you're hurt."

Fantomex started to lift a hand to swat him away, but a searing hot pain shot up his back when he tried to move his arm. All right then, that was probably broken. His back and maybe his other arm too. Perhaps his body wasn't yet returned to its full level of durability. He used to be able to take a fall like that without nearly so much damage.

He was considering passing out for a spell when more footsteps approached. A pale-skinned blonde woman wearing all black stepped into his field of vision, her arms crossed and a scowl plastered on her face.

"Next time, you should think about dodging," Emma Frost said helpfully.

The other head of this pseudo-school, she'd made scant appearances in his hospital room over the past few weeks, but it was obvious she'd been observing the simulation this whole time. Lovely.

"I'll bear that in mind," he said through gritted teeth. E.V.A. floated above him, still in her small spherical form, scanning him and relaying the extent of his injuries –

everything bruised, nothing broken – to Triage, who nodded thoughtfully. Fantomex could already feel the young man aligning his energy and heartbeat with his own. He remembered this from when he was floating in the void. He hadn't been fully aware of it until the end, but Triage truly had helped him, guiding his recovery when he was too weak to do it for himself.

Cyclops was right. He probably owed the man his life.

He didn't like owing anyone anything.

Even the healing process itself was pleasant, now that he knew not to fight it. The fiery pain in his back and arms cooled to a dull ache, but even that faded after a moment, leaving behind only a faint stiffness and a soft echo as Christopher's heartbeat slowly faded.

"All right, you should be good to go," the young man said, helping him to sit up.

"What were you doing just watching that thing come at you?" Emma asked, unwilling to let him off the hook.

"If you must know, I was attempting to use an ability that up until recently was second nature to me," he said in a clipped voice, trying to communicate with his glare that he didn't want to discuss the matter further. He pointed at Lockheed, who was circling above them, watching the scene. "I didn't see Puff the Magic Dragon doing anything either," he added sullenly.

A gout of flame kissed the back of his neck. Fantomex flinched from the heat. "Point taken," he said, saluting the creature as he staggered to his feet. He gave Christopher a curt nod, acknowledging the healing. "Now, if you wouldn't mind…"

"Yeah, sure, I remember this part." The young man turned and headed for the door before Fantomex could order him away. "I'll show myself out while you all discuss... whatever that was," he said, throwing a wave over his shoulder.

When the Danger Room doors hissed shut behind him, Fantomex turned to find Emma eying him speculatively. "What?" he demanded.

She shrugged. "If you were to ask my opinion–"

"Which I didn't."

"You and Triage both possess substantial healing abilities," she continued, unfazed. "Or at least you used to – maybe they ended up in another brain, along with your manners, reflexes, and hand-eye coordination."

He gestured to the floor. "Would you like me to lie back down while you kick me, or am I fine here?"

"I'm saying he could learn from you, and maybe–" she widened her eyes in mock horror "–you could learn from him, if you'd put your pride and that substantial ego aside for a minute."

"I've been suggesting the same to him for the past several weeks," E.V.A. said. She'd shifted back to her humanoid form and joined them.

On the wall behind her, a large screen replayed the combat simulation at half speed so he could watch himself get punched into oblivion in slow motion, stunning high definition. As much as he wished it were otherwise, the footage didn't lie. He'd obviously lost a step, his body healing slower than it used to. It was galling.

He shot a glare at E.V.A. "I told you it would be a waste of time," he snapped, rolling his shoulders in agitation. "We're only staying here long enough for me to get back to fighting form. This arrangement is temporary."

They stared at each other, but E.V.A.'s expression remained neutral. "Very well," she said.

"At any rate," Emma cut in, "we need to talk about what happened here." She made a gesture, freezing the simulation at the moment he was trying and failing to use his misdirection power. "Up until this point, everything looked good. Your strength and fighting style were all consistent with what we've seen from you in the past."

He frowned, though she probably couldn't tell behind the mask. "As I said, I was trying to use my misdirection ability to throw it off. With it, I manipulate all of the target's senses and emotions, planting an illusion in their thoughts that's so convincing they can't distinguish reality from the artificial state that I've created for them. It's worked on Sentinels in the past, so that's not the issue."

His jaw tightened. The issue was that the misdirection ability had obviously been connected to one of his other brains, so now it resided with one of the imposters.

Which left him significantly diminished. Everyone in the room had seen it.

"It's possible that your powers were not so concretely associated with your individual brains as you believe," E.V.A. said, sensing his frustration. "With time and sufficient practice, you could learn to reproduce your misdirection ability in your current state. It might not have the same strength and effectiveness, but I'd be happy to–"

"I don't need help," he said, cutting her off. Tension knotted the air as he turned away from them and strode to the door, but neither of them tried to stop him. "I'll be sure to sign up for another pummeling session tomorrow," he added, waving to Lockheed, who had landed near the door and was watching him with what looked like a quizzical expression. Hard to tell with a dragon.

Fantomex strode blindly down the dank gray hallways with no thought of a particular destination. He just needed to walk, to give his seething anger and humiliation a chance to subside.

He wasn't surprised when E.V.A. caught up to him, falling smoothly into step beside him. But, for once, her aura of calm didn't make him feel any better. If anything, it made things worse.

"You blame me for your current situation," she said after a moment of silence. Her tone was matter of fact, but as he glanced at her, he could see the pinched skin between her brows. She was difficult to read, even in her human form, processing and experiencing emotions in ways he would probably never fully understand. But that didn't mean she was immune to being hurt.

"If you hadn't intervened, I'd be permanently dead," he said. "The fact that I was able to be resurrected after having my heart cut from my chest is nothing short of miraculous." He sighed, the air hissing between his teeth. "I've done a poor job showing gratitude for that. I apologize."

"You have been through a traumatic experience," she said. "It will take time to adjust. You should be patient with yourself. No one here thinks less of you for what you've been through."

Her words only served to draw attention to the fact that every time they passed groups of students in the hall, voices hushed, and eyes darted furtively in his direction. No doubt that when they thought of him at all, they viewed him as a sort of curiosity, a science experiment gone awry, as Christopher had so bluntly pointed out. But they weren't far wrong.

Not that any of it mattered. He didn't care what a group of teenagers thought of him. His only concern was getting as much of his strength back as possible so he could leave this place.

And go where? And do what? What was he, in this diminished state?

He pushed those questions out of his head. He'd figure them out later. What he needed right now was a distraction.

"Perhaps exercising your mental faculties will put you in a better frame of mind," E.V.A. suggested. She was holding a piece of paper in her hand, skimming her finger down what looked like a list. "Did you know that in addition to combat training, the school offers lectures on a myriad of subjects: world history, advanced mathematics, art – even French history and culture," she added lightly.

"What are you looking at?" He plucked the list out of her hands. "How did you get a class schedule?"

"I asked for it," she said, an edge of exasperation in her voice. "The people here are quite accommodating if you give them a chance."

"Everyone is so determined to make me socialize," he muttered. Even though he hated to admit it, it was a sound strategy. When you're weak, you find protection, cultivate allies, try to blend in with the herd so you don't get picked off by predators. Play nice, in other words.

He looked at the description of the French history and culture lecture that was starting in twenty minutes. Barely enough time for him to shower and change and–

No, forget that. He would go exactly as he was. Let the people here think whatever they wanted about him. He was Fantomex, and they may as well get used to it.

"It should be amusing at least, seeing if this instructor, whoever they are–" the class list didn't say "–has anything new to teach *me* about French culture."

"That's the spirit," E.V.A. said with a long-suffering sigh. "What could possibly go wrong when the student goes in thinking they know more than the teacher?"

# CHAPTER FOUR

Avery sat in a circle of chairs with a small group of fellow students while their instructor, Magneto, took a seat near the front of the room. Most of the students looked surprised to see him, but she'd heard someone whisper that he'd been the only one available today to teach this session. She'd never been to one of his lectures before – the students were all intimidated by him, though she'd never seen him use his powers – and she hadn't really wanted to come to this one, but it was better than sitting in her room stewing.

She'd spent the last hour trying to get her psychometric powers to work using various objects that Magik had placed before her. An old pocket watch. A pearl brooch. A black and white photograph of a pair of children scowling at the camera. All of the objects had a history that was just waiting to be revealed.

To someone, maybe, but not to her.

One after another, she'd drawn a blank. Nothing had triggered her powers.

Just like always.

Magik had urged her to be patient, that progress often came slowly with mutant powers like hers. But Avery had been here for what felt like forever, and she hadn't made any progress at all.

Seeing her downcast expression after the session, David Bond had convinced her to attend the French history and culture lecture with him. Avery still wasn't quite sure how he'd talked her into it. Probably it had been the promise that there would be discussions of art, something that would make her feel for a moment like she was back in California in an art history class with Jane, doodling in her sketchbook all the while.

She missed drawing, too. For some reason, she couldn't bring herself to do it while she was within the Institute's walls. The dark interior of the place didn't exactly scream inspiration. The overall lack of color was distressing.

So here she was, trying to capture some inspiration, and she immediately regretted her decision.

Magneto leveled a dead-eyed stare at the costumed man positioned on the opposite side of the circle from him, the man who'd just laughed heartily when he'd started off the food portion of the lecture talking about Paris.

In the wake of that laugh, the room had gone absolutely silent.

"Did you have something you wished to contribute to this discussion?" Magneto asked, and even though the question wasn't directed at any of them, the students visibly shrank in their chairs. Forget about his powers, Avery was convinced Magneto's tone could make the bravest mutant on the planet shrivel up and die.

Avery had no idea if the masked man in the white and black costume was the bravest mutant on the planet or not, but his eyes held a hint of cold amusement as he regarded Magneto. He sat back in his chair, hands clasped behind his head, one ankle resting on his opposite knee. Full manspreading. He wasn't fooling anyone, though, or at least he wasn't fooling her. Avery could see the tension in his shoulders, the restless tapping of his right foot, as if it was all he could do to keep his butt planted in that chair. He would rather be anywhere but here.

So why *was* he here?

It felt like everyone in the room was holding their collective breath, waiting for the man to respond to Magneto's question.

Next to her, David whispered, "It's like the scene in the old western movies when the outlaw walks into the saloon and everyone freezes right before they run for cover."

She had to admit, that was pretty accurate. All they needed was an Ennio Morricone soundtrack.

Finally, the man in the costume broke the tension by sighing, long and loud. Way too much drama. Avery rolled her eyes.

"I was willing to give you a chance," he said, and Avery thought his accent sounded French, but only in the vaguest way, "but I refuse, simply refuse to entertain a discussion of French gastronomy that doesn't lead off with Lyon. We should be plumbing the sweet depths of the Rhône Valley, basking in the glory of the charcuterie of the Monts du

Lyonnais. Now that, pupils, is true cuisine. Who's with me?"

He looked around at the rest of them, his gaze coming to rest for whatever reason on Avery, as if he actually expected her to agree with him.

Yeah, she was definitely wasting her time here.

"You do realize this is only an hour-long class?" she asked in exasperation. "We don't have a whole lot of time to 'plumb the depths' of anything here, so maybe you need to dial back the enthusiasm a bit, or whatever it is you have going on over there."

Chuckles, quickly smothered by coughs, echoed from different parts of the room. Even Magneto flicked her a glance that held something like approval. "An astute point," he said, dismissing the man in the costume with a sniff.

"Are you really Fantomex?" David asked, surprising Avery. Maybe he was emboldened by her attitude, though that hadn't been her intention. She'd just wanted the man – Fantomex, whatever – to shut up. "We've heard stories about you," he went on. "Wild stories."

"They're probably all true," Fantomex drawled. "Except the ones that aren't."

Avery rolled her eyes again.

"I saw that," he said, without looking in her direction.

"That's enough," Magneto barked. "Fantomex, no matter how much he might wish otherwise, is not the subject of this lecture."

"But shouldn't we at least get to know him?" Fabio Medina asked tentatively. "He's new. We all introduced ourselves on our first day, so shouldn't he do that too?"

"Indeed, professor, shouldn't I familiarize myself with your pupils?" Fantomex's eyes twinkled. Magneto looked like he wanted to familiarize Fantomex's face with the business end of a shovel.

"Is it true you have something like twelve functioning brains?" David asked, taking the opening.

Fantomex swung to face him, the mischief in his eyes vanishing. "What? No, that's not–"

"And three stomachs?" asked Eva Bell, who was sitting on Avery's other side, leaning forward eagerly in her chair. "Is that why you're so obsessed with food?"

"I'm not obsessed with food, and no, three stomachs are ridiculous!"

"Cows have four stomach compartments," Avery pointed out. "Are you saying cows are ridiculous?"

"Yes," he deadpanned. "Cows are ridiculous, except when I'm enjoying their cheese."

Fabio raised his voice to be heard over everyone. "*I* heard that he has an advanced central nervous system that functions outside his body and somehow attained sentience so that it now takes on human form!"

Everyone stopped talking and turned to stare at him.

"OK, that one really is ridiculous," David said, chuckling. "Where'd you even hear that?"

Fantomex threw up his hands. "All right, I can see I'm going to have to educate everyone in the room on–"

His words were drowned out by an ear-splitting shriek and crunching sound as the metal chair he sat in crumpled and twisted into a tight ball, depositing him on his backside on the floor.

The room went silent again. The only sound was Magneto's harsh breathing, his nostrils flared as he lowered his outstretched hand. "Class dismissed," he growled.

So much for French history and culture.

Avery angrily shoved her notebook into her messenger bag and followed the rest of the students out of the room. Instead of learning anything useful about her powers or anything interesting about the world in general, she'd had to watch some mutant wannabe-elitist strut and showboat his way through an hour of her life. The whole day had been a complete waste of time.

Automatically, she started walking toward her next class, but her steps faltered as her anger grew, and she found herself darting into the nearest restroom instead. She bent and looked under the stall doors, but there was no sign of feet. Good. No one else was using the place as a sanctuary.

Some sanctuary, though. Rust stains in the sinks, mildewy tile and bare, flickering bulbs providing a depressingly small amount of light. Avery had never been inside a prison, but she imagined that the bathrooms probably looked a lot like these.

And this was supposed to be a school.

She rubbed her hands up and down her arms as she paced in front of the grimy mirror. What was she doing here? A couple of months ago, she'd been studying art in California with Jane. If she were there now, they could be attending a life study class or something else equally fascinating. They'd grab a pizza on their way back to the apartment they shared with twenty-seven roommates, or whatever weird college housing arrangement they'd worked out. She'd fall asleep on the couch with her head in Jane's lap while they binge-watched Jane Austen movies, because of course Avery had a girlfriend named Jane who was in love with Jane Austen movies.

Avery wiped her face with the backs of her hands, but she couldn't stop her shuddering breaths or the knife-like pain in her chest.

She needed to get out of here. Just for a little while, she needed to be somewhere where she felt more like herself. Someplace comforting.

The painting. She needed the painting.

And Jane. She needed to talk to her before that relationship slipped away.

Maybe she would even confess everything this time, tell her the truth.

*Jane, I'm a mutant. I should have told you. I'm sorry for keeping it from you.*

Also, I might be in love with you, and that terrifies me.

One thing at a time. First, she had to calm down. She checked her face in the mirror to make sure her eyes weren't red and puffy. She felt washed out, her brown skin looking sallow. Actually, that was probably just the terrible lighting. Either way, it was time for a change of scenery. She'd waited long enough, and she didn't care who disapproved.

Avery left the bathroom on a mission. She strode down the hall, making a left, then two rights, winding her way to where Scott Summers had his office.

She knocked briskly on the door and waited. A moment went by while she fidgeted, clutching the strap of her messenger bag. Where was he? Impatient, she knocked again.

The door opened, and a young man walked past her, giving her a brief nod. Avery blinked, momentarily nonplussed. It was a younger version of the Scott Summers who co-ran the school, right down to the ruby quartz glasses.

Then she remembered. There were mutants here who'd been displaced in time, including the younger Scott Summers. Who'd apparently been in a meeting with the older Scott Summers. Or something.

Yeah, she really needed to get out of this place for a few days.

"Come in, Avery," Cyclops called to her, and she went inside.

"I need to go to Edmonton again," she said without preamble. "Just to clear my head."

If he thought her abruptness was strange, he didn't show it. He only nodded, considering her. "Did something happen?"

"No. Well, it depends. I was in class with that guy Fantomex just now and–"

Scott groaned, and somehow Avery knew she would be on her way soon. "Alright," he said. "We'll make arrangements to get you to Edmonton."

# CHAPTER FIVE

E.V.A. was waiting for him outside the classroom when Fantomex finally extricated himself from the metal pretzel that had once been a chair.

"How did it go?" she asked, a hopeful note in her voice.

He held up the chair by way of explanation.

"Ah," she said. "Why did you bring the chair with you?"

He shrugged. "A trophy?"

One of the students coming out of the classroom stopped beside him and slapped something into his free hand. "Great class," he said, rubbing his goateed chin and chuckling to himself as he walked away. "One for the books."

"What is that?" E.V.A. inquired, staring at the dubious object the young man had placed in his hand.

He held it up. It was a package of beef jerky with the words "Made in Monts du Lyonnais" scrawled on the package in black permanent marker. He'd even spelled it correctly.

Fantomex groaned. He really didn't want to like these youths, and yet...

"Are you smiling?" E.V.A. asked, leaning toward him as if trying to peer through his mask. "Does that mean it wasn't a total waste of time?"

"Oh, it was definitely a waste of time," Fantomex said. The chair was getting heavy. He tossed it aside with a loud clang. "I'm ready to leave now."

Crossing her arms, E.V.A. fell into step beside him as he walked down the hall, trying to remember where Emma Frost's office was. "I thought we had discussed – at length, with charts and graphs to illustrate my points – several reasons why that wouldn't be a wise course of action at this time," she said.

"And you were right, as always," he said, not slowing down. "I'm talking about a temporary leave of absence, a mission, an outing. We're going to track down my counterparts, starting with Cluster." He glanced over at her to gauge her reaction to his proposal. He did his best to pretend that he'd been planning this all along, when, in reality, it had only occurred to him out of desperation while he was sitting in that torture chamber that could only loosely be called a classroom.

E.V.A. pursed her lips in thought. Good, at least she wasn't dismissing the idea outright.

"It's true that I would feel better if we knew more about what the former parts of yourself were doing, seeing as how we've had only silence since your revival," she said carefully. "As long as we proceed with caution and accept whatever aid the Institute is willing to offer, I think it's a good plan."

"Excellent," Fantomex said, doubling back and turning down a short hall to stop in front of a thick metal door. He knocked three times. "Let's see if we can get that aid."

"What do you mean, you already know where she is?" Fantomex demanded, as Emma Frost stared at him across her rather impressive oak desk and even more impressive computer, with its multiple holo screens floating in a crescent around her.

"Just what I said. We have a lead." Arms folded on the desktop, she was as unflappable as ever, while he felt like a child being lectured by a bored parent.

"W- When were you going to inform us of this development?" he sputtered.

"We weren't keeping the information from you, if that's what you're implying," Emma said calmly. "We were upfront that we would be attempting to locate Weapon XIII and Cluster after E.V.A. brought you here. It proved difficult at first to track them via the usual channels. We believe both of them integrated similar telepathic intrusion-blocking methods into their costumes, just as you have." She gestured to his ceramic-plated mask. "We still haven't located Weapon XIII, but we recently got a blip on Cluster in America. We followed up and discovered she's been quite busy, actually."

Fantomex and E.V.A. leaned forward as Emma activated a holoscreen in front of her and swiped to rotate it so they could see. A profile of Cluster flashed onto the screen, accompanied by an image of a costumed white woman in her early thirties, with long brown hair and a duster jacket similar to his. In fact, the whole outfit was much like his only... better somehow. That needled him.

He studied her face, fascinated and absorbed by the

similarities. It wasn't like looking into a mirror, more like finding a photograph of yourself you hadn't seen in years. The familiarity, the nostalgia, as if no time at all had passed since that frozen memory, yet you clearly feel the sting of knowing you will never again be the person in that snapshot.

That was how he felt, gazing at his counterpart.

E.V.A. was watching him. He could feel it. He dragged his attention away from the image of Cluster to the accompanying text. There were snippets from a handful of news outlets detailing a series of thefts at art museums both famous and obscure in different parts of the world.

He flicked a finger to scroll through the accounts, and was treated to some recorded surveillance footage that showed Cluster apparently casing one of the museums during the day. She walked through a room full of statues, this time dressed in leggings and a gray hoodie, a backpack slung over her shoulder as if she was posing as a college student.

"That was the first hit we got on tracking her, the only time she wasn't wearing her mask," Emma said. "It seems Cluster has taken up the family business, so to speak." She narrowed her eyes at him. "You have any idea why she might have had the sudden urge to go on a crime spree just a few months after coming back from the dead?"

"Not really," he lied. Actually, he could think of a very compelling reason, but he wasn't keen to share it with her. If Cluster was struggling as much as he was with this new reality, then turning to one of their favorite pastimes was only natural. If he'd thought of it first, he probably would have done the same thing.

"Where is that?" he asked, pointing to the long, cavernous

gallery she was walking through in the footage. She even walked the same way he did. It was uncanny. "I don't recognize that museum." And he'd visited his fair share.

"It's not a true museum," E.V.A. put in, and he could tell by the flicker in her eyes that she was analyzing the footage, running it through her own advanced processing systems. "It's a temporary exhibition space meant to house a travelling display of art and artifacts from a selection of museums around the world. The exhibition is called *Limitless Imagination*. The surveillance footage is sourced from the exhibition's current location: an island in Lake Michigan, accessible via the city of Chicago, in the United States."

"Yes, that matches what we found as well," Emma said. "The building it's housed in is a replica of the Musée d'Orsay in Paris."

"Fascinating, I'm sure, but I'm more interested in what she stole from the exhibition," Fantomex said, scrolling faster to try to find the information

E.V.A. came to his rescue. "According to surveillance footage and police reports, she stole a piece of one of the statues – an arrow from the Diana of Versailles from the Louvre."

"She defaced a priceless statue?" Fantomex could hardly entertain the idea. Taking the arrow would surely have done incredible damage to the statue. He didn't respect much in this world – not authority, not other mutants, certainly not people who refused to aerate their wine – but he respected art. Had his counterpart changed so drastically?

"The statues are not originals," E.V.A. said, pointing to a line in the report. "It would have been too risky and too costly to transport them to different locations around the world, so replicas are being used. The rest of the pieces in the exhibition: paintings, pottery, arms and armor, textiles, and jewelry, are all authentic."

But she hadn't touched those. All those temptations at her fingertips, and instead she'd stolen a piece of a replica statue and got herself caught on surveillance footage without her mask. A smile twitched at his lips. "Well, then, what are we waiting for? Let's go to the exhibition and have a closer look at what remains of this statue."

There was a brief silence as Emma and E.V.A. shared a glance.

"What?" he demanded, feeling a spark of anger stirring inside him. "If it's a question of my physical capabilities, your own Danger Room simulation proved I'm almost returned to full strength. I can't do anything about my lack of a misdirection ability, but maybe if I can get Cluster to talk to me, I can find out her physical state as well and that might give us more information to work with."

He didn't add that if he had to stay in this dank, dismal place with people he didn't know staring at him and whispering every time he walked down the hall, like he was a guest star in some inane teenage dramedy show, he was going to lose his mind. Although he didn't say it aloud, he was pretty sure Emma could read the desperation in his eyes as he glared at her.

However, she remained unfazed. "I'd feel better if we had more intel going in about these thefts," she said, "but it feels like the authorities – and S.H.I.E.L.D., if they're involved – are keeping things quiet. They probably realize it's a mutant behind the thefts, but they don't want to cause a panic by making it public knowledge."

Or reveal that a mutant was outsmarting them and their best museum security systems all around the world, Fantomex thought with a surge of pride. Was it strange to feel pride in one's self in this way?

No, he had to stop thinking of them as part of himself. Seeing Cluster's activities laid out for him over the past several months reinforced that. They were completely independent beings now, with their own separate drives, desires, and powers. The question became, what were their intentions and goals now?

There was only one way to find out.

He surfaced from his musing in time to catch E.V.A. watching him thoughtfully, but she spoke before he could question her about it. "I think we should do as Fantomex suggests," she said. "According to the new reports, the exhibition is only going to be on the island for one more day, so we should proceed immediately. We'll get answers for you and fill in the blanks about what Cluster has been up to."

Emma nodded, though she still seemed reluctant. "All right, but keep in touch," she said, looking to E.V.A. "I assume that won't be a problem for you?"

"Not in the least."

"Then be careful, be subtle, and if you're tempted to reveal the school's location to anyone, take a moment to remember who healed you – and who has a record of all your weaknesses." With the warning hanging in the air, she waved a hand, clearly dismissing them.

When they were outside her office, Fantomex steered them back toward the dismal quarters he'd been given. He needed to retrieve what gear he still possessed. Already his body hummed with excitement. He hadn't realized how much he needed this task to focus his energies.

His excitement dimmed somewhat when he noticed that E.V.A. was unusually quiet. "Were you lying to her just now?" he asked, needing to know how she truly felt. "Do you think this mission is a bad idea?"

She glanced over at him in surprise, but she was stopped from replying when they encountered a group of students coming down the hall from the opposite direction. Two of them waved and called out as they passed.

"Hey, Fantomex!"

"What's up, François?"

He scowled as the rest of the students laughed. "This is what I've been reduced to," he muttered as they turned a corner, leaving the group behind. "Packs of children mocking me." He looked at her, seeking support, and found instead she was biting her lip to keep from grinning. "Et tu, Brute?"

"They don't appear to be acting out of maliciousness," E.V.A. said, ever the diplomat. "Their jokes seem good-natured, and they're not children, despite the obvious age difference."

She was probably right about the age thing. At this point, he wasn't exactly sure how old he was. Where did one start with a new body? Anyway, it didn't matter. They all looked like children to him. "They're annoying."

"Consider this, then," she said, gesturing at the dank gray

walls and the depressingly utilitarian light fixtures above their heads. "You loathe the atmosphere of this place, but many of them have been living here far longer than you have."

Well, when she put it that way, it did give him an unwelcome stab of pity for them. "What's your point?"

"You're probably the most excitement, of a benign sort, that they've seen in quite some time," she said. "You, your situation, your... *mystique*, I suppose is as good a word as any."

Now he was suspicious. "You're softening me up for something. I can tell."

She sighed. "I believe you could easily make friends and allies of them, if you'd put forth minimal effort. It would be good for you, but since I know you won't believe me perhaps you'll instead do me the favor of telling me the real reason you want to find Cluster."

He stopped in the middle of the hallway. Luckily, they were in a less-traveled section of the facility, so there was no one around to eavesdrop. "What makes you think I have any other motives?"

She looked at him with something like pity in her eyes, which put his hackles up. "Because despite all the other things you have recently lost, I am still here, and I know you better than anyone else in any reality. Go ahead and try to deny it."

He couldn't, and she knew that very well, so he did what he did best and dodged the question. "Since we're probing motivations, let me ask *you* something. Why are you here with me instead of either of my counterparts? I'm assuming they were just as injured as I was after the separation. Both of them likely would have welcomed your presence, so why focus on me when you could be off gallivanting around the world with Cluster right now? Surely that's the more appealing assignment?"

He'd been broken into three pieces. Why had she picked up this one?

She stared at him, a complicated expression on her face. He found himself anxious to hear her answer and at the same time dreading it. Why was he feeling this way? His memories weren't in the best shape, but he was certain he never used to doubt himself so much.

"It's true that you were all experiencing varying degrees of... distress upon awakening to your new reality," E.V.A. conceded. "But in your case, it was different. You were..." She trailed off, as if struggling to find a way to explain.

Or trying to protect his feelings. Like a blow to the chest, he knew, suddenly, what she was holding back.

"I was the most broken," he finished, sparing her the burden of saying it. "That's why you stayed with me."

She believed he was the weakest. Just as he'd feared.

"Fantomex–"

"We should hurry," he said, and resumed walking, as if the conversation had never occurred. "We have a lot of work and planning ahead of us and not a lot of time. We'll need to secure floorplans for the exhibition space, determine a point of entry, analyze the security systems, all the usual strategizing."

She caught up to him. He could feel the weight of her regard, how much she wanted to say something, but in the end she stayed silent as he chattered inanely about the work ahead.

Inwardly, he was planning. The mission had just become more than a distraction, more than a way to get out of this dank place for a few hours. Now he couldn't wait to re-unite with Cluster. They'd see who the weak one was soon enough.

# CHAPTER SIX

Avery was back in her happy place. She was surrounded by art, with Jane's voice in her ear.

Maybe it wasn't the perfect date. Jane was still thousands of miles away, connected to her only via the wireless earpiece Avery wore, but if she closed her eyes and shut out the rest of the world it still felt like Jane was standing right behind her, and any minute she would walk up and put her arms around Avery from behind, hooking her chin on her shoulder. It was one of Avery's favorite things, and Jane knew it.

A blush warmed her cheeks. No one seemed to be paying attention to her, but Avery still ducked her head and adjusted the earpiece so it wasn't too obvious. Technically, the Edmonton Art Museum allowed phones and pictures – no flash – but the visitors tended to frown on people strolling through the galleries talking loudly on their cell phones, so she was trying to be discreet. But she'd been wanting to give Jane a tour of her favorite museum ever since they'd met. Someday, maybe she could even bring her here in person.

Someday.

"I'm passing into the miniatures room now," Avery said, keeping her voice down as she strolled into the warmly lit gallery with its assortment of viewing windows, behind which were detailed displays of moments from places and times long past, captured by the artisans in a reduced scale. She felt like a giant peeking into the windows of history. "The gallery is on the way to my painting, so I always take a quick detour around here," she continued. "Reminds me of when I had dollhouses as a kid."

Jane chuckled, the sound making Avery's chest tighten. There was no better sound in the world than Jane's laugh. "I bet you were a cute kid," she said. "Can I see baby pictures of you?"

"Absolutely not," Avery snorted. "You'd set them as wallpaper on your phone."

"Yes, I would. So you'll send them?"

Avery sighed. "Sure, I'll dig some up." She didn't mention what a Herculean effort it would be. Most of her family's belongings were packed away in storage or locked in safe deposit boxes, things too fragile to take with her after her dad passed away, but things she couldn't bear to part with either.

Someday, she wanted to have a home where she could display her mother's degree from Harvard Law School, and the picture of her accepting a special commendation from the United Nations, one of the first Black women to receive such an honor for her work in human rights issues. They would hang next to the pair of Rembrandt sketches her father had purchased right before he'd gotten sick. He'd been so proud of them.

One day she would have a place for all of it.

But she didn't want to think of that now, especially when she was giving Jane a tour of her favorite part of the museum. She passed into the familiar gallery and counted: first, second, third, fourth painting on the right, with a lovely little padded bench sitting a few feet away, as if it'd been placed there just for her. She sank down, letting out a sigh of happiness.

"Listen to you. You sound like a smitten teenager," Jane said. "Should I be jealous of a painting?"

The words were teasing, but Avery thought she detected a hint of wistfulness in Jane's voice. Surely she didn't think that Avery cared more about the painting than her?

"Never," Avery said firmly. "It's just one of those paintings, you know? A painting that reminds you why you wanted to be an artist in the first place."

"Oh, I definitely get that. Talk to me about her. The woman in the painting."

The invitation was impossible to resist – this was her favorite subject, after all – but Avery found herself, as she always did, lacking the proper words.

She started by listing the facts on the little placard next to the painting, even though they hardly told the whole story. *The Woman and the Tower*, artist Ruby Alano, oil on canvas, 1940, signed lower right, origin New York. Then she moved on to describe the painting itself. She could have done so with her eyes closed, in fact. The woman in the painting was a lovingly rendered figure of Cubist influences and nods to Pre-Columbian art. She shared the canvas with a tower of weathered stone, with finger-sized slits for windows that put Avery in mind of eyes. Yet, instead of being ominous, the tower's presence spoke to a yearning reflected in the woman's eyes. A yearning for change. At least, that was how Avery thought of it. All these things she described to Jane, but that was where she stopped. What she really wanted to tell her was what the painting represented, and how it had changed her life. Those were the words that she couldn't force past her lips.

Avery had first visited the museum in middle school with her father, the day after she'd told him she wanted to be an artist.

He'd given her one of his lopsided smiles and touched her cheek with his large hand. "Well, love, if that's the case, I'd better start introducing you to the family. You'll need to know the history and what you're getting into."

It was one of the things she'd loved most about her father. He was a restorer, and his work had taken him and their little family all over the globe, so he'd come to think of all artists as one big family, connected through the centuries, no matter how well known or obscure. Yet he was a particular champion of the obscure artists. He'd spend days on the phone, talking to collectors, getting that starry-eyed gaze as they described what they had squirreled away in their homes. Then he'd drive around, meeting with them and crawling into their attics to unearth forgotten treasures, works by artists whose talent hadn't gotten the recognition it deserved while their creators were alive. He brought them into the light, and she loved him for it.

And he'd kept his promise to her. They were living in Edmonton for his job at the time, so he'd taken her to the Edmonton Art Museum, where he was consulting. He was four years away from ultimately dying of a heart attack, right before she graduated high school. But that shock and pain was still in the future. Back then, it had just been a daytrip of bliss, surrounded by art. Her father had given her the same tour Avery was giving Jane now, though Avery hadn't told Jane that, either.

They'd been separated briefly while her father went to the restroom, and Avery was left alone in this very spot, the Arts of the Americas, Gallery 214. She'd stared at the Ruby Alano painting, mesmerized by the image of the mysterious tower and the woman, the fractured planes of her face, her eyes locking with the viewer when you looked at the painting just right.

To this day, Avery wasn't sure why – she wasn't the type of person who broke the rules – but she'd reached out, almost by compulsion, and let her fingertips barely graze the surface of the canvas over the place where the artist had signed it, the first time she'd ever touched a painting in a museum in her life.

The moment had been like an out of body experience, but luckily Avery realized what she was doing and had snapped out of it. She'd jerked her hand back, breaking into a cold sweat as she imagined alarms going off around the building and security guards converging on her, tackling her to the ground for daring to put her hands where they didn't belong. But nothing had happened. By some miracle, no alarm had gone off. No one had seen her brief, reckless touch.

But in that terrified moment, her mutant abilities had manifested.

She'd fallen into a trance. It was the only way she could

describe what happened next, what was happening to her even now, while Jane's voice still echoed in her ear. She could no longer feel the ground beneath her feet. Yet she wasn't afraid. Somehow, she knew she was safe. The colors of the painting ran together, woman and tower blurring, and she felt as if she were being pulled toward the painting by a string attached to her ribcage. The heady smells of paint and turpentine filled her nostrils, and then just as suddenly were replaced by the odors and traffic sounds of a busy city.

Avery blinked her vision clear and looked around, a sense of wellbeing and belonging settling around her shoulders like a warm blanket. It was as if a door had opened in her mind, allowing her to step back in time to stand in the artist's studio. Ruby Alano was right across the room from her, a stooped, white-haired woman humming softly as she ran her brush over an unfinished canvas with such soft, delicate movements that it hardly seemed she touched its surface at all.

The hands were what always struck Avery, the ochre skin with deeper brown cracks and lines of age, yet they were steady as a surgeon's and moved with a precision and grace that took her breath away. It hit her, as it did every time she fell into her visions, that she was seeing the creation of *The Woman and the Tower* before her eyes, a painting that would one day be viewed by millions of visitors every year at the museum.

But the psychometric visions encompassed more than that. If Avery walked to the window, she could look out and see the busy New York City streets, people crowding the sidewalks outside the window, old cars jockeying for position in the constant press of traffic.

She hadn't ever tried to leave the studio, to see how far she could take the vision. In truth she'd never had a desire to. This vision was more than enough for her. In it, she could keep one part of her mind in the past, while another stayed dimly aware of what was going on in the museum, and she could still carry on a conversation with Jane.

No one else could see her or hear her in the artist's studio. She was little more than a ghost bearing witness to a moment in the past. Even so, the scene was vibrant and alive to Avery, touching all five of her senses.

It should have been impossible. But that was psychometry. Or so she'd been told.

When she'd finally come out of that first vision, she hadn't known what happened or what to do. But after that day her ability had never manifested for any other objects she'd touched.

Once she was able to drive herself, she'd gone back to the Edmonton museum and visited the painting. This time, she hadn't even needed to touch it for the vision to manifest. But again, instead of frightening her, standing in Ruby Alano's studio had been a comfort, like coming to visit an old friend, even if the artist could not see or acknowledge her. She'd stayed at the museum the entire day, surfacing from the vision only to eat or draw in the sketchbook she always carried with her. Her desire to draw, to create, was always strongest when she came out of the visions. Watching Ruby Alano at work was inspiring, and made Avery feel a part of the art world in a way she'd only felt when she was with her father, watching him work and express his passions.

She must have looked strange to the tour groups passing by, sitting and staring dreamily at the same painting all day long, punctuated by periods of concentrated sketching in between. She worked fast, almost feverishly, pouring out everything she felt and saw from the vision onto the paper. Even if she would never be as talented as Ruby Alano, the connection was there, and that was what was important. She was a part of something bigger than herself. It was a heady, intoxicating feeling.

"I'd love to see the painting in person someday," Jane was saying, and Avery felt a stab of longing deep inside her.

"I'd love to show it to you," she murmured, as she watched Ruby Alano move her brush in a gentle curve over the canvas to fill in her subject's thick fall of dark hair.

In the grand scheme of mutant powers, Avery's felt like a harmless gift. She wasn't afraid of it, and at first she'd felt certain she could keep it a secret for the rest of her life if she had to. But the doubts kept creeping in.

What if it got worse? So far, only the Alano painting had triggered her visions, but what if eventually every old object she touched sent her thoughts spinning into the past? What if someday she could no longer control it?

Some of that anxiety came from the stories she'd heard about dangerous mutants with world-shaking powers. She hated that the fear and ignorance of the world had infected her as well, but she couldn't help it. Even without those influences, she'd known on some level that she should get advice from other mutants about her powers, just to make sure. Yet the idea of exposing herself even that much... what if someone found out?

Fortunately, that didn't happen. She wrote a letter, of all things, to a Professor Charles Xavier. She'd half-expected him never to receive it, but he had, and shockingly, he wrote back right away. After they'd exchanged a few letters and she'd been able to answer some questions he'd posed to her about her abilities, he'd eventually been able to meet with her in Edmonton. She hadn't told her dad what she was doing. She hadn't wanted to put any more strain on him and his health.

So many things could have gone wrong, but they hadn't.

She'd met with the professor, who'd described to her his theory that she had psychometric powers. He'd even given her an old coin to use as practice, hoping it would trigger a vision. She hadn't been able to get anything to happen when she touched it, but that didn't stop her from trying every day, even now. He'd also offered her a place at his school to investigate the extent of her abilities.

She'd had to refuse, of course. She didn't want to put her dad through that fear and uncertainty, not after everything he already had to deal with at work and with his health. The professor had understood, but he hadn't wanted her to feel like she had nowhere to go if her abilities ever escalated. He'd given her names and phone numbers of people to reach out to if she ever changed her mind and wanted to explore her abilities further at the school.

When her dad had passed, she'd stayed in Edmonton and gone to college, studying art while grieving. Between the inheritance and life insurance, her dad had left her enough money to be comfortable and to pay for school, so at least she hadn't had to worry too much about finances. Time passed, and she'd gradually gotten used to being alone. Then she'd embraced it. No attachments meant there was little chance her secrets would be revealed. The isolation felt safe.

The tradeoff was she ached with loneliness.

During that time, the painting was her solace, her refuge. She went to the museum every day it was open, falling into the visions, and watched art being created before her eyes. She felt connected to Alano and her work like never before, and that studio was like her own private world. A place where she could forget everything, even herself.

It had become irresistible. And people began to notice.

At first, it was innocent. The guards started recognizing her and saying hello. Then the docents and some of the students who came there regularly. But when they realized she only ever came for one thing, one painting, the strange looks and the whispers began. For the first time in a long time, Avery was afraid. What if they saw through her somehow? What if they guessed what she was?

That's when she left. She didn't just leave the city, she left Canada altogether and transferred to art school in California.

Then she met Jane.

Together they embarked on a year of a happiness she hadn't known in a long time. It was a new start, a chance to leave the pain, grief, and uncertainty of her past behind her.

She wasn't alone anymore.

But she couldn't get the painting out of her head.

It still called to her. She saw the tower in her dreams at night, her hands reaching toward the windows that stared at her like eyes. Waiting. The dreams were so vivid, they should have frightened her, but they didn't. She'd wanted to tell someone about them, but it was the one piece of her life she didn't dare share with anyone, not even Jane.

After months of those restless, dream-filled nights, she'd finally taken out the list of names and numbers and started calling. She learned, to her sorrow, that Professor Xavier was gone, but surely someone out there could still help her, so she kept calling.

Scott Summers had been the one to finally answer.

Now she was back where she started in Canada, even though leaving Jane was one of the hardest decisions she'd ever had to make.

She'd been away long enough that the guards and docents no longer remembered her, but she was still careful to change her hair and clothing style, and to make sure she spent time in other parts of the museum as well, so she wouldn't draw undue attention to herself. So here she was, comfortable and stuck, lying to Jane about a study abroad program while she tried to understand herself and her strange abilities.

Avery hesitated. Yet here was the perfect opening to confess everything.

*Just say it. Just tell her what you are.*

The idea of it made her lightheaded with terror and the promise of relief. To finally have it out in the open, no more secrets. She'd be unmoored and unburdened. Maybe she could even tell Jane she loved her.

But there the lovely fantasy wobbled and came crashing down in her head. What if Avery told her, and Jane said she didn't want anything to do with mutants? Scott's warning rang in her head, the gentle reminder that even people you cared for deeply could let hate and fear twist them up inside. They could disappoint you.

They could abandon you.

She swallowed a lump in her throat. Staring at Ruby Alano, she found herself wishing she could talk to the artist and ask for her advice. It was silly, of course. She was just an image, a scene from an old movie repeating itself. But Avery needed guidance. She had to tell Jane the truth, but she didn't know if she had the strength.

And in that instant of misery and uncertainty, Ruby Alano's brush stilled on the canvas, and the artist raised her head and looked Avery right in the eyes.

Avery froze. Her awareness of the museum vanished. Jane's voice on the other end of the phone faded, replaced by a high-pitched ringing in her ears. Ruby Alano's lips moved as if she were speaking, but no sound issued from her. There was only that ringing that felt like an ice pick grinding against her temples.

"Wh- What's going on?" Avery stammered. "What are you trying to say?"

No, no, no. This wasn't right. This couldn't *happen*. The visions were supposed to be harmless. She wasn't supposed to be able to interact with them. The professor had told her so.

What if he'd been wrong?

Gasping, Avery squeezed her eyes shut, snapping herself out of her vision. The sounds of the museum filtered back into her consciousness all at once. She was grateful she was sitting on the bench. No way her trembling legs would have been able to hold her upright.

"Avery?"

She jumped at the sound of Jane's voice. That's right. She was still on the phone with Jane. How long had she been sitting there, lost in her vision?

"I'm here," she said, her voice coming out choked. "Did you say something?"

"Nothing important," Jane said, but she sounded subdued. "Are you all right, Avery? I thought we lost the connection."

"I'm sorry," Avery said, scrambling for an explanation for her strange behavior. Her heart was beating so fast she thought she was on the verge of a panic attack. "You're right, the... reception's not very good in here. I think I lost you for a minute."

"Or I lost you," Jane said softly, making everything inside Avery contract. "Listen, if it's OK, I think I'm going to bail out a little early on the tour. I have a lot of studying to do, and I'm meeting some friends later for dinner."

"Sure, I understand." Avery's voice sounded hollow in her ears. She felt the same way she did just before a trance, but not in the usual comforting way. She was lost, couldn't feel her feet pressing into the ground. "Can I call you tomorrow?" she asked, hope straining her voice. "We could pick up where we left off." She'd planned to stay in Edmonton another day anyway. One more day before she had to go back to the frozen wasteland. That way she'd have time to think, to figure out what had happened with her visions. She could handle this. She just needed time.

Jane hesitated, and Avery held her breath. "Let me text you," she said finally, "and we'll go from there. All right?"

The uncertainty in Jane's voice was killing her, but she reminded herself that anything was better than outright rejection. "Of course it's all right," Avery managed. "Have a good evening, Jane."

"You too, Avery."

"I miss you so much."

"Yeah, I miss you too." There was a soft beep as Jane severed the connection.

Avery took the earpiece out of her ear and sat staring at the ground a minute.

She was a coward. That's all there was to it. But she was a coward who still had a girlfriend. At least for now.

She took a steadying breath to try to calm her racing heart. Then she glanced at her cell phone clock. There were still a couple of hours before the museum closed. She could sit in Alano's studio for a little while longer, if she wanted.

But when she looked up at the painting, a chill passed through her body. She tore her gaze away before the vision could sweep her up.

What was happening to her?

# CHAPTER SEVEN

"Passing over Chicago now. We should be arriving at the island in the next five minutes."

In her ship form, E.V.A.'s voice echoed all around him. Fantomex sat in a chair in the center of the cockpit, a narrow console to his left and right, a VR unit covering his eyes, offering him a direct connection to the ship's navigation and weapons systems should it become necessary for them to engage in aerial combat. Not that he thought they'd need to on this mission. They were coming in under cover of darkness, and E.V.A.'s stealth systems were second to none, but one could never be too careful.

"Why did they decide to set the exhibition out in the middle of nowhere on the lake?" he wondered aloud. "It's only accessible by air and water. Hardly makes it easy on the droves of tourists coming in to see the art."

"The city is well equipped to transport tourists via their many water taxi services," E.V.A. said. "As for why the decision was made to put the exhibition on the island, according to my research, there was some concern about size. The building and grounds take up quite a number of acres. There were also concerns about security following a recent incident at the Grace Museum of Natural History."

That piqued his interest. "What sort of incident?"

"It dealt directly with a pair of students from the Institute, as a matter of fact," E.V.A. said. "I questioned Cyclops about it, but he appeared reluctant to discuss the details. Triage was in the room at the time, and I sensed the incident involved him in some way, which would explain Cyclops' reluctance to speak. Perhaps if you asked the young man directly, he may be more forthcoming."

Or perhaps he also liked to keep his own counsel. Fantomex could respect that.

What he could not respect was the architectural nightmare coming into view on his VR unit as they approached the island. No wonder he hadn't recognized the museum at first.

"They managed to achieve the train station look of the d'Orsay, but they forgot all of the elegance and history," he grumbled.

"I have observed that human beings tend to find comfort in the familiar," E.V.A. commented. "Perhaps the building is a reflection of that impulse."

More likely it was a reflection of someone's impulse to create a giant warehouse with an atrium pasted on it with all the care and consideration of a two year-old. Just looking at it was making his head hurt.

"Any sign of Cluster?" he asked as they drew closer.

"The exhibition is closed for the night, and I'm not detecting any heat signatures inside the facility itself," E.V.A.

said, putting up a larger view of the island and exhibition grounds across his screen. "There are guardhouses with two occupants each in the front and rear of the building. Preliminary analysis indicates the guards also periodically make a sweep of the area on foot. If I hover above the facility for an hour or so in stealth mode, I can collect data on their exact movements so we know how long we have to accomplish our mission. There will be minimal risk."

"Where's the fun in that?" Fantomex scoffed. "Take us to the roof and we'll head inside from there. I promise you they'll never know we were here."

"As you wish."

They glided silently down, hovering above the barrel-vaulted atrium that ran the length of the building. Fantomex deactivated the VR unit, waiting while it peeled back from his face. He put on his mask, making sure the ceramic dampening plates were snug in place. He checked his weapons, then strode to the hatch in the floor at the center of the cockpit. It slid back at his approach, and a cool night breeze blew across his body, bringing with it the smell of the lake and the distant sounds of fretful night birds gliding above the water. He looked down to gauge the distance, then stepped off casually, letting his body drop through the hatch.

He landed lightly on the atrium's surface, gripping the metal ridges along the glass for balance. E.V.A. glided soundlessly down to hover next to him, and then transformed into her humanoid form, perching gracefully in front of him in a charcoal costume and mask that covered just the upper part of her face.

He nodded to her, and as one, they slid down the side of the atrium, clinging to the metal ridges until they ran out of handholds. They dropped to a level portion of the roof, landing with barely a sound. Fantomex went into a crouch, listening. It was so quiet out here on the lake, they couldn't afford to make any noise.

They waited, but there was no stirring or shouts from the guards on the ground, only the sound of waves lapping the shore nearby.

Carefully, he stood, his coat swishing around his hips. He was in his element now, the anticipation of a heist thrumming through his veins, even though technically they weren't here to abscond with anything.

Well, he would never rule out a little window shopping, and if he found something that he simply couldn't live without...

"Over there," E.V.A. whispered, pointing to a door roughly thirty feet from where they stood. Keeping low and in the shadows, they moved swiftly across the roof.

Fantomex examined the lock on the door critically. Based on their pre-mission research, he'd expected keycard entry and an intrusion detection system, and that was certainly what this looked like, but it wasn't as sophisticated as he'd hoped. He would have relished the challenge of something state of the art.

Reaching into a hidden pocket of his costume, he pulled out a metallic green keycard, a precise match to the one used by the security company – Atlas Tech Services – that had been hired to guard the temporary exhibition. A part of him had wanted to try to foil the security system the old-fashioned way, but he was anxious to find out what Cluster was up to, and it had seemed easier to have E.V.A. fabricate a keycard from the company and stroll in as if he belonged there.

Which, this being a museum, was a given.

He swiped the card, waited a beat for the lights on the keypad to go green, then tried the door. It creaked a bit louder than he would have liked, but not enough for the sound to carry all the way down to the guards' station. They were in.

"Can you hack the surveillance systems?" he asked as they proceeded down a short flight of stairs that ended in another door requiring another swipe.

"I can," E.V.A. confirmed. "Their server room is onsite. I was planning to upload standard looped video footage from the last hour to cover our movements. May I proceed?"

He started to tell her to go ahead, but then an idea occurred to him. Cyclops and Emma Frost would not like it, of course, which made it all the more tantalizing. "Do it, but bring the cameras in the main sculpture gallery back online just before we leave," he said.

"You want to appear on the surveillance footage?" E.V.A. couldn't keep the surprise out of her voice. "But why risk capture just to–" she stopped. "You want Cluster and the rest of the world to know that you were here. That you're back."

He'd forgotten how perceptive she was. "Never hurts to leave a calling card."

"It's entirely possible you'll draw the attention of organizations like S.H.I.E.L.D."

He shrugged. "Life is full of risks. Let's go. We're wasting time."

They set off again, moving quicker this time. He knew he was being reckless, that he was putting them both in unnecessary danger, but the thrill of it was impossible to ignore. Yes, he was back, and he did want the whole world to know it.

Especially Cluster and Weapon XIII.

He'd studied the exhibition's interior layout from maps that E.V.A. had acquired online, though it had hardly been necessary. This space was also loosely patterned after the Musée d'Orsay, a place he knew as well as he knew any building in the world, save perhaps for the Louvre. Being in familiar territory was useful for their mission, he had to admit, but the stab of disappointment remained. All this was just a pale imitation, a replica. There was nothing original to gasp at or be surprised by.

Another overpowering irony. The universe really did have a sense of humor where he was concerned.

The statue gallery was on the first floor. They found the main stairs at the north end of the building and proceeded down, keeping to the shadows as much as possible. There was enough illumination from the emergency lights and the subtle moonlight filtering in through the atrium to guide their way.

The ground floor of the museum once again loosely mimicked the d'Orsay, with a central nave flanked by galleries overlooked by the second-floor terraces, which were lined with paintings and pottery. The sculpture display in the nave was the centerpiece, though it wasn't a large collection, and it was again painfully obvious that these were replicas, but still, if he squinted, he could pretend he was in Paris, walking among the giants of art. It was always important to be able to pretend.

"There she is," E.V.A. said, pointing to the far corner. "Diana of Versailles."

From a distance, the statue was luminous in the moonlight and appeared entirely untouched, with no signs of tampering. Even as they drew closer, Fantomex struggled to see how Cluster had defaced the statue. Diana the huntress stood in the familiar pose, ready to spring after her chosen prey, a small deer prancing at her side. Her right arm reached for her quiver, ready to draw an arrow.

An arrow that was no longer there.

"Extraordinary," he said, stepping closer. The arrow right beneath the huntress's fingertips, the one she intended to bury in the heart of her prey – that was what Cluster had taken – but it should have been impossible. Fantomex studied the statue from every angle, but there was no damage. It wasn't as if the stone arrow had been ripped from its nest, leaving cracks and scars behind. The arrow was simply missing, as if it had never been there at all.

A strange foreboding sensation lifted the hairs at Fantomex's neck. It wasn't just the missing arrow that unsettled him. Something about the statue itself was strange and… wrong somehow, beyond its being a replica. But he couldn't put his finger on the source of the strangeness.

"Will you analyze this, please? he asked E.V.A., his attention still fixed on Diana's quiver. "Scan every inch of it and tell me what you find."

"What is it you suspect?" E.V.A. asked, watching him.

"I don't know, but I don't think this statue is simply a

replica," he said. "There's something different about it." Which meant there was much more going on here than he'd thought.

He was still staring at the statue when the Belleek vase came spinning out of the darkness, aimed right at his face.

His body reacted on instinct. He caught the vase by the neck, briefly juggling it from hand to hand to soften the impact before tucking it under his arm. In one smooth motion, he drew a knife and sent it flying back at the shadow that had thrown the porcelain missile. The figure ducked, and the knife buried itself in the far wall, inches from an 1899 Intimist painting.

Cluster stepped into the wan light, holding a second Belleek, this one larger with an olive glaze. If he'd been disconcerted at seeing her image before, her appearance in the flesh threw him even more off-kilter. She was a walking shadow, apart but tethered to him, her gaze assessing him even as he studied her. Her long brown hair was tied back from her face. Once again, she wore no mask, but otherwise her costume was quite similar to his, though her white and black coat was sleeveless, and she carried a large, thoroughly modern composite bow in her free hand that would have consumed Diana with envy.

He pulled himself together. "About time you showed yourself," he said. "Care to explain all this?"

"Please keep a respectable distance and don't interact with the art," she replied, in a chirruping imitation of a tour guide, "so future generations can enjoy the same beauty we do today."

He scowled at her. "*You* were the one who threw the vase at *me*."

Her eyes danced. "True."

She chucked the second vase at him.

He caught that one too, and quickly set both vases on the floor, remaining in a defensive crouch. "E.V.A., weapons systems?"

"Available," E.V.A. offered, though she didn't sound happy about it.

Cluster turned to E.V.A. and smiled warmly. "Hello, old friend. I've missed you very much."

"And I you," E.V.A. said, her amber gaze flicking uncertainly between her and Fantomex.

"Don't worry," Cluster said. "I just need to have a word with our boy for a minute." She turned back to Fantomex, drawing an arrow with a strange-looking tip from a quiver on her back. "Surely, he's not afraid of some light sparring, one on one?"

Now that was a tantalizing invitation, and a few short minutes ago he would have jumped at the chance. But the statue had changed things, thrown him off his purpose. Right now he wanted answers, so he found himself, for once, being the voice of reason. He really hated that.

"This isn't the time, Cluster," he said. "You know the minute we start fighting, the guards are going to show up and end the party before it gets good."

She tilted her head, pasting an innocent expression on her face. "Are they, though? Shouldn't they have been here by now? I think they're probably asleep at their posts, poor dears."

He gritted his teeth. Of course, she would have to one-up him by taking out the entire security force singlehandedly.

"What are you playing at here?" he demanded. "It's uncouth to target the same venue twice in a row. I assumed you'd have more class. What is it you want?"

She leveled the strange-looking arrow at him. "That's a rude way to greet someone who's practically family."

"Are we, though?" he mimicked, snatching up one of the vases and holding it in front of his chest like a shield. It was a calculated risk, but he didn't believe she would wantonly destroy any of the true art or artifacts here. She'd known he would catch the vases, just as he'd known his knife wouldn't have touched that Darawey painting.

Out of the corner of his eye, he noticed E.V.A. stepping back, giving them space. It was obvious she wanted no part of this squabble. Not that he blamed her. Divided loyalties didn't even begin to cover this situation.

Still, it stung.

Cluster eyed him thoughtfully. She let the bow dip. "You know, I've actually been trying to come up with a good word for what we three are now," she said. "Any thoughts?"

"How about, I'm Fantomex, and the rest of you are imposters."

"Oh, you're no fun at all." Cluster glanced at the Diana statue, briefly arranging her body in a similar pose. "Mine's much better."

"What's yours?"

She flashed him a grin as broad as the Cheshire cat's. "Obviously, I'm not telling you after you called me an imposter."

In a lightning move, she loosed the arrow at him.

Well, not *at* him precisely, a fact he realized as soon as he dove out of the way, careful to keep his Belleek shield from smashing on the tiled floor. She fired at the ground, and the weighted tip of the arrow burst, sending up a wall of smoke that billowed outward in a small mushroom cloud and completely filled the nave.

In seconds he lost sight of both Cluster and E.V.A. It was a good tactic, separating them all, but Fantomex could take advantage of being hidden just as well as his counterpart.

Drawing another knife, he backed up until his shoulders brushed against the paneled wall near the stairs. Sliding into a crouch, he carefully set the Belleek vase aside as he squinted into the smoke, searching for signs of movement.

"You know, I was hoping you'd be fun when we met again," came Cluster's voice from somewhere within the white fog. "I've been wanting to check on you for months. I missed you – more fool me – and now look at us, fighting like children."

He knew that to answer would risk giving away his position, but he couldn't let that jab pass. "I didn't start this fight!" he called out, using the echoing space to help shield his location. "I came to see why you stole a piece of the Diana statue. I came because you *invited* me!"

There was a little silence from within the smoke, which was beginning to dissipate now. Before it cleared, Fantomex took the opportunity to move along the wall, keeping low to the ground, working his way nearer to where he thought her voice had come from.

"How do you know I wanted you here?" Cluster asked. She'd moved again. It sounded like she was on one of the second-floor terraces now.

"Oh, please," he scoffed. "You let yourself get caught on

surveillance footage without your mask. If you'd turned to the camera and winked, you couldn't have made it more obvious that you wanted this place to stand out amongst all your other heists. You wanted me here, and I came, so tell me what's going on. You should never have been able to steal an arrow from that statue. How did you do it?"

He adjusted his grip on the knife, but there was no response. For a second he thought she wasn't going to answer. Then a soft *swishing* sound made him freeze in place. He held his breath, ears straining. There it was again, the swish of fabric, followed by the lightest footfall.

Coming up behind him.

He spun, grabbing blindly, and his hand landed on Cluster's upper arm. He yanked her forward, hoping to throw her off balance, but she compensated by slamming straight into him with all her weight, driving them both to the ground. He managed to bring his knife up, the point hovering just shy of her stomach. A grin spread across his face – an instant before he felt her own blade rasping over the fabric of the mask that covered his throat.

She was also smiling. "You got me," she said. "I was hoping you'd come." She gripped his wrist with her free hand. Her fingers shifted, pinching his skin.

The move tickled. "What are you doing?" He tried to wiggle free, but she had a secure grip on him.

"Checking your pulse," she said, and had the nerve to shush him. "Hang on, I'm counting. Good, it's right where I'd expect it to be after that much exertion."

"Exertion!"

She ignored him. "E.V.A., has he been eating enough?"

"What are you going on about?"

E.V.A. stepped out of the clearing smoke. "According to him, the food at the Institute has been nutritional but... lacking in substance," she said.

Cluster made a noise in her throat. "I'm sure he said it less politely than that. So, you're a picky eater, are you? Don't be. You're going to have to get more protein to build back that muscle quicker."

He gave her his best dead-eyed stare, the one that usually sent his enemies running for the nearest exit. "Did you forget I have a knife to your gut?"

She tsked. "Don't be crude, and no, I didn't forget. Why didn't you use your misdirection power on me during our fight?"

Oh, she aimed right where it hurt. "Because I no longer have it," he snapped. "Why didn't *you*?"

The flicker of regret in her eyes was answer enough.

"I see," he said. "So our goth brother was the only one to retain that ability."

"Among other things." To his shock, Cluster lifted her knife away from his neck and sheathed it on her belt. "Truce?"

He studied her, searching for a deception, but also because he was deeply curious. Up close, she looked nothing like him and yet... and yet there was a recognition, a knowledge that went deeper than the surface. Even if he had never seen her before, he could have picked her out of a crowd of thousands. Something in her was still a part of him. They were connected, just as he and E.V.A. were connected. What did that make them? What did it make him?

It was the strangest feeling, staring at something that used to belong solely to him. Something irretrievably lost.

He wasn't sure how long he lay there, staring up at her, but at some point he realized she was examining him too, and maybe something of those same thoughts flashed in her eyes, but then she blinked and looked away, dispelling the moment.

Cautiously, he drew the knife away from her, and they got up. Fantomex felt suddenly uncomfortable, as if he'd given away too much, even though he hadn't said a word. That, in turn, made him irritated. Striving for a distraction, he marched over to the Diana statue. "So how did you do it?" he asked, pointing at the huntress's quiver. "How did you take the arrow, and why?"

She joined him at the statue, circling it slowly, studying the elegant figure. He was struck again by how similar she looked to the goddess of the hunt. "How I did it is easy," she said. "You've already realized this isn't a normal statue. Have E.V.A. and the others at the Institute study the data you've collected tonight. It might take a bit, but you'll see what I'm talking about."

"Or you could save me the suspense and explain it," he said dryly, knowing full well that she wouldn't.

She smiled faintly. "As for why I came here, I wanted to know that you were all right after everything that happened." A shadow crossed her face. "I imagine the last few months have been difficult for you."

There was that feeling inside him again, that hollowness. He couldn't escape it, no matter how many distractions were put in front of him. Then, as her words sank in, he realized something else. All of that, just now, the fighting and throwing of vases, the cat and mouse game in the smoke, had been a performance. She'd been testing him, seeing how he was physically.

Checking up on him and scolding him like he was a child who was unable to take care of himself.

He nodded to the statue. "Is this some kind of test for my mental faculties, then?" He sneered. "A little puzzle you devised to play with me? If so, you can save your energies. I don't need anyone looking after me."

She sighed, her smile fading. "I thought you'd be difficult, but really, I was hoping for more support than this. It's going to make things so much harder going forward." She folded her arms. "If you don't want me looking out for you, that's fine, but don't rebuff the Institute so casually. Stay there and get stronger. I need help, and I need you at your best when the time comes."

"Well, that's suitably cryptic," he said. "What does that–"

He cut himself off. He caught the way her gaze shifted, not meeting his. She'd subtly placed the statue between them while they bantered, and she was fiddling with something attached to her wrist, some sort of device.

He lunged for her, just as an oval of bright light spun into being behind her. The flash of radiance temporarily blinded him, and he stumbled. By the time he'd righted himself, the light – portal, actually – had already swallowed her up and collapsed in on itself.

Her disembodied voice left him a brief farewell. "We'll see each other again soon, Fantomex, if you do what you're told. Be safe."

Then she was gone, leaving him and E.V.A. alone in the

silent gallery. As Cluster had promised, no guards stormed in to investigate the noise they'd made during their fight. It was obvious Cluster had taken care of them and any other obstacles that might have gotten in her way. She'd probably been waiting here for him for hours.

His hands balled into fists. Even though he'd held his own in their fight, it still felt like she'd gotten the better of him in every possible way.

He rounded on E.V.A., who was standing silently by the statue. "Thanks for stepping in there to stop her from leaving. Always a comfort to know your partner has your back."

She didn't react to the biting words except to incline her head in acknowledgment, which, instead of appeasing him, only ratcheted up his anger.

"Come to think of it, I'm surprised you didn't accompany her." He gestured to the space where the portal had been. "Since you missed each other so very much. It was truly a touching exchange. I nearly cried."

Still, she said nothing. Her silence, and the quiet censure in her eyes, were far worse than if she'd just called him an insufferable pig and stomped off.

"Did you know that was what she was doing?" he pressed, unable to let it go. "Checking up on me, testing me?"

"I suspected," E.V.A. said, "but I didn't know for sure." She added, "Believe it or not, I am also finding it a challenge to adjust to this new state you find yourselves in. You are as different and as alike to me as you are to each other. I have no desire to hurt or be hurt by either of you."

Yes, he was definitely an insufferable pig. "We should

head back," he said gruffly. "Our gracious hosts will likely
be getting nervous since we haven't reported in lately." He
looked at her, wondering what she was thinking, but once
again that mask of impassivity was firmly in place, her amber
eyes refusing to give anything away. "Do you have the data
on the statue?"

"I need time to analyze it. Whatever she wants us to find,
we'll find it," she assured him.

"What would I do without you?"

She walked past him and said over her shoulder, "Before all
this, I would have said without your central nervous system
you'd most likely expire on the spot, which is why I never get
a vacation." She hesitated, her voice dropping. "Now I find it
much harder to predict what you will and won't do, and what
the consequences will be."

He'd like to think the person he used to be wouldn't have
acted so snappish, so insecure, but maybe he was giving his
former self too much credit. He kept forgetting that he wasn't
the only one who'd lost something vital in all this. E.V.A. had
been affected by everything he'd gone through as well, and
she was adjusting to this new state of being as best she could.

Looking after him. The weakest one.

"What if we found a lovely wine bar with a terrace view
and stopped for a drink on the way back?" He extended
the apology tentatively as they made their way up the steps
toward the roof. "There have to be some decent vintages
somewhere in this city, after all. Food and clothing shops
too. I could use a refresh in the wardrobe department, and
there's nothing worth eating back at that dreary facility, so
we could take care of that problem, too."

"No doubt we could," E.V.A. said, pausing to examine a Batista as they ascended. "But none of these places you mention will be open at this hour."

She was right, of course. It was nearly two am. He stretched, cracking his knuckles. "That's never been a hindrance to me before, remember?" Some things didn't change, even with a split resurrection. "What about a Beaujolais and a late-night snack? I'm sure we could find something exquisite, and I could beg your forgiveness in more detail."

This time she gave a soft laugh, and he felt a bit lighter.

# CHAPTER EIGHT

They arrived back at the Institute just after dawn, flying over sheets of rippling snow that had been shaped into jagged crescents by the overnight wind. Defiant bursts of orange and yellow sunrise pushed back the gray light over the desolate landscape, creating a breathtaking canvas for the arriving day.

The facility was quiet when they landed, the hangar bay deserted and echoing. Most of the students and faculty must still have been in bed. Taking advantage of the absence of prying eyes, Fantomex deposited two large boxes and some paper bags in the kitchen, pushing their contents to the back of the pantry and refrigerator to conceal them. Then he returned to his room, which, though it was in the dormitory wing with the other students, stood blessedly apart from the rest of the occupied rooms.

He knew this wasn't done for his benefit. Cyclops and Emma Frost didn't trust him, so they didn't put him too close to the other students. Despite E.V.A.'s assertion that he could find friends and allies here, in the end, he knew what he was, especially in their eyes. He couldn't blame them for being cautious. How could they be sure of him or his intentions when he wasn't sure of himself anymore?

And after the encounter with Cluster at the exhibition, he'd come away feeling even more adrift.

He lay down on the ridiculously uncomfortable bed to try to get a few hours' sleep, but it was fitful, full of dreams invaded by statues.

No, that wasn't right. Not true statues.

Replicas. Simulations. They marched before him like he was in a hall of mirrors that endlessly reflected his face. As he watched, trapped in the dream, they changed shape, their eyes glowing with sinister light. They melted into Cluster's face, then E.V.A.'s, even Weapon XIII, before disappearing into a shadowy void where he could hear distant voices laughing and whispering his name.

"You are what they made you to be."

"A perfect killer."

"An image, a replica cobbled together from bits of history and story."

Suddenly, he was staring at a statue of his former self, battered and torn by the Skinless Man, the artist capturing him in the instant of death. The moment was frozen perfectly in white marble, a morbid copy, but the eyes… oh, the eyes were still alive and terrified, the soul within knowing full well its fate.

If he were awake, he would have scoffed at the heavy-handedness of the metaphor, but in the way of dreams, his mind pulled back from the safety of reality, denied the release of waking, until all he could see were those terrified eyes.

He couldn't help it. The fear infected him too.

The marble around the statue's chest began to bubble and melt. Fantomex watched, unable to look away, as his duplicate's eyes bulged, as he tried to scream but couldn't. A perfect marble heart, quivering and bone white, rose up out of the wreck of the statue's chest and pulsed once, before exploding into a thousand gritty shards. Still there was no sound, only the pain in those eyes that held him captive as spidery cracks appeared in the statue's head. Wider and wider, jagged and black, until the marble shattered into three chunks and fell to the ground. He looked down at them, but the eyes were gone, and the broken statue was unrecognizable as anything that had ever been alive.

"Will there be anything left of you when the world has had its fill?"

The whispers faded, and Fantomex let the void take him.

When he woke again, a headache pressed at his temples like a vise. He refused to blame the dream for it. Too much good wine late at night. That's all it was.

The clock on the wall of the dormitory said it was half-past ten in the morning. He'd slept much longer than he'd intended. Cyclops and Emma Frost would be impatient for their debriefing.

He sat up and moved to the edge of his bed, letting his hands dangle between his knees. He turned them over, looking at the white skin, thinking of marble, and searching unconsciously for cracks.

"You look like death," Emma said, handing him a cup of coffee. "Haven't you been sleeping for the past several hours?" *While we waited on you.* She didn't say the last bit aloud, but it was heavily implied by the arch of her pale brows.

"Lovely to see you too this morning," Fantomex said, raising his coffee cup in salute.

Emma rolled her eyes and sat back down across from him. She was in costume this morning, the intimidating black coat, gloves, and boots giving off an unmistakable *Don't mess with me* aura. He respected her for that, if not for the coffee, which was a watery travesty that coated his taste buds like sediment. Ah, what he wouldn't give for even a basic pour-over system, a grinder, and some beans from Café Mirai. He should have thought to acquire them last night, along with an espresso machine.

They had gathered around a large, scarred table in the Institute's war room for the debriefing. E.V.A. was sitting to his right, out of costume and dressed for comfort and warmth in a new black sweater with coordinating jacket and slacks. One of their many acquisitions last night. Cyclops was at the other end of the table, freshly shaven but casual in jeans and a button-down shirt with the sleeves pushed up. For himself, Fantomex had opted to go sans costume as well, but he'd skipped the shave, which he regretted, and the shower had been another tragedy, the hot water only lasting for a scant few minutes. This place really was like a prison. No wonder the inmates – sorry, students – were starved for pleasure and entertainment.

At least his wardrobe was back in form, and he was proving it with his luxury lamb wool trench coat and trousers, not that anyone in the room but E.V.A. would appreciate it. In fact, the food, the fashion, and the wine had been the only part of last night's escapade that hadn't felt like a failure.

With perfect recall, E.V.A. had filled them in on what had happened and relayed the data she'd collected on the Diana of Versailles statue. A holographic image of it hovered above the table, turning slowly, while a separate close-up of Diana's quiver appeared next to the image.

"It is extraordinary," Cyclops mused, leaning forward to look at the image. "If you didn't know a piece was missing, you'd swear it hadn't been tampered with at all." He glanced at Fantomex. "But if she went to all that trouble to bait you into going to the exhibition, I don't understand why she wouldn't tell you what she's up to."

"Maybe because this is all for fun," Emma interjected before Fantomex could answer. "Maybe she wants to waste our time."

Fantomex couldn't immediately argue with that logic. It had felt like that was exactly what Cluster was doing during their combat last night. Wasting his time.

And humiliating him.

To his surprise, E.V.A. spoke up. "I believe there's more to it than that," she said. "I think Cluster truly does need our help, even though she's being cagey about asking."

"What makes you say that?" Cyclops asked, and Fantomex looked at her expectantly, also curious about the answer.

"It involves speaking candidly about your physiology," E.V.A. said, looking to Fantomex. Her eyes asked permission.

He nodded for her to speak, even though he was getting an uncomfortable feeling in his gut.

"I have spent a fair amount of time analyzing Fantomex's personality and behavior, both before and after his separation," E.V.A. began.

"Not a job for the faint-hearted," Fantomex drawled, taking another drink of sediment.

E.V.A.'s lips twitched, but she was the consummate professional. "This was necessary to maintain the strength of our connection and to anticipate his actions in combat so that we might work successfully in tandem."

"Naturally." Emma sounded impatient. "You're referring to the use of your neuroweapons system."

"That and more," E.V.A. said. "It also helps me anticipate when his body requires healing and when he will make a decision that I would otherwise deem… unwise."

"So she can keep me from getting into too much trouble when I do something foolish," Fantomex translated helpfully. He wasn't sure he really wanted to know where this was going.

"Fantomex, in his previous form, displayed personality traits and inclinations that I could often link to neural activity in the frontal lobe of a specific brain," E.V.A. explained. "One brain represented his sense of morality, duty, and even a certain nobility that flourished under the right circumstances, while another brain was largely responsible for his worst impulses and his most selfish desires." She hesitated, then looked pointedly at Fantomex. "The third brain was hardest to interpret, as it occupied that liminal space between those warring states, the mischievous, often sarcastic and sometimes fatalistic side of Fantomex."

"Black, white, and shades of gray," Cyclops said

thoughtfully, exchanging a glance with Emma. "Id, ego, and superego?"

"Not so concrete as that, but yes, it's an adequate analogy," E.V.A. said.

"As much as I enjoy being an 'adequate analogy' for everyone," Fantomex said, "let's get to the point." He held up his hands like a set of scales. "If I'm the sarcastic fatalist, and we assume by his attire that Weapon XIII is the dark, selfish one, then you're saying that leaves Cluster to be the noble one?"

"That's my theory, yes," E.V.A. said. "If I'm correct, I believe Cluster is acting in good faith, even if she pretends otherwise. Therefore, I think we should proceed as she instructed and investigate the statue to the fullest extent possible."

"I still want to find her and have a direct conversation, but after last night's escapade her trail's gone cold," Emma said. She speared Fantomex with a look as he started to speak. "If the next words out of your mouth are 'pun intended', I will end you."

He closed his mouth.

She was right, though. They could stare at the image of the statue all day long, and at the end of it they might pry some secrets from it, but they still wouldn't know how to find Cluster again.

Except… maybe that wasn't the case. Something tickled Fantomex's memory as he replayed in his mind their little dance around the statue. E.V.A. might have been right. Maybe they were nothing more than archetypal personalities at their core. Maybe that's what their creator had intended – no nuance needed for a killing machine, just a balanced trio working as one – but he didn't want to believe it was quite so clear-cut as all that. Cluster was like him, in several specific ways. She prevaricated like he did, dropping half-truths and hints.

Her eyes when she'd said she needed help – she had been telling the truth, but there was more she wasn't saying. And when she'd told him he'd see her again, if he did what he was told… maybe that also held an element of truth.

What had she asked of him?

To stay at the Institute, to get stronger and be ready when she needed him. Did that mean she would contact him here, that he was supposed to sit patiently like a puppy waiting for its master to come home?

Not going to happen.

Or could it be something more banal than that? Something right in front of him?

He sat up straighter in his chair. "What are the closest major cities to the Institute?" he asked, looking to Emma.

"Calgary and Edmonton," she supplied. "Why?"

But E.V.A. was already with him. "There are multiple art museums in both cities." She paused, sifting through data. "None of them have yet been a target of Cluster's."

Not yet, but that was going to change. Fantomex would bet serious money on it. "Hack the surveillance footage for museums in both those cities," he told her. "She'll show up again. I know it. That's what she meant when she said I'd see her soon if I did as I was told. If I stayed here, she'd come to the Institute's backyard."

"How does she know the Institute's location?" Cyclops demanded, color rising in his face.

"She doesn't," E.V.A. assured him, then amended, "at least, not the exact location. She wasn't present for my conversation with Kitty Pryde, but I did reveal that the facility was near Edmonton and Calgary. Nothing more than that."

Cyclops nodded, but he didn't look happy. This was all news to Fantomex, and he wondered why E.V.A. hadn't mentioned any of this before now. He resolved to ask her for more details later, but right now the trail on Cluster was hot, and he intended to follow it.

Emma turned to the computer set into the war room table. E.V.A. joined her and put her hand on the console. "May I?" she asked. When Emma nodded her permission, E.V.A.'s amber eyes flashed as she connected to the Institute's systems. She worked fast. He could see that even Emma seemed impressed, though she tried to hide it. Less than a minute, and scenes flashed on the holo projector above the table, replacing the statue. Museums in Calgary and Edmonton, galleries and pottery collections and sculpture gardens and textile rooms went by in a dizzying blur. E.V.A. scanned the faces as the pictures went, faster than Fantomex could follow, but she had no trouble working through them.

"Here." She froze the image on one particular gallery at the Edmonton Art Museum, gallery number 214, the Arts of the Americas. "The footage is time-stamped this morning, right after the museum opened."

Cluster wasn't wasting any time or bothering with sleep Fantomex noted, as E.V.A. zoomed in on a familiar figure in a hoodie and jeans. This time she made no effort to hide her presence. As the footage rolled, she looked up at the camera, smiled and winked. Despite himself, Fantomex chuckled.

"So, the game is on," he murmured, feeling the familiar excitement of a challenge stirring within him, eclipsing a bit of his earlier malaise. "Freeze it there. I want to see that painting behind her." Everything she was doing was calculated. He refused to believe it was merely chance that she stopped with one painting perfectly framed over her left shoulder as she stared into the camera.

"The painting is Ruby Alano's *The Woman and the Tower*," E.V.A. said, as the image filled the screen. "Painted in New York in 1940."

Fantomex studied the lines and angles, admiring the colors and the Cubist influences at work. It was a lovely painting, but beyond beauty it had little in common with the Diana of Versailles statue other than the fact that both featured female figures.

"We need to get our hands on that painting before Cluster does," he said.

"Agreed," Cyclops said, his tone all business. "The museum is too close to the Institute for comfort, and the more Cluster draws attention to herself with her thefts, the more we risk exposure."

"So let's acquire the painting and bring it here," Emma said, swiping the console to zoom out and let the security footage resume.

"And how do you propose to do that," Fantomex asked, amused, "without drawing the same negative attention to ourselves?"

"By perfectly legal means," she said, crossing her arms, her expression all innocence. "A few phone calls will get me in touch with the museum's board of directors. I'll present myself as an eccentric collector – hideously wealthy, of course – who wants to display the painting during a private party. A slight mental manipulation here, the promise of a sizable donation there, and I should have the painting by tonight."

Cyclops considered the proposal. "I like it. Let's make it happen, nice and quiet, with the lightest touch possible."

"Not a problem. Now, do we–" Emma paused, her attention drawn back to the surveillance footage. She froze it again, this time on a figure sitting on a bench near the painting. "Is that… Avery Torres?" She shot a questioning look at Cyclops. "You let her go to Edmonton again?"

"She asked to leave for a few days. Apparently there was a disruption in one of her classes that put her on edge." His ruby quartz lenses turned ominously in Fantomex's direction.

"What?" Fantomex was indignant. "I didn't do anything to her. We were simply engaging in a spirited debate… and then Magneto tried to crush me with a chair."

"At any rate," Cyclops said, in the tone of an exhausted parent, "it seemed important to her, so I asked Magik to teleport her to Edmonton. None of the students are prisoners here," he reminded Emma.

"Despite all evidence to the contrary," Fantomex muttered. He glanced at the figure and winced. Avery Torres, his loudest critic from that disaster of a lecture. He hadn't been paying much attention to her that day, but he remembered. Seeing her now, he couldn't help but note she was a faint reflection of the woman in the painting, with a similar thick fall of hair down her back, though hers was done in small cornrows and gathered into a ponytail. She was dressed in jeans and a white cable knit sweater. In the footage she alternated between staring at the painting and tapping on a cell phone she had clutched in her hands.

"Typical." He dismissed her with a sigh. "The art isn't enough to keep her attention. She needs the million and one distractions of her tiny rectangular supercomputer to keep her happy."

Emma cocked an eyebrow. "Says the man who travels with a techno-organic being who puts the power of supercomputers to shame."

E.V.A. inclined her head, accepting the compliment.

Emma wasn't done with Cyclops. "I don't mind Avery coming and going," she said, "although this teleporting back and forth carries its own risks, and you know it. It's more that I worry about her commitment. Does she want to learn to control her powers or not? That takes time and patience, and if she's distracted by something out there–" she made a vague gesture to the museum gallery where Avery sat "–then she's not going to accomplish anything here, and she's wasting everyone's time, especially her own."

"You say that as if it's a simple matter to sever ties to the life she was leading before her whole world upended itself," Fantomex found himself saying. When the others looked at him in surprise, he realized he'd just defended the girl. What on earth was getting into him?

He stood and headed for the door, signaling a rather abrupt ending to the meeting, but he was tired and bored with these prosaic concerns. Why should he care whether Avery Torres, a girl who had no patience for *him*, succeeded in her education here or not?

"Let me know when you've secured the painting," he said on his way out. "I'm going to follow Ms Torres' example and go out for the day myself. Fresh air's good for the recovery and all that." He didn't give them a chance to reply. He just walked away.

He went back to his room long enough to retrieve his costume and change. He immediately felt more secure slipping the mask over his face, the ceramic plates shielding his thoughts from prying telepaths.

E.V.A. waited for him in the hall outside his room, but he shook his head when she started to speak. He wanted a moment to survey the area and make sure there were no students nearby to listen. When he was confident they were all either in their dormitories or in class, he began walking down the hall in the direction of the hangar. "I meant what I said in there. We're going out, if you're amenable?"

"I am," she replied, though her expression reflected curiosity. "I confess I was surprised you were so accommodating to Emma Frost's method of acquiring the painting."

"Was I?" He hummed in his throat. "I suppose I thought it best not to antagonize our hosts too much."

"True," E.V.A. said. She hesitated. "I was also glad, as it shows a willingness to work with the X-Men that I think will be beneficial to us both."

"Ah. Yes, well." He rubbed the back of his neck. "I feel like I'm about to disappoint you then. Again."

E.V.A. stopped, forcing him to stop too. She folded her arms. "You're going to steal the painting anyway, aren't you?"

"We're leaving right this moment." Conveniently, they'd stopped just outside the hangar door. But E.V.A.'s expression was as unyielding as a roadblock.

"Is this about Cluster beating you last night?" she asked bluntly.

"She didn't exactly *beat* me," he said defensively. He put his hands to his chest in mock agony. "But, as usual, you deliver the blow right to the heart."

It was the hands on his chest that triggered it. Without warning, a cold sweat broke out on Fantomex's skin. The Skinless Man was suddenly in front of him, just like in his dream, a ghost holding a knife to his tender flesh. Ready to carve. Fear was a bitter taste in his mouth.

He dropped his hands to his sides, clenching and unclenching his fists. His heart raced as the fight or flight instinct warred inside him. He closed his eyes, forcing himself to breathe deep and slow to calm himself.

There were memories surrounding his death that he was missing, and others that were hazy, almost as if they'd happened to another person. Why did this one, this pain, have to return to him with perfect clarity whenever he least expected it?

When he opened his eyes, E.V.A. was leaning against the wall, watching him. There was no pity in her eyes, only calm strength and patience. He nodded, letting her know he was all right. She nodded back. She always knew how to react, how to handle him.

The weakest one.

"It's a matter of necessity," he said, picking up their conversation as if nothing had happened. "After dropping that obvious a clue for us, Cluster won't wait to make her move. If we sit here and do nothing, she'll have the painting in her possession long before Emma Frost can execute her more bureaucratic approach. Cyclops was right. That will bring the authorities and possibly other unwanted attention – like S.H.I.E.L.D. – closer to the Institute. We'll be doing everyone a favor by quietly removing the painting from the museum first. If everything goes as I plan, no one will ever know the painting has been taken, and no one will know I was anywhere near the museum. Everyone wins."

"Nevertheless, they won't like us leaving like this, without a word to anyone. Why not share your intentions and trust them to see the wisdom of what you propose?"

"Because I am not a person they are ever going to trust!" he said, his voice rising in frustration. With an effort, he calmed himself. "Nor should they, truth be told. I'm not like them."

"Is that true, or is it that you fear having to rely on them? On anyone, for that matter?"

"I rely on you," he said, with perfect honesty. "That hasn't changed. Can I rely on you now?"

He waited for her to argue with him further, but it seemed that, having delivered her warning, she was willing to let the subject drop.

She strode to the middle of the hangar, away from the stealth helicopter and jet that took up much of the space. She spread her arms, preparing to shift into her ship form. "You should know I took the liberty of recording a slice of their security footage at the museum," she said breezily. "I should have no trouble re-uploading it once we arrive and looping the footage to cover our time inside the building."

Taken aback, Fantomex tried to bury his surprise. "You knew I was going to choose this course of action?"

"I knew it was one of several possibilities," E.V.A. said. "As I explained before, I do try to be prepared for anything."

He smiled sheepishly, though she wouldn't see it behind the mask. He should never have doubted her. "Thank you for your confidence, my friend." A thought occurred to him. "Can you upload the footage a bit earlier, to overwrite Avery Torres' time at the museum today as well? I don't anticipate anything going wrong, but if it does, there's no reason to risk exposing her identity."

"Of course." E.V.A. inclined her head in acknowledgment, then her form shifted and grew until a large spherical silver ship sat in the middle of the chamber, resting on insect-like landing gear. A door slid open in the sphere, and a set of metal steps emerged, inviting entry. Her voice echoed from all around him as he stepped inside the ship and took the command seat in the cockpit. "It has been some time since we conducted a heist in broad daylight. This will take delicacy."

Delicacy, discretion, and a level of forethought and planning that normally stretched over days instead of hours, but the challenge once again sparked him, made him feel alive.

Cluster wasn't going to get the better of him this time. He would take the painting, return it to the Institute for safekeeping, and then find a way to flush her out of hiding.

"We'll work out the details and stop for any supplies we need along the way," he said, letting the VR unit settle over his eyes to access the flight controls. The hum of the ship powering up settled into his bones, making him feel at home.

It was almost enough to make him forget the Skinless Man, and the hollow feeling in his head and heart.

Almost.

# CHAPTER NINE

Well, this wasn't good. It wasn't terrible, but it certainly wasn't the way Avery had planned to start the day as she sat in the museum's café with a cup of coffee and a warm sesame bagel.

She'd arrived at the museum right after it opened and followed her usual routine of strolling casually through some of the other exhibits before she'd made her way to the Arts of the Americas gallery. It was a new day, and she was determined to get to the bottom of what was happening with her visions, preferably before she spoke to Jane again. But when she reached the gallery, there was a woman sitting on the bench – Avery's bench – in front of the Alano painting.

Avery knew she'd been one of the first people to enter the museum. The crowds were sparse at this hour, so she'd taken it for granted that there wouldn't be anyone here, but obviously she'd dithered too long in other areas. Still, it struck her as odd that the woman had had the same notion to come to this gallery first thing in the morning.

The woman wore ripped jeans and a hoodie, and she hadn't even looked up when Avery entered the gallery, so focused was she on studying *The Woman and the Tower*.

No one did that.

Sure, sometimes people hogged the bench because they were resting their feet or checking their phones or even sketching, but no one ever just sat and looked at the painting the way Avery did. It was a smaller canvas, for one thing, and tended to be overlooked in favor of the larger Alano and Tamayo works that dominated the rest of the gallery. It was also considered to be a minor work, produced late in the artist's career, so it never drew a crowd.

Seeing the woman show so much interest now had Avery on edge in a way she couldn't quite explain. She knew it was ridiculous. It wasn't *her* painting, after all. She was fine if others loved it as much as she did. That was a good thing.

To prove that she wasn't bothered, she'd come back down to the café for a quick breakfast, determined to enjoy the rest of what the museum had to offer. There would be plenty of time to go back and visit the Alano painting later.

But she also hadn't heard from Jane.

She'd promised to text today. True, she hadn't said when, and Avery was determined to give her space, but the silence was nerve-racking. She had a sinking feeling in her stomach that made the coffee bitter and the bagel taste like paper.

At times like this, she wished she could talk to her dad. Or maybe yell at both her parents for choosing to go the only child route. An older brother or sister would have been great right now too, someone to tell her how to confess that she was in love and that she was a mutant, all in the same day.

To be fair, no matter how many family members she wished for, they would probably be lost on how to navigate that last one.

Her text notification chimed.

Avery jumped, spilling lukewarm coffee across the table. Grabbing a wad of napkins from the dispenser, she mopped up the mess with shaking hands. She'd been waiting for this all morning, but now that the moment had come she was totally unprepared. She clutched her phone and stared at the little pop-up text bubble as if it might bite her. Her stomach churned. Maybe she should wait until after she finished her breakfast before she checked the text. Besides, she didn't want to seem like she was just waiting by her phone, ready to pounce. She wasn't a stalker.

But she wasn't going to be a coward either, not this time. Don't overthink it. She just had to face it, whatever *it* turned out to be.

She picked up the phone.

*Jane: Hey you. Sorry I took so long, overslept.*

*Avery: It's OK! I'm sorry our date got awkward yesterday.*

There was a long pause, which usually meant Jane was typing a novel in text form. It was one of the reasons Avery started the Jane Austen jokes. Jane loved a long, twisty text thread. Avery did too. And Jane wrote such lovely texts. They were poetry as far as she was concerned.

Finally, the expected block of text popped up.

*Jane: Yeah, I'm sorry too. I think it boils down to I miss you, and I feel like things are changing between us. There's stuff you aren't telling me, and I don't know why. The long-distance thing is tough. We knew that when we decided to*

*give this a chance. But this feels different. I think you're
keeping secrets. Why won't you tell me how long you're
going to be participating in this special art program?
Why won't you tell me about the friends you're making?
What are your teachers like? What are your classes like?
You don't tell me anything, unless it involves the museum
or the Alano painting. I know it means the world to you,
but it feels like there's no world beyond it. I feel like we're
stuck, and I don't know what to do. What should we do?*

Avery read the text three times, searching for the words
to reply, to confess what she needed to confess. If she told
Jane she was a mutant, she would no longer technically be
keeping secrets from her. But what about the rest?

She had no good answers to Jane's questions. She still
couldn't tell her girlfriend how long she'd be at the Institute,
because she had no idea how long it would take to learn to
use her powers properly. Especially after that strange vision
yesterday, when Ruby Alano had seemed to be trying to talk
to her. Were her powers changing? Growing stronger? What
if it got to the point where she couldn't control them?

She couldn't even talk about any friends she might
make because she had to protect the identities of the other
students. Was telling Jane she was a mutant really going to
solve any of the problems in their relationship, or would it
just create more? Was it worth the risk she took revealing
her secret?

Jane was right. They were stuck. As Avery sat there
clutching her phone, she could see it suddenly so clearly,
their entire relationship scrolling out on different paths in
different directions, all the various possibilities for their

future. Down one road, she confessed everything to Jane, told her the truth about being a mutant – and was rejected. Down another, she confessed and was accepted – but now Jane was in danger because she was in a relationship with a mutant. The people in this world who hated and feared them weren't going to care if her powers were harmless. It was her very existence that they despised.

She tried to make herself see the possible futures where she could be accepted by Jane and feel safe about continuing their relationship. But each time she went there, a voice inside her whispered that she was being selfish. Those hopes were unrealistic, those futures a fantasy.

Hadn't the same thing happened with her and her dad? Before he'd gotten sick, Avery had been happy, planning for her future and following her passion for art. Then he died, and it was as if the world had stepped in and pulled the rug out from under her.

Now she was setting herself up for the same thing to happen all over again.

Besides, it wasn't fair of her to dump all of her baggage into someone else's life. She'd heard inklings of how some of the other mutants had come to discover their powers, the trauma they'd gone through. Jane had her own problems and worries, and this would just make everything worse for her.

Eyes burning, throat tight, Avery began typing out the very words she'd been afraid to hear from Jane. She knew it was terrible to end things this way, and she would have given anything to talk to her in person, but Jane had made it clear yesterday that she wasn't up to talking right now, and Avery had to respect that. And, if Avery was being honest with herself, she needed the shield of the text thread as much as Jane did right now.

It took her several attempts to say what she needed to say. Her hands shook so badly she could barely get the message typed. By the time she hit send, there was a flood of tears rolling down her face. She was bawling in the middle of the breakfast rush at the museum café, but she couldn't bring herself to care.

*Avery: You're right. About everything. There are things I've been keeping from you, but I swear I'm not doing it to hurt you. I only want to protect you. I'm so sorry, Jane. You're right, I don't think this is working anymore, the long-distance thing. I think it's better if we go back to being friends. I don't want to lose you, but you deserve someone who can be there for you, and right now that's not me. You deserve every happiness in the world.*

She'd poured out her heart – as much as she was able – but right then, she couldn't bear to read Jane's response, not here in front of all these strangers. Avery stood up so fast from the table her chair scraped loudly on the floor. People were definitely looking at her now, but she kept her head down, gathered her trash, and dumped it in the recycling bins near the café exit.

On the walk up the stairs to her gallery, Avery's sorrow morphed into something hotter, more dangerous.

It wasn't fair. She hadn't asked for any of this to happen, hadn't wanted this power that was unreliable and unpredictable. She hadn't asked to lose the last of an already tiny family. And now the world wasn't even going to let her build another one.

Fine, then. The world better not mess with her today. If that woman was still in the gallery, sitting on her favorite bench, Avery was ready to boot her off.

Fortunately, the bench was unoccupied, but the woman was still in the gallery, this time standing in front of the Alano painting. Oddly, though, her back was to the canvas, and she was looking at something high on the opposite wall. Curious, Avery followed her gaze, but there was nothing there but the ever-present eye of the security camera.

Maybe she didn't like being watched. Avery didn't particularly care. She marched right past the woman and sat down on the bench. She dropped her messenger bag beside her, pulled out her sketchbook and deliberately spread herself out as much as possible, claiming her territory. When she looked up, the woman was still standing there, and from this position, they were directly facing each other, just a few feet apart. Well, that was super awkward. Still, Avery wasn't giving ground. She deliberately looked past the woman and fixed her attention on the painting.

Out of the corner of her eye, Avery noticed the woman was watching her and, infuriatingly, she was smiling.

Avery put on her best *approach me at your peril* face and ignored her.

But the woman was not to be ignored.

"It's a lovely piece, don't you think?" She gestured to the painting. Her voice was lightly accented – French, maybe, though it was hard to tell. "So small and easy to overlook amongst its fellows. Imagine all the things people are missing by not taking the time to see the finer details of the world around them."

Avery had to admit she often had that same thought about the painting herself. Against her will, she felt her stiff shoulders relax slightly, and she breathed out a quiet sigh. Maybe the woman wasn't so bad. She couldn't be if she could see the beauty in Ruby Alano's work.

"It's my favorite painting in the whole museum," Avery confessed. Normally, she would never say such a thing to a complete stranger, but the woman's eyes were kind, and right then she needed to feel something, anything, other than her heart being ripped out of her. "My father's family is Portuguese, and our name, Torres, means 'tower.'"

That was Jane's favorite story about the painting. When her father had seen how much she was taken by it, he'd said, "Look at the tower, Avery. Looks intimidating, doesn't it? But don't let it fool you. I think Alano wants us to see strength and change there. We are the tower, love, and that strength is in us too."

This wasn't helping. Avery tried to shrug the memories off, to pretend her eyes weren't filling with tears again. "Anyway, I just like the connection," she said. "Probably sounds silly to you."

"Not at all," the woman replied. Her voice, with its light accent, was oddly soothing. "Connections are important. Sometimes they're all we have to ground us." Avery thought she detected a hint of regret in the woman's expression as she spoke. She turned away from the painting. "My apologies. I'm disturbing you."

And just like that, she was gone. Avery watched her retreating back, thinking that somehow the woman looked familiar, but she couldn't think why. She must have seen her around the museum. Maybe she was a regular or a volunteer.

Now that she was alone, Avery reluctantly pulled out her phone to read the response from Jane to her breakup message. Her heart was pounding so loudly in her ears, it drowned out the sounds of the other patrons moving through the museum.

She pulled up the text thread.

Nothing.

There'd been no response, even though almost ten minutes had gone by since Avery had sent the text.

Well, what had she thought was going to happen? That Jane would calmly accept the inevitable? You know what, Avery, you're absolutely right, let's go back to being friends and it'll be like none of this relationship stuff ever happened.

Avery held the phone so tightly in her hands she was afraid she would break the screen. She knew she'd hurt Jane deeply. She didn't deserve that, either. That's why it was better this way, better that she was alone. That way she wouldn't disappoint anyone, and no one would disappoint her. The pain would pass eventually, and she'd get used to being alone again.

Still, the anger and frustration at the unfairness of it all flared hot inside her again, and she repeated her earlier mantra.

*No one better mess with me today.*

# CHAPTER TEN

Fantomex surveyed the site of his intended heist with satisfaction. The Edmonton Art Museum was an impressive steel and glass structure with a unique curvilinear canopy running through the heart of the building. Modern instead of classic, striking yet welcoming. And original. That was the most refreshing thing. No pale imitation here, no warehouse replicas needed. It wasn't his preferred style, but he could appreciate the boldness and fanciful imagery the design evoked when one stood a distance away to marvel at the feat of architecture, as he and E.V.A. were doing now. The sun was shining, and the sky was so blue it created the perfect backdrop for the building, allowing him to imagine it as a fantastical ship putting out to sea.

It was, in fact, the perfect place and the perfect day for a heist.

But then E.V.A. stepped in to interrupt his moment of joy, his oneness with the universe. "This plan of yours has a certain element of..."

"Derring-do?" he suggested. "*Je ne sais quoi?*"

"Flying by the seat of one's pants," E.V.A. said. "That's the colloquial expression, I believe. It relies on a great many things going right."

"Personally, I think it's inspired, but if we'd stopped for proper coffee, maybe I could have come up with something better," he huffed as they crossed the busy street arm in arm. "Now, we have to prepare to play our roles. This is the fun part, remember?"

This was their stage. Today they were acting the part of the busy, ultra-privileged couple who worked together in the financial sector and were taking a long lunch break at the museum. E.V.A. had shifted her pupilless amber eyes to a warm brown shade with amber flecks and was dressed in a black and white pants suit with matching overcoat and gloves. To complement her, he had chosen a slim-fit gray suit in virgin wool, a small laptop bag slung casually over his shoulder.

They entered the museum as if they owned it and, more importantly, as if they routinely donated large sums of money to its upkeep, so that when the volunteer at the coat check started to say something about taking his laptop bag, Fantomex gave the young man a cold stare that made him swallow the words. They showed their museum passes and were detained no further.

"This way, darling," he said, steering E.V.A. away from the elevator bank where she'd been headed. "We'll go by the stairs, get some exercise, get the blood flowing."

She raised an eyebrow. "I fail to see how we require any further exercise, seeing as how we circled the museum twice studying its entrances and exits and walked several blocks away in order to properly view the building – all of this at your suggestion, I might add."

"Now we're studying the interior," he said, projecting what he thought was a casual aura.

She wasn't buying it. "We both already know the layout by heart, which is how I know you're taking us on a circuitous route through the museum that will doubtless sweep us past the miniatures room, a place you never fail to visit whenever you find one in any museum in any part of the world," she said, a note of triumph in her voice at having caught him at his game.

"Fine," he grumbled. "It'll take five minutes, I swear."

She snorted. "We'll be twenty minutes, no less."

"I'll take that bet," he said as they ascended the staircase, following the flowing metal ribbon that sailed through the building as part of the architecture. "Besides, you shouldn't make fun. They're fantastic designs, meticulously crafted and so lifelike–"

"They're almost like looking at the real thing," E.V.A. finished for him, giving his arm a teasing poke. "I don't make fun of the miniatures. I'm making fun of you for turning into a ten year-old child whenever you get in a room with them."

"But just feast your eyes!" he declared, aware he was proving her point as he practically dragged her into the gallery and up to the wood-framed viewing windows where the miniatures were on display behind secure glass. "Every room a tiny replica in a tiny world! Where else can you find a Tudor great room sitting shoulder to shoulder with a French boudoir and traditional Chinese fretwork?" Without waiting for an answer, he pulled her to another window and pointed at a fully laid English dining set. "Look there, not a fork out of place. There's even a tiny butter dish with tiny butter on the table!"

"Well, what person can be cynical in the face of tiny butter?" She smiled at him fondly as they moved from one room to the next.

What person indeed? He glanced around at the tourists filing through the room with their guide maps and cell phone cameras ready. Most people who walked through the gallery no doubt looked on the pieces as nothing more than curious little novelties, and maybe that's all they were, in the end, but yes, he had a soft spot in his soul for these clever imitations. Maybe that made him a hypocrite, but in his mind they weren't anything like the cobbled together, cheap knockoff Musée d'Orsay out on that island. These miniatures were creations that managed to be so perfect they transcended the original and became their own form of art.

Hadn't he staked much of his hopes for his own existence and meaning on that same belief? That Fantomex, who had been created as the perfect imitation, the perfect killer, could transcend that and become something unique unto himself?

And yet, a traitorous voice whispered inside him, how could one strive to be greater, to make themselves better, when the world kept tearing little pieces of you away?

They had reached the end of the room. E.V.A., as if sensing the shift in his mood, looked around warily. "Did you see something? Is it Cluster?"

"No sign of her yet." He nodded to a room across the hall. "That's number 214, I believe."

He forced his doubts aside as he led her across the hall. He had no time for distractions now. His mind was already working the space, taking in every detail of the scene, noting the number of tourists, museum volunteers, and guards who moved around them like extras in their play. The museum wasn't terribly crowded at this time of day, which was good for them. It meant fewer variables to control, fewer players complicating the scene.

"Ready?" he asked, glancing at E.V.A.

"Always," she murmured, but her eyes were on a specific subject. "Avery Torres is still here. She just exited the gallery."

"What?" He looked, hoping she was mistaken, but no, it was definitely Avery crossing the hall in front of them. She had a blazing look in her eyes, as if daring anyone to speak to her. He turned his back as she went past so she wouldn't notice him and suppressed a sigh of exasperation.

The surveillance footage they'd been viewing back at the Institute had been captured several hours earlier. With the girl's attention span, he'd have expected her to be long gone from the museum by now, or at least to have moved on to a different wing. Didn't she know there was art all over the building?

"What do you want to do?" E.V.A. asked. "Abort?"

"Absolutely not," he growled, striding purposefully toward the gallery. He was not about to let Avery Torres be the wrench in his entire plan for getting the better of Cluster. "We go now, while she's away." With luck, she was finished trolling the place anyway.

E.V.A. said nothing as she followed him into the room, but he could feel her misgivings like a force radiating from her.

"Go ahead," he said, sighing, "lodge your complaints now before we get on with the show."

"I'm afraid we don't have time for all of them at the moment," E.V.A. said. Sliding her hand from the crook of his arm, she arranged herself off to the side of the nearest painting, pretending to read the small placard next to it. She would continue to move through the room in this unhurried way until she was standing near the wall directly opposite the painting.

Taking his cue, Fantomex wandered the other side of the room, giving a perfunctory glance at each painting, when really what he was doing was studying the stage and readying for his own part to begin.

Besides the two of them, there were a couple of twentysomethings in the gallery looking at the paintings together, but it was clear they were far more wrapped up in studying each other. They held hands and kept their heads bent close, whispering and giggling. Second or third date, he guessed, not that it was relevant. But as extras in this scene, they would do nicely.

He spared another glance at the gallery entrance, searching for any sign of Cluster. An ambush would not be a welcome twist, and he wouldn't put it past her to concoct one just to keep him on his toes. But if she was lying in wait somewhere for him, she was keeping herself well hidden.

The only other person in the gallery at the moment was the guard, who wore comfortable shoes and looked to be on the grayer side of fifty, with a dashing handlebar mustache that went nicely with his uniform. His blue eyes were soft but alert. Fantomex guessed that he'd been working at the museum a long time. The man knew his job and liked it. Hopefully, that meant he was competent at it as well. Competent was exactly what they needed. Someone who wouldn't lose his head in a crisis.

He waited for the guard to catch his eye, and when he did, Fantomex offered an easy smile and the oldest conversation opener in recorded history. "Beautiful weather," he said. He'd dropped his French accent, going instead for blandly American.

The guard nodded at the rectangles of sunshine pooling on the floor from the nearby windows. "Enjoy it," he said. "Snow coming again tonight."

"Is that right?"

"What I heard, anyway."

And so the play began.

"I don't know about you, but I could handle some snow. Feels hot in here right now." Fantomex slipped off his suit jacket and loosened his tie, putting a slight wheeze in his breath. "Gosh, I'm sweating." He rubbed his chest, his face creasing in discomfort. For an instant, he worried that his act would trigger an actual panic attack, but the thrill of the heist was strong. It overcame the haunting memories, so he continued the scene. Impatiently, he checked his watch, as if he couldn't wait to get out of there.

"You feeling all right, sir?" the guard asked. He was watching Fantomex closely, a look of mild concern making his magnificent mustache droop.

"Oh, yes, just something I ate disagreeing with me. Terrible thing to get older. When I was in college I used to be able to eat anything."

The guard chuckled. "Just wait until you're my age. It only gets worse."

Good. All the guard's attention was diverted. Across the room, with the timing of the most graceful dancer, E.V.A. reached her mark. She was standing exactly three feet from the wall opposite the Alano painting. She reached into her handbag and pulled out a tiny holographic projection device, no bigger than a thumbnail, tinted the exact shade of eggshell paint on the walls.

Casually, she looked down at her left shoe and frowned, as if noticing a scuff or a stain. In a quick motion, she braced one hand on the wall behind her and lifted her left foot to brush the invisible mark off the shoe. No one else was looking at her, but if they had been they would have seen only that motion – not the instant when she pressed the projection device to the wall until the adhesive took. He blinked, and she was standing upright again, moving on to read the placard beside the next painting.

There was barely a visible change when the device activated three seconds later. It was only the merest flicker in the air, easily attributable to the clouds passing over the sun outside and shifting the light in the gallery for just an instant. Sometimes the universe did you a favor like that.

Now it was time to earn his award.

Fantomex coughed, rubbing a hand over his chest again, and this time with the grimace of pain he added a stutter in his step. The guard lifted his hand but checked himself, his eyes sharpening.

"Sir, are you sure you're feeling–"

Now.

Fantomex dropped to his knees, drawing in a ragged breath. The guard was at his side seconds later – for all the creaks to his step, the man was quick.

"Darling, are you all right?"

They both looked up as E.V.A. came gliding across the room, the perfect picture of composure and concern. She knelt on his other side and immediately took his wrist in her hand to check his pulse.

"Did you take your medicine this morning?" she pressed. "I'm a doctor," she added for the guard's benefit. "My husband has a congenital heart defect."

That changed the guard's expression from one of concern to alarm, and it brought the young couple scurrying over to pepper them with questions.

"Oh, wow, can we help you, sir?" The woman put a hand on his shoulder to offer support.

"Do you need some water?" Without waiting for an answer, the young man produced a water bottle and brandished it at him like a sword.

E.V.A. cast a pleading look to the guard. "If we could just have some room, I'll get his medicine," she said. "That should take care of things."

The words worked like a charm. The guard knew exactly what his job was and was thankful that it didn't involve calling an ambulance.

"All right, now, I need you folks to clear the gallery," he said, taking the young couple by the elbows and gently guiding them up from the floor. Quickly, he ushered them out and shooed away some others who had wandered up to the gallery entrance when they heard the commotion.

Grabbing the retractable band from one of the two stanchions on either side of the doorway, he pulled it across the opening to bar entry. By that point, other people were gathering, so he had to usher them away too, at the same time grabbing a walkie-talkie on his belt to report the incident.

While he was occupied controlling the crowd and answering questions from the person on the other end of the walkie talkie, Fantomex and E.V.A. were for that moment alone in the gallery.

"Hurry," Fantomex whispered. "He's got everyone away from the door. No one's looking." He let the strap of the laptop bag fall from his shoulder and unzipped the bag. Inside was a blank canvas in an unadorned frame. Perhaps if he'd had more time, he could have tried his hand at making a replica, but their cruder method would have to do for now.

Smoothly, E.V.A. stood, took the canvas from the bag, and walked to the painting, which, even in its frame, was no bigger than an average laptop screen. The laser alarms trained on the painting would go off if the canvases weren't switched perfectly, without breaking the beam, but E.V.A. never faltered. She shifted her vision so she could see the lasers, lifted the painting off the wall, and slid the blank one in its place with not the slightest disturbance.

And the holographic projector on the opposite wall displayed a perfect image of *The Woman and the Tower* over the blank canvas. It was as if the painting had never moved at all.

E.V.A. brought the real painting back over to where he crouched and slid it into the laptop bag. Fantomex zipped it shut, his head buzzing with the rush of adrenaline. He flashed E.V.A. a quick smile.

"Always a pleasure working with you, my friend," he said.

"Hey!"

He looked up, just in time to meet the furious gaze of Avery Torres, who was standing on the other side of the roped-off gallery entrance.

And then everything went sideways.

# CHAPTER ELEVEN

Every fiber of Avery's body seethed as she watched the woman take the Alano painting off the wall and slip it into the bag Fantomex held open for her.

"Hey!" The word was out of her mouth before she'd even considered speaking.

Fantomex lifted his head and locked eyes with her. For a moment, she was surprised at how... alive those eyes were, compared to when she'd observed him in the classroom. Full of mischief and daring. Infuriatingly smug. The standoff between them lasted seconds, but Avery read the challenge in his gaze clearly.

Your move, he seemed to be saying. How do you want to play this?

She suspected she was dipping into a game that he had already mastered, when she wasn't yet aware of the rules.

"Miss, I need you to move back. We want to keep this area clear."

The guard had returned, stepping in front of her so that

he cut off her view of Fantomex and the woman. He didn't touch her, but he still managed to gently herd her back with his outstretched hands, making small talk all the while, with the practiced ease of someone who handled crowds every day.

"But–" The words she wanted to say jumbled in her throat. What was she going to do? Tell the white guard that the affluent white couple having a medical emergency were actually stealing the Ruby Alano painting? It was still there on the wall, or at least a copy of it was. Avery wasn't sure exactly how they'd managed to make it look like the real painting was still in place, but she would never convince the mellow guard that there was something wrong when everything appeared normal.

And even if she did convince him, was she willing to risk exposure of herself and two other mutants from the school? That had been the challenge in Fantomex's eyes, Avery realized. He'd been asking her to consider her actions carefully.

By now, the guard had herded the crowd about ten feet back from the gallery. Over his shoulder, Avery could see Fantomex coming out of the room, the laptop bag with the painting held unobtrusively against his side. He disappeared around the corner, and a second later, the woman followed. She walked over to the guard and touched his shoulder to get his attention.

Avery couldn't hear all the words they exchanged. The hall had filled with curious onlookers, and the noise swelled, echoing off the cavernous walls. But the woman was saying something about her husband feeling better, that he'd forgotten his medicine this morning and that it was just a scare. Then it looked like she thanked him, a sheen of tears in her eyes. Avery shook her head in grudging admiration as the woman turned and hurried away. It was an award-winning performance.

But they weren't going to get away with this.

Avery turned and pushed through the crowd, heading for the bank of service elevators in the back of the hall. They were technically for museum staff only, but she'd ridden in them once with her father when he was doing consulting work on a project for the museum. They were mainly used by janitorial workers and volunteers, so they didn't stop at any floors that needed special keys or security codes to access. And lucky for her, they came out right in the middle of the wide, light-filled atrium where Fantomex and the woman would exit to the street.

With the crowd distracted, she easily slipped through the large metal doors and impatiently tapped the button for the first floor.

She knew every inch of this museum because her dad had shared it with her and had loved it as much as she did.

She wasn't letting anyone mess with that.

And Fantomex wasn't taking her painting.

By the time the doors slid open on the first floor, Avery's anger had reached a peak, fueling her steps as she darted into the lobby, dodging families and school groups lining up at the café. She scanned the crowd, searching for Fantomex and his accomplice. She knew they hadn't beaten her down here. She had to get to them before they left the building and she lost them for good.

Then, suddenly, there they were, strolling across the lobby, their heads bent together, talking and laughing like a normal couple out on a date to the museum. As if they didn't have a care in the world. She knew they were playing a part, but even so, something about that carefree, remorseless attitude made Avery's blood run hot in her veins.

She'd give them something to care about.

Striding across the lobby beneath the brilliance of the sun-dappled atrium, Avery put herself right in their path, forcing them to stop.

"Give it back," she said without preamble.

Fantomex looked down at her, pasting a bland smile on his face. "Well, hello, Avery," he said politely. "I didn't expect to see you here, out of *school.*"

Avery wasn't in the mood for games. "I don't know what you think you're doing, but I'm not letting you steal that painting," she hissed, stepping closer. Her gaze dropped to the bag. "I saw you."

Beneath the bland expression, his eyes assessed her. The woman glanced around the atrium, keeping watch on the crowd. "I don't think you know quite what you saw," Fantomex said. "The painting's still in the gallery, is it not?"

"Nice try." She made as if to reach for the laptop bag. "How about you prove it?"

He twisted away from her but made the action look smooth and casual, nothing that would draw attention to their tense little group.

"I can guarantee there's more going on here than you realize," he said. "Things sanctioned by the Institute where we're both enrolled. I'm sure you wouldn't want to jeopardize that."

Sanctioned by the Institute. His words made her falter. Could that be true? Was she unknowingly interfering in some kind of secret X-Men mission? But if that was the case, why hadn't Cyclops warned her that something like this was going to go down while she was visiting the museum? Why had he let her come in the first place?

Avery stared at Fantomex, and this time she glimpsed the wariness in his expression, the hint of guilt that he quickly buried. He wasn't good at hiding his emotions when he wasn't wearing his mask.

"You're a liar," she said. "Give me that bag, or I'm going to make a scene right in the middle of the lobby."

The woman snapped her attention back to them, her eyes narrowing in alarm. "That would be unwise," she said.

"You're bluffing," Fantomex challenged her.

"You really want to find out?" Avery spread her hands, raising her voice slightly. "Even if they think I'm crazy, if I shout enough times that you have a stolen painting in your laptop bag, sooner or later, someone's going to ask to see inside. Then what will you do?"

"You think that's the way to handle this?" Fantomex said. "Do you want everyone to see us, to risk finding out that we're mutants? Is that what Scott Summers had in mind when he trusted you to leave the Institute on your own with full knowledge of the place's location, its status as a sanctuary, its secrets? Do you think this is what he would want?"

The words hit Avery right in the gut. Oh, he was good.

In addition to being arrogant, elitist, and annoying, he knew how to manipulate people. Her hands clenched into fists at her sides, but she knew striking out at him wouldn't do any good either. She wasn't a fighter. By her own choice, she wasn't a trained member of the X-Men. He probably knew that too.

She didn't think she'd ever despised anyone as much as she despised him in that moment.

Was she really just going to let him walk out of here?

The woman, as if sensing her inner turmoil, put a hand up in a placating gesture. "Come with us," she invited. "Back to the Institute. We'll explain our actions there, and you'll see for yourself that we mean no harm. I assure you, there is a reason for what we're doing."

"I'm not going anywhere with him," Avery said, jerking her head at Fantomex.

He shrugged. "Then it appears we have nothing more to say to one another."

Fantomex turned and began walking across the lobby toward the exit. He was calling her bluff, testing to see if she would actually make good on her threat to cause a scene.

Rage coursed through her like poison. How dare he underestimate her? How dare he think he could walk in here and take what didn't belong to him, as if he were smarter than everyone else?

She opened her mouth to call out, to tell every person in the room what a fraud and a trickster he was.

But she couldn't do it. The words simply wouldn't come because, as much as she despised him, she knew he was right. She wouldn't risk exposing herself, the Institute, or anyone associated with it. The students there – she had the barest idea of what their lives were like, what powers they were trying to learn about and control. They needed that school, dark and dismal and neglected as it was, to keep them safe. She had no right to jeopardize that.

Then why did she feel so terrible, so helpless, as she watched them carry the painting away from her? It felt like her connection to it was being shredded. Her stomach churned with unhappiness.

"*No, please don't,*" she whispered. But there was no one around to hear her. No one around who cared.

Suddenly, out of the myriad of voices and ambient noise of the lobby, there came a soft but insistent thrumming sound. Like a distant roll of thunder, it passed through the atrium, vibrating the glass ceiling above them and streaking through Avery's body like a brief surge of flame. But it wasn't the kind of flame that burned.

Within it, something whispered back to her.

"*No, please don't.*"

Avery had a brief instant of vertigo, and when it passed her knees were weak and wobbly. She wanted to sit down right in the middle of the lobby. She glanced around, sure that someone must have felt that strange thunder, heard the voice…

Nothing had changed. The people in the lobby carried on with their conversations. Diners at the café ate and laughed in peaceful oblivion.

Avery put her hands up to her ears. The thrumming came again, stronger this time, drowning out the voices. She felt like she was being swallowed up. The whisper repeated those same words in a cacophony in her head, her own plea given back to her over and over.

*"No, please don't."*

*please don't.*

*please don't*

*please don't*

Someone grabbed her arm and spun her around.

Avery blinked up into Fantomex's furious blue eyes. "What are you doing?" he demanded.

"The surge is growing exponentially," the woman said, coming up beside him. She was now holding the laptop bag, cradling it against her chest. "If we don't do something, it's going to detonate in less than a minute."

"What?" Avery found her voice when she heard the word "detonate". "What's happening?"

"The painting," the woman said, speaking low and fast. "It's emitting an energy surge that's dangerously unstable."

"It's a bomb," Fantomex said curtly. "The painting is one giant bomb and its countdown clock started going the second we walked away from you." Still holding her arm in a painful grip, he looked her over, turning her left and right, as if searching for something she had hidden on her person. "It has to be because of you. What are your mutant powers? What can you do?"

She jerked out of his grip. "Don't touch me!" she snapped, loud enough to draw some uneasy glances from one of the nearby café tables. But more concerning, the thrumming noise got louder with her anger. Avery could feel the atrium windows bowing outward with the strain, though no one else seemed to be aware of it.

Except Fantomex and the woman.

"Avery," she said, her voice gentle, soothing. "You have to calm down. Whatever is happening, I believe it's connected to your current emotional state." Her warm brown eyes, flecked with amber, were kind. "You feel it, don't you? The connection between you and the painting?"

"I'm not doing anything!" Avery insisted, staring at the woman helplessly. "I can't… I can't help it!"

The woman nodded, processing this. She glanced down at the bag in her hands, then back at Avery. Stepping forward cautiously, she held out the bag. When Avery hesitated, confused, she gently took her hands and wrapped them around the bag, putting its weight into her arms.

Avery gave an involuntary sigh, and just like that the thrumming noise ceased, the whispers dying away in her ears, replaced by the ordinary sounds of the crowd in the lobby. But the experience had left her shaken and sick.

The woman seemed to sense it. She touched Avery's forehead with a cool hand. "You need rest and some water," she said. "You're slightly feverish. It's the stress of your powers."

"I need some answers first," Fantomex cut in, staring at Avery as if he'd never seen her before. "What just happened? Were you really going to blow up the building over a painting?"

"She doesn't understand what's going on any more than we do," the woman chided him.

Blow up the building? Did they think she had that kind of power? Then the scarier thought flashed through her mind: would that really have happened? Was she truly the cause of that strange surge that pushed against the building itself? If so, it was everything she'd feared might happen with her powers, what had fueled her choice to stay at the Institute.

Reflexively, Avery held the painting tighter, though any sane person would probably have flung it away and run. This all felt like a dream. There was nothing about the painting now that felt dangerous. She was just holding a normal bag, and inside, a normal stolen canvas and frame.

If this was a dream, she was ready to wake up any time.

# CHAPTER TWELVE

Fantomex stood in the atrium lobby and stewed. This was not how the day was supposed to go, by any stretch of the imagination. Avery Torres, the unexpected thorn in his side, had just changed the game entirely.

What was she? E.V.A. was right, the girl didn't seem to know what was going on any more than they did. Was this Cluster's doing? The painting had seemed normal enough in the limited time it had been in his hands, but maybe she had rigged it to explode if it left the museum grounds. Perhaps Cluster and Avery were working together. Or was it possible that what was happening with the painting was unconnected to Avery, that it was pure coincidence that they'd walked away from her when the mysterious energy surge started? There was the obvious way to test that theory, but he had no desire to do it here in a crowded building. No, for now he had to assume that her mutant powers, whatever they were, were somehow causing the painting to become volatile.

So, if she needed to stay near the painting, he'd make sure she did.

"We're getting out of here," he said, addressing both of them, but specifically Avery. "You're coming with us." He held up a hand before she could argue. "Yes, I know, you'd rather die than go anywhere in my company – point taken. I won't try to take the painting from you again, but we need to get it away from any crowds and back to the Institute where we can figure out what's happening to you and to it. Can we at least agree on that necessity?"

"I'm not going anywhere unless you tell me why you're stealing it in the first place." She eyed him warily, as if searching for a trick or a trap, still clutching the painting protectively. Against his better judgment, he was impressed. She faced him down without any apparent fear, all while holding a potentially deadly weapon in her hands. This wasn't some misguided sense of doing what was right, he realized. The painting truly meant something to her.

And right now, she had all the leverage she needed to get the answers she wanted. He had to accept that she was part of the game now, whether he liked it or not.

"We're stealing the painting before someone else arrives to steal it first," he confided. "There's a woman who's been targeting artifacts at museums around the globe."

Remembering the image of Avery and Cluster on the surveillance footage together, he added, "Perhaps you've seen her." He gave a brief description, and some of the color leached from Avery's face.

"I thought she just liked the painting as much as I did," Avery said faintly.

"Apparently, she does." Now, more than ever, he needed to know why, and they were wasting time here.

He was starting to entertain the idea of a short neuroblast to render Avery unconscious when she nodded. "OK," she said. "I'll go with you. I don't have a car, so we'll have to take yours."

The ghost of a smile curved E.V.A.'s lips. "That won't be a problem. We'll just–"

She never got a chance to finish. Her eyes went briefly unfocused, and there was a flash of amber light in them that had Fantomex cursing under his breath and glancing around to make sure no one had seen.

"E.V.A., what–"

"He's coming," she interrupted, her hand falling on his wrist in a tight grip. "He's coming! You have to–"

The hairs on the back of Fantomex's neck prickled, and he instinctively looked up, just in time to see a dark shape whip past the glass ceiling of the atrium. He lost the figure for a second in the sunlight glittering off the window panes, but then it was back, landing with an impact that shook the building's frame and shattered part of the ceiling.

Fantomex grabbed Avery and E.V.A. by their shoulders, yanking them to the floor and against his sides. He spread his wool coat over their heads as best he could to protect them from the glass shards raining down all around them.

Screams echoed through the lobby, and people were suddenly running for the exits, tripping over each other in a mad rush to get away.

Fantomex stood, shaking the glass off his coat. E.V.A. placed herself in front of Avery and the painting. They all stared at the figure who had landed in the middle of the lobby about thirty feet away. All this time, they'd been worried about Cluster showing up to thwart their plans. Once again, they'd been caught flatfooted.

The man was similar to Fantomex in height and build, dressed all in black, with white accents on his costume that truly did make him a strange, dark mirror to Fantomex's own costume, which he was sorely missing at that moment. He felt naked facing down his double this way.

That sense of disquieting familiarity washed over him again. Weapon XIII moved with the same catlike grace he did and held himself with the same confidence and swagger. If anything, this imposter was even more a shadow of him than Cluster – except for the eyes. There was some spark of life missing in those eyes. Soulless, he might have called them, if he believed in the concept of souls.

"Weapon XIII," he said, offering a mock bow, while at the same time assessing his options for a quick escape route for Avery. He gestured at the chaos and wreckage his twin's entrance had caused. "You could have just called and said you wanted to meet for lunch."

"Give me the painting," Weapon XIII said, his hand out.

"Now, where have I heard that before?" Fantomex folded his arms and adopted a relaxed stance. In his periphery, he could see Avery edging backward, still mostly shielded by E.V.A. Good. When the fighting started, she'd be ready to run, and if her earlier actions were any indication she wasn't going to lose her head in a crisis. Again, he found himself grudgingly impressed. This new batch of mutants at the Institute were turning out to be tougher than he'd expected.

But his double was no fool either. He drew a rather large gun from a holster hanging from his belt and leveled it at them. "We can do this quick and clean, or it can be bloody," he said. "Your choice."

Fantomex heaved a disappointed sigh. "Why does it have to be hard at all?" he asked, taking a step forward. "That's not rhetorical, by the way. I'd actually like to know why both you and Cluster feel the need to come at me weapons first. Well, technically, she came at me vase first, but still, I thought we shared something, that we had a connection–"

The roar of the gunshot made him flinch, but when he looked down there was no gaping hole in his gut. Well, that was good. A quick glance told him E.V.A. and Avery were unharmed, but one of the sliding doors at the museum's entrance had shattered and was dripping glass everywhere. Screams echoed through the building as its few remaining occupants ran for cover.

"Move again, and I'll put the next one down your throat," Weapon XIII promised. "Give me the painting."

Fine, so he wasn't going to get anywhere with guile and banter. He was flexible.

And E.V.A. was just waiting for his signal.

He didn't give it in words. She would hear it in his voice. They were a part of each other, after all.

"Whatever you say."

He squeezed his eyes shut against the burst of energy that erupted from her. Grunting, Weapon XIII fired again, but his aim had been disrupted by the blinding flash. Before he could recover, Fantomex bull-rushed him, and they both went down on the carpet of glass shards on the lobby floor.

He grabbed Weapon XIII's gun arm and slammed his hand down onto the glass repeatedly until his fingers went slack, releasing the weapon.

He spared a glance at Avery. She was already halfway across the lobby. She darted into the café, weaving among the tables until she'd gotten behind the counter. She stumbled once, then kicked open the swinging door that led to the back food prep area and disappeared.

He had to hope she knew where she was going because he had no more time to worry about it. Weapon XIII's bloody fist slammed into the side of his face, causing his vision to erupt in twinkling stars. Did he really punch that hard? That, or his double had been working on his upper body strength exclusively for the past several months.

Fantomex rolled them across the floor, feeling the glass shards digging painfully into him even through the heavy wool coat. He forced Weapon XIII onto his back and straddled him, but his double wasn't going to be distracted by the pain. His hands found Fantomex's throat and squeezed.

Well, now he was mildly concerned. Dark spots popped in the corners of his eyes, looking disturbingly like a tunnel. A neuroweapon blast would be good right about now. What was E.V.A. doing?

"Fire," he croaked, bringing his arms up, fast and hard, breaking the chokehold. "Don't worry about the proximity, just fire!"

Weapon XIII lifted his booted foot and planted it on Fantomex's chest, kicking out and sending him sailing backward. He landed in another sea of glass. Glass everywhere. And pain.

"E.V.A.!"

But there was no energy burst.

Looking around wildly, he caught sight of her across the room near the door where Avery had disappeared. She was on her knees, looking frantic, her hands moving over the empty air as if there was something invisible there that she was holding onto.

Oh no. He'd witnessed people in that state before – he'd been the one to put them there. Whatever she was seeing, it was an illusion planted in her mind, a false reality that would be utterly convincing to all five of her senses.

Well, that confirmed where his misdirection power had gone.

Terrific.

He dove behind the nearest café table, pulling it down behind him so he'd have a bit of cover while he drew his gun and knife. Reaching over the top of the table, he fired until he'd emptied his clip. He needed to distract his annoying duplicate, get him to drop the illusion.

A return volley of gunfire answered him, pinging off the metal table.

He couldn't help thinking this would be a marvelous time for Cluster to make a dramatic entrance and join the fight – preferably on his side, but any sort of distraction right now would be welcome.

Reloading, he came around the side of the table this time and opened fire. Weapon XIII had been moving through the café, but he ducked behind a column, part of the metal ribbon that ran throughout the building. He was moving steadily toward E.V.A. and the door where Avery had escaped.

E.V.A., crouched on the ground with her back to him, was helpless.

A cold terror gripped Fantomex, but it wasn't just worry for his friend's safety. No, it was the thought that Weapon XIII might actually hurt E.V.A. To Fantomex, the idea was unthinkable, abhorrent. She was a part of all of them, even though she'd chosen for now to travel with him. Hurting her would be like stabbing himself in the gut.

But these people – Weapon XIII and Cluster – were not a part of him anymore. These were not perfect mirrors of himself. And watching his strange duplicate come after them like a hunter scenting prey, Fantomex felt a sharp twist of betrayal.

It wasn't supposed to be like this.

We are...

What were they now?

It didn't matter. He would sooner let the Skinless Man carve his body into small pieces than allow E.V.A. to be hurt. It was a line Weapon XIII should never have crossed, and he would make the imposter pay.

He jumped up from behind the table, firing again to plant Weapon XIII firmly behind the column. Charging forward, he flung his smallest knife at E.V.A. It skimmed across her outstretched hand, just a small cut, but hopefully the brief pain would bite deep enough to penetrate the fog that Weapon XIII had woven around her mind. She looked down at the cut, the thin trail of blood running across her palm, and shook her head as if to clear it.

"Glider!" he shouted, praying that she heard him and understood.

He ran out of bullets, so he moved on to the café chairs, seizing two and hurling them at Weapon XIII in quick succession when he popped out from behind the column, gun leading. The metal clanged off the column, and outside the building there came the distant, muted sound of screams.

Of course. People could see them fighting from the street. Museum security hadn't turned up yet, but that was likely because they knew they were outmatched. No doubt the entire city of Edmonton was mobilizing a force to take back the museum from the two mutants so obviously making it their battle ground.

Probably they had already summoned whatever Sentinel presence was currently in the area as well.

He made it to the column just as Weapon XIII reached around it with his gun. Fantomex seized his wrist and twisted it, slamming it against the column so that the gun went flying. He followed with a high kick that connected with the other man's jaw, sending him backward and over a table.

Energy blasts filled the air, striking Weapon XIII, not powerful enough to kill but strong enough to knock him into the far wall.

The tide was turning.

Fantomex whirled in time to see E.V.A. transform into a much smaller, sleeker version of her ship form, vaguely shaped like a metal boomerang. He ran to the glider and hopped on. The surface was large enough for one person. Well, maybe two.

"Let's finish this somewhere a bit less public," he said as Weapon XIII jumped to his feet and launched himself at Fantomex again. But instead of trying to drive him back,

Fantomex grabbed him by the lapels of his long coat and shouted, "Go!"

E.V.A. went, straight up through the gap in the shattered atrium ceiling, out into the crisp afternoon air.

"Take us–"

He never got the chance to say. Weapon XIII drove his shoulder into Fantomex, the momentum knocking them off the glider, sending it spinning away, and both of them into a freefall. They landed hard on the museum roof, rolling along the metal ribbon. Luckily, E.V.A. hadn't gotten much altitude or the fall would have ended badly for both of them.

But Weapon XIII was still attached to him like a burr, his hands inching toward Fantomex's throat again.

"You're… incredibly… needy… you know that?" Fantomex punctuated the words with a series of punches to the head.

"I was hoping you'd be useful to me," Weapon XIII growled. His face was so close, one eye half-closed from the punches, that Fantomex could see the similarities in their features were striking. "But you truly are… the least of us."

"Well, this has been an engaging therapy session." Fantomex shoved him back against the ridge of metal, but his muscles were beginning to burn with fatigue. "The military is likely going to break it up soon, no?"

E.V.A. drifted into his line of vision, still in glider form with weapons primed, momentarily blocking the sun. "Get the girl," Fantomex told her. "We're about to have company."

# CHAPTER THIRTEEN

Avery ran blindly through the café's kitchen and out the rear door. A set of grimy stairs led down to two more doors, one of them marked as the underground parking garage. The other one had no sign at all. Only the door to the parking garage was unlocked, so she hooked the laptop bag and her messenger bag over her shoulder and pushed through that one.

Outside, it was cold and dark. To her right were several rows of parked cars, while to her left, across the garage, a ramp led up to the street-level exit. Beyond it, she could see the flashing lights of about a dozen police cars and a handful of more heavily armored military vehicles.

"It's fine. It's going to be fine," she whispered to herself as she limped across the garage. She'd sprained her ankle somehow in her desperation to get away, and now it throbbed painfully with every step she took. "Cops everywhere, rogue mutants trying to kill each other upstairs, and I have a stolen painting in my bag."

She needed to hide.

She wasn't picky. A gray SUV sat parked halfway down the row nearest her. She dropped to her belly and slithered underneath, trying to ignore the freezing cold concrete and dirty, slushy puddles around its tires.

Her hand reflexively clutched the laptop bag, trying not to jostle it, but there were no energy surges emitting from the painting now. Whatever threat had loomed upstairs seemed to have passed now that the painting was safe with her.

Was it possible she had imagined those strange energy surges up in the atrium? Could Fantomex have been lying to her about the painting being a bomb? She wouldn't put it past him, but what did he gain from telling her that? He'd seemed genuinely worried when he'd confronted her.

What were the odds that so many different people wanted the Alano painting? Were willing to fight to the death over it, by the sound of all the gunfire coming from the lobby.

None of this made any sense. But Avery knew she had to get out of here. She couldn't be caught with the painting. Maybe she could hide it in a trashcan or something. Then she could slip out of the parking garage and blend in with the crowds outside until she could safely come back for it later.

But even as she considered that idea, she felt a strange quiver from the bag, like something stirring. Her heartbeat quickened. So much for this being a figment of her imagination.

Biting her lip to keep from whimpering in fear, she forced herself to put her hand on the bag and pat it awkwardly.

"OK," she whispered. "OK, I won't leave you behind. Just don't… you know… explode. Please."

Now she was talking to a painting. She was definitely losing it.

Across the garage she heard a door open and slam shut, then footsteps pelted down the row of cars. They were moving away from her, but Avery held her breath, tucking into a ball and holding absolutely still.

The footsteps eventually stopped, then started again, then stopped. As if someone was looking for something.

"Avery."

Looking for her.

"Avery, where are you?"

Avery stayed where she was, frozen, but gradually the woman's voice penetrated the fog of fear that had wrapped around her mind. It was the woman who'd been with Fantomex. E.V.A., he'd called her.

She weighed her options. She could stay hidden and hope that the police didn't sweep into the garage in the next few minutes to search the area. Or she could trust that the woman was here to help and didn't mean to harm her.

She and Fantomex had both been welcomed at the school, at least as far as she knew. That meant Cyclops must trust them, as far as that went.

She didn't see any better options, so, reluctantly, she crawled out from under the SUV and stood on legs that were trembling. "Over here," she said, her voice strained and quiet. She thought there was no way the woman could have heard her, but the footsteps paused, and E.V.A. doubled back down the row to join her.

"I'm glad you're safe," the woman said, laying a hand on Avery's arm. "We need to get out of here quickly."

A loud, shrill siren cut off any reply Avery might have made. Ducking behind the SUV, they risked a glance through the back windows of the vehicle. At the top of the exit ramp, an armored military vehicle was pulling in, blocking the way out.

"I was hoping to avoid this," E.V.A. said, her forehead creased in worry. Taking Avery's arm, she pointed to the opposite end of the parking garage, where another ramp led up to an exit on the south side of the street. "When I give the signal, run as fast as you can toward that exit."

Avery doubted her injured ankle and shaking legs could carry her far, but she nodded. There was no other choice. "What's the signal?"

"This." E.V.A. turned and lifted her hands. Her right arm elongated and hardened, shifting into a scythe-like weapon from her shoulder down. Her left arm began to glow with energy, a brilliant ball of amber light gathering between her fingertips that she hurled at the oncoming armored car.

Avery turned and ran.

Behind her, there was a loud boom as the energy blast hit the side of the car. Avery risked a glance over her shoulder and saw E.V.A. follow up the strike with a swing of the scythe in a wide arc that tore the entire front end off the car and left a nasty, jagged gash in the windshield. The driver and passenger spilled out and took cover behind the rear bumper, but E.V.A. was done with them, it seemed, and she'd done enough. Armor or not, the car wouldn't be going anywhere. She began running after Avery, who turned her attention back to the exit.

A cold knot of dread settled in her stomach. Two more police cars were approaching, their lights flashing, sirens wailing.

She wasn't going to make it. Her ankle throbbed, she was weighted down by bags, and she was limping more than running. They were going to cut her off.

Panicked, Avery glanced back. E.V.A. was coming full speed ahead. If Avery hadn't been so frightened, she would have been deeply impressed to see the woman running all out in a business casual suit and two-inch heels with a scythe for an arm. But she wasn't going to make it out either.

And then the woman jumped, drawing her knees up to her chest. For an instant, time slowed, or maybe the woman simply defied the laws of gravity. Whatever was happening, Avery had never seen anything like it. E.V.A.'s body pulled in on itself, the scythe shrinking and reforming rapidly into a spherical mass of metal surrounded by spinning rings with spindly, insect-like legs.

No, not legs, Avery thought, but a kind of landing platform. The woman had transformed into a flying saucer.

And she was now moving very, very fast.

A hysterical laugh bubbled up in Avery's throat, but she didn't have time to lose it like she wanted to. E.V.A.'s voice rang out in the parking garage, amplified and deep. Becoming a ship must do that to you.

"Turn around and jump!"

Seriously?

Avery stopped, turned, and saw a doorway slide open in the sphere, just like in all the movies she'd ever seen about aliens and flying saucers. The ship was barreling right for her, ready to scoop her up.

Well, it was the military on one side or… this. Summoning her courage, Avery waited until the ship was almost on top of her.

She jumped.

The ship took her, smooth as silk, into its interior, though the landing left something to be desired. Avery banged her shoulder on a hard metal surface, landing with her bags wedged between her hip and the floor. Quickly, she rolled off the painting and sat up, hoping it hadn't been damaged. The door in the side of the ship slid shut and blended seamlessly with the wall.

Trapped now. Wherever they were going, Avery was along for the ride whether she liked it or not.

Don't panic. Don't panic.

"For your safety, it would be best if you came up front and strapped into one of the cockpit chairs," E.V.A.'s voice, tight but calm, echoed through the ship. "We're going to have a bit of a bumpy journey getting out of here."

At that moment, something large and heavy slammed into the side of the ship, throwing Avery to the floor again.

"You call that bumpy?" she yelled.

"Apologies."

Scrambling up on all fours, she crawled to the front of the ship and threw herself into the center chair, which was flanked on either side by a pair of control panels and some kind of VR unit that looked almost… organic. Avery shuddered and focused on strapping the laptop bag into the chair next to her and then securing herself.

Not a moment too soon. The ship tilted sharply, throwing her against the harness and knocking the breath from her body.

"What's going on?" Avery shouted when she managed to suck air back into her lungs. "What's hitting us?" She gestured wildly to the blank wall in front of them. "Put it on the main viewer or something!"

"This is not a science fiction television program," E.V.A. said dryly. But, in a fair imitation of one, the metal wall in front of Avery peeled back, revealing a bank of darkly tinted windows that gave a panoramic view of the outside.

Avery was sorry she'd asked.

They'd cleared the parking garage, but in front of them was a wall of armored vehicles and a pair of Sentinels. Avery had seen news footage of the robots – mutant hunters. They were even more frightening up close. Very close. One of them had grabbed onto the ship and was trying to yank it out of the air. E.V.A. maneuvered frantically to try to break its grip.

"Weapons systems locked," E.V.A. said, and a burst of amber energy erupted from the ship, filling the windows with a blinding glow that had Avery throwing up an arm in front of her face. When she could see again, hope surged within her.

The Sentinel had been blown backward, crushing one of the military vehicles beneath its weight.

"Nice!" Avery shouted, punching the air with her fist. Wait, was she actually enjoying this a teeny bit?

"Hold on!"

Before Avery could react, the ship surged straight upward,

leaving her stomach behind. Cold sweat broke out on her forehead and neck. Nope, she'd changed her mind. She definitely hated this. Clamping her lips together, she squeezed her eyes shut, praying to the gastrointestinal gods that she wouldn't throw up, and praying to anyone who would listen that they wouldn't be blown out of the sky.

Nothing happened. The shuddering sensation in the ship eased as they leveled out, and her stomach steadied with it.

She risked opening her eyes a crack. They were flying high above the city now, and the museum was a speck of gray metal and glass below. But before Avery could be suitably relieved to be out of reach of the scary robots, the ship was turning, angling back toward the ground. No no no. Avery didn't want to go back down there. She wanted to stay up here where it was safe and smooth and there was no one trying to kill them. "Where are we going?" she asked.

"We have to get Fantomex," E.V.A. said.

She groaned, hoping E.V.A. wouldn't hear her. "Where is he?"

"I have a visual."

Avery leaned forward to look. Below them, the museum's sculpture garden spread out like a maze, the statues and installations covered in a light blanket of snow.

Right in the middle of that peaceful scene it looked like someone had taken a huge shovel and scraped it across the ground, tearing up the landscape and knocking over three of the modern art sculptures.

Anger flooded Avery. She gripped the arms of her chair. "Don't they even care about what they're destroying? I thought your friend was supposed to love culture and art?"

"He does," E.V.A. said, and even amidst the tension Avery recognized the edge of worry and sadness in her voice. "But he's never had to fight this kind of battle before. He can't prevent the collateral damage, and I'm not entirely sure he can win, no matter how hard he tries."

# CHAPTER FOURTEEN

A less confident man might say he was losing this battle.

The fleeting thought passed through Fantomex's mind as he tumbled across the snow-covered grass, fetching up against the base of a large statue of a human hand rising from the ground, fingers splayed, as if reaching to pluck something out of the sky.

Fantomex pushed himself to his feet as Weapon XIII stalked toward him, stealing a precious few seconds to take stock. He was bleeding from at least three serious wounds, one of them a gunshot to the calf, but he was fairly certain the bullet had passed cleanly through, so he could hold himself up a little bit longer.

The military and the Sentinels were another matter, but, luckily or unluckily, depending on how you wanted to look at it, Weapon XIII had noticed them as well and thrown a misdirection that had two of the Sentinels turning on their masters. Now a group of soldiers and robots were tied up in a pitched battle near the museum's south loading dock. There was another battle going on near the parking garage, which, if he had to guess, was what was delaying E.V.A. from coming to rescue him from this fight, which had devolved into a punishing bout of hand-to-hand combat.

*Ah, here comes some more punishment.*

Fantomex surged forward, landing a satisfying upper cut that snapped Weapon XIII's head to the side, but he was too tired to follow it up and just took that opportunity to breathe. A fire burned in his lungs.

"What's so important... about... it?" he gasped, trying to distract his single-minded enemy. "The painting? Why are you... and Cluster... after it?"

And why was it a time bomb set to go off at the whim of a college student? So many questions, but it was getting increasingly difficult to concentrate – or care – about any of the answers. He really needed to rest. Or fall unconscious.

Weapon XIII, predictably, said nothing. He hadn't said anything since he'd demanded the painting from them. He wiped the blood out of his eyes and did a spinning kick so fast Fantomex barely had time to register the movement before it connected with his solar plexus. His back hit the statue of the hand, and with a loud crack the sculpture split, falling to the ground in a spray of snow and dirt.

Fantomex fell with it, and he knew he was done. All the helpless rage in the world wasn't going to get him back on his feet. Either Weapon XIII was going to try to parley with him for the painting again, or he was going to kill him.

A spray of energy blasts tore up the ground around Weapon XIII, two of them catching him in the back. He screamed and fell to his knees, giving Fantomex enough hope and energy to pull himself up on shaking legs as E.V.A.

glided fast toward him, the ship hovering inches above the ground. A doorway in the sphere slid open, and he dove inside.

He felt them rising into the air, fast and smooth, away from the museum and the city. Or at least he assumed they were. He couldn't move or even lift his head to look out the wall of windows off to his right.

After a moment, he was dimly aware that someone crouched before him. He cracked an eye open. Avery hovered over him, examining his wounds.

"He's bleeding a lot," she said, directing the statement to E.V.A. "Do you have any first aid onboard this… er, I mean, you?"

He reached up with a trembling hand and took hold of Avery's wrist. She looked down at him in surprise.

"Let her concentrate… on flying," he said. He pointed Avery in the direction of a metal cabinet attached to the back wall of the ship. "In there."

She nodded and went where he pointed, opening the sliding door to reveal a kit of bandages, gauze, disinfectant, and other first aid supplies. After a moment of indecision, she brought everything back and scattered it on the floor beside him.

He helped her as best he could, grabbing the gauze and pressing it against the wound at his hip while she worked on the one at his calf.

"Can you go into a healing trance?" E.V.A. asked. "It will be some time before we reach the school."

"I don't think so," he said roughly. He was teetering on the edge of unconsciousness as it was. If he tried to relax and enter a meditative state, he might pass out instead. Much as he hated to admit it, he needed Christopher Muse's help, just like last time, in order to repair himself. He'd lost too much of his healing ability in the separation.

He gritted his teeth against the pain. Would he always be forced to rely on other people now? People who might abandon him at the first sign of trouble?

It was very possible that that circumstance had already happened. Once they returned to the Institute and Cyclops and Emma Frost learned what had transpired at the museum.

Assuming they didn't already know, of course.

He groaned.

"Am I hurting you?" Avery asked, her brows drawn tightly together. Her hands where they were pressed over the wound at his calf were trembling. He knew he should have thanked her for her aid, but as his gaze fell on the laptop bag sitting on one of the cockpit chairs nearby, the scene in the museum lobby rushed back to him.

If Avery Torres hadn't swooped in with her righteous anger and a painting that she'd somehow transformed into a Cubist thermal detonator, they might have made it out of the museum without any fuss or damage. Instead he was bleeding out on the floor of the ship, and his pride had taken a number of blows it might never recover from.

"*You*," he said, using his most intimidating tone, but it came out so faint that it lacked any punch. "We need to have a *discussion*."

As it turned out, he wasn't the only one who wanted to have a nice long chat punctuated by some yelling. As soon as they arrived back at the Institute and E.V.A. and Avery helped him to the infirmary, Cyclops descended upon them in all his ruby-eyed wrath, with Triage trailing behind and looking as if he wanted to be anywhere but here.

"What did you think you were doing?" Scott ranted, as Fantomex shifted his body onto the examining table so the young healer could take a look at his leg, which seemed at the moment to be the biggest concern and the greatest source of blood loss. "Minus Avery, your faces are on the Edmonton news, amateur footage of your battle is all over social media, and I'm fairly certain S.H.I.E.L.D. is having meetings right now to decide how best to deal with the problem." He jabbed a finger at Fantomex. "If they decide it's worth sending a unit sniffing around up here, it puts us in an incredibly dangerous position. This is everything I was trying to avoid!"

Maybe his bellowing would have had a greater impact on the students, but Fantomex was more affected by the shooting pain in his leg as Christopher manipulated it into position to start his healing process. "I highly doubt Weapon XIII cared whether or not he exposed this place," Fantomex growled. "He would have come for the painting, likely in the same very public fashion, whether we had been there or not. But if we'd gone with Emma Frost's plan of securing it, we'd be sitting on our hands watching news footage of his theft right now."

And they'd be no closer to figuring out why Cluster – and now Weapon XIII – were stealing these artifacts. Although he had a pretty good idea it was tied somehow to Avery's strange reaction with the Alano painting.

Speaking of which...

He gestured at Avery, who had been trying to sidle quietly

out the door while they were arguing, the laptop bag slung over her shoulder. "Not so fast," he snapped, causing her to freeze in place and turn to glare at him. "Don't look at me like that. Perhaps you'd like to share with all of us just what's going on with you and that painting you're trying to sneak out of here."

All eyes in the room, even Christopher's, swung to Avery, but instead of shrinking under the attention, she raised her chin slightly in defiance. "I was only trying to protect the painting from you," she said. She shot an accusing glance at Cyclops. "I didn't know they were stealing it on your orders."

"He wasn't following anyone's orders, and it's a lot more complicated than that," Cyclops said. He glanced between the two of them. "What exactly did happen at the museum, and how did Avery get involved?"

Judging by the stubborn set to her expression, Avery wasn't going to be volunteering to lead the retelling of their daring exploits, so Fantomex launched into the story, leaving nothing out and putting particular emphasis on the moment when Avery had interfered in their attempt at a clean escape, somehow transforming the painting into a bomb.

When he'd finished, Cyclops stood tense, thinking. Triage was focused on his healing, but even he seemed unsettled. And Avery, despite her defiance, was unable to hide the fear in her eyes.

Fantomex felt a stab of regret. He'd taken his frustration out at her expense, but he hadn't meant to make her feel afraid. Here among the X-Men was probably the last place she would face rejection, but if she was new here, she couldn't be expected to know that.

She spoke before he could try to reassure her. "I didn't make the painting do whatever it was it did," she said, then, biting her lip, "at least not on purpose."

"We know that," Cyclops said, his voice gentling. "So let me try to understand. When you met with Professor Xavier all those years ago–" his jaw tightened, but whatever emotion he felt was gone so quickly, Fantomex thought he must have imagined it "–he thought you had psychometry powers, but he never saw you do anything like this. Is that right?"

She shifted uneasily. Hesitating for an instant, she pulled the laptop bag around to unzip the zipper. Carefully, she lifted out the painting. There was a hairline crack in the top of the frame, but otherwise it was undamaged. Fantomex was impressed she'd been able to keep it so protected during their escape from the museum.

"I first discovered my powers when I touched this painting at the museum when I was in middle school," she said. Fantomex shot her a look of disapproval, but she only rolled her eyes. "You have no room to be self-righteous, Mr I Stole a Painting in Broad Daylight and I'm Not Even Sorry."

"Ignore him," Cyclops said. He walked over to take the painting from her. "What happened when you touched it?"

"I saw into the past," she said. "I had a vision I was in her studio – Ruby Alano's. At least, I think it was her. I watched her working on the painting, and I felt a connection to her and to her art, but it was always like I was witnessing something that had already happened. I think that's what made the Professor think I was using psychometry. I could never interact with the vision until…"

"Until?" Scott prompted.

Her gaze shifted uncertainly to the painting. "Yesterday, I was having a vision. Everything was the same as always, but then, all of a sudden, Ruby Alano looked up at me. I can't explain it, but somehow she knew I was there. She tried to talk to me, but there were no words coming from her mouth." She lifted her shoulders helplessly. "That's never happened before."

So, he'd been right. Avery did have a personal connection to the painting. Fantomex hadn't had the opportunity to examine the work up close, but now that he did he felt that familiar rush of emotion he always experienced when he was in the presence of a piece that moved him. The colors, the angles, even the stones of the tower were rendered with such love and care that it took his breath away.

"Art is what separates us from the monsters," he murmured.

"Since you came to the school and started practicing your abilities, how many similar experiences have you had like the one with the painting?" Cyclops asked, pulling him from his musings.

Avery hesitated. "None."

"None?" Cyclops was taken aback. "But I thought…"

"That something would have broken through by now," Avery interrupted. "Yeah, so did I, but it's only ever been with that painting."

The way Avery looked at the painting, Fantomex could tell that its beauty pierced her heart the same way it did him. Another mark in her favor, as far as he was concerned.

She was still a nuisance.

"This can't be a coincidence," Fantomex said. "Weapon XIII and Cluster interested in the same painting that triggered visions for Avery and then a volatile reaction when we forcibly tried to separate her from it? Is it possible Avery's powers were mischaracterized?"

"As much as I hate to say it, I agree with Fantomex."

He looked up. Emma Frost stood in the doorway. E.V.A. was with her. They both wore similar worried frowns, and that made him uneasy.

"What's wrong?" Cyclops asked.

"We've been analyzing my scans of the painting and comparing them to the data we collected from the Diana statue," E.V.A. said. "We found something. We need to speak to Avery."

"Alone," Emma said, when Fantomex scooted to the edge of the examining table. "Stay here and finish getting patched up." She glanced at Cyclops. "You set him straight yet?"

"I was getting to that part, but we got sidetracked." He handed the painting back to Avery, who slipped it into the laptop bag. She followed Emma and E.V.A. from the room with all the enthusiasm of a prison inmate on death row.

When she'd gone, Triage gave his healed wounds one last look, then nodded in satisfaction. "You know, there were plenty of artists in history who were also terrible people," he said. It took Fantomex a second to realize he was referring to his earlier comment about art and monsters. Before he could reply, the young man added, "I'm all done here. Try not to get banged up again so soon, will you?"

Fantomex flexed his healed leg and rolled his shoulder, marveling that there wasn't any sign of scarring or stiffness. "Thank you," he said. "The pain is completely gone. This is excellent work."

Christopher's brows lifted in surprise at the compliment. "You're welcome."

When he too had left the room, Fantomex glanced at Cyclops and then raised his hands and gestured to himself. "Let the yelling commence," he invited.

But Cyclops didn't look like a man on the verge of yelling. He'd gone quiet, and stared at Fantomex so intently he found he would have preferred a round of shouting.

"Do you remember what I told you when you first woke up here?" he asked. "That if you harmed any of the students at this school, we'd have a very different conversation?"

"I recall it, yes." So, he was about to be cast out of the Institute. He couldn't say he was surprised, but the fear and disappointment tightening his gut was something he hadn't expected.

"The only reason you aren't flying away in your ship right now is because you kept Avery safe," Cyclops said. "We checked the surveillance footage starting from the beginning of the day up through your little escapade. You replaced all the footage."

"Well, technically, E.V.A. did, but that's because she's much less ham-fisted than I am."

Cyclops seemed to hold onto his patience with an impressive effort. "My point is that Avery doesn't appear on the footage anywhere near the heist, so her identity is protected. As far as we can tell from the news reports, no civilians were hurt on the museum grounds either. There was significant property damage, of course."

Which had mostly been caused by his body impacting various art pieces in the sculpture garden. Fantomex winced at the memory. "Believe me when I say I am more upset by that circumstance than anyone here." He respected art. Despite appearances to the contrary, he suspected Cluster did too. Obviously, Weapon XIII was the most changed of their strange trio, especially since he'd appeared to have no qualms about ending the life of one of his counterparts.

"I know you think you have something to prove," Cyclops continued, "but there are more things at stake here than your pride. If you keep up the lone wolf antics, someone's going to get hurt. This isn't the X-Force. Not everyone here is trained, and some of the students are just here to learn about their powers and have a safe haven. I won't ruin that for them, and I won't let you ruin it either."

Fantomex stood up, facing Cyclops squarely. "You think this is about my pride? You think I don't want to find out what's going on with these… other selves… as much as you do? I want it more!" Deliberately, he took a calming breath and lowered his voice. "You have no idea what it's like to have two vital parts of yourself ripped away, to be left behind to figure out what sort of meaning is left in your existence."

Cyclops let out a sharp breath and stepped back, almost as if he'd been punched. He recovered quickly, though. "I understand more than you think," he said quietly, "but if anything like this happens again, you're gone." He turned and walked out of the room, slamming the door to the infirmary behind him.

# CHAPTER FIFTEEN

Avery had never been in the Danger Room before. Oh, she knew what it was, and she'd heard the other students describing the simulations – how intense they were and how they helped in their training as X-Men. But she had never had any desire to be one of the X-Men, so she'd asked to be excluded from those sessions. Instead, her training had been focused on trying to understand her powers. She'd still taken part in self-defense classes and things like that. It was always good to know how to defend yourself, whether you were a mutant or not. But right now she was wishing she'd taken part in at least one Danger Room session before today. She was feeling alone and out of her depth, and she had no idea what was about to happen.

Her palms were sweaty as she stood clutching the bag with the painting inside and watching Emma Frost and E.V.A. discussing something across the room, something that was obviously about her but that they didn't want her to overhear. The waiting and wondering were doing nothing for her nerves.

Behind her, the doors to the Danger Room hissed open, and two familiar faces strode in: David Bond and Christopher Muse. They were heading in her direction. For some reason, she was relieved to see them, though she wasn't quite sure why. It wasn't like she knew either of them well.

Emma looked up with a faint scowl. "This is a private meeting, gentlemen," she said. "Whatever you need, it'll have to wait."

Christopher raised his hands in a placating gesture. "Won't be a minute, I promise." He pointed to Avery. "I didn't get a chance to heal her ankle while she was in the infirmary."

Avery blinked in surprise. She hadn't realized he'd even noticed she was hurt. The pain in her ankle had subsided to a dull throb, but she could feel it was swollen beneath the cuff of her jeans.

"He would have, but he was too busy treating François," David added with a smirk.

"I see." Emma's scowl didn't lift. "And what are you doing here, David?"

"Moral support," he said breezily, as he came to stand next to Avery. "And … well, literal support." He offered his arm, as Christopher went down on one knee to examine her ankle.

"Can I have you lift your foot off the ground, please?" he asked her politely. "It'll be easier if you're not putting weight on it while I work."

Taking David's arm to keep her balance, Avery lifted her foot and pulled up the cuff of her jeans to show the swollen ankle. She was curious about how his powers worked, but she didn't really want to see them up close right at the moment. She was nervous enough about why she was here, and she'd seen her fill of mutant powers in action for one day.

"Don't worry," David said, pitching his voice low so the two women across the room couldn't hear them. "We've all been here. Your first Danger Room session can be a shock. Just remember that no matter how real it looks, it's all an illusion."

"Good advice, but it's easy to forget it in the moment," Christopher said, wincing as if at some memory. He glanced up at her. "Is it all right if I touch your ankle for a minute? I promise it'll be quick, and it won't hurt."

Appreciating that he'd asked, Avery nodded for him to go ahead. "I am scared," she confessed. Her throat tightened, the words coming unwillingly. "I don't know what's going on with my powers, and I don't want to hurt anyone." It was hard to admit, but she had to share her fears with someone. Jane was gone – Avery hadn't even been able to check to see if she'd answered her breakup text – and these were the only people who had any idea what she was going through.

David cast her a look of understanding. Avery silently thanked him for not pitying her. She couldn't stand that. "Remember where we are," he said, reaching behind him with his free hand to bang on the wall of the Danger Room. The metal was rock solid, absorbing the impact like he'd merely tapped his finger on its surface. "This is an old military base."

"Among other things, if you believe all the rumors," Christopher said. His hands moved carefully over her ankle. As he'd promised, it didn't hurt it all. He was good at this.

David snorted. "Some of those are too wild to be true. But one thing that is true is that this place was built to be a fortress. It can take a beating and not show a scratch. Also, there are people here who've probably dealt with far worse than whatever it is your powers can do. Trust them, and trust us." He shot her a grin. "We don't let anything happen to our friends, even the temporary ones."

Avery chuckled at that. She couldn't help it. How she was able to find any bit of humor in this was beyond her, but for the first time since her message to Jane she felt less alone.

"All right, I'm done here," Christopher said, hopping to his feet. "Take it out for a spin," he said, as if he were showing off a new car.

Avery put her foot down and gingerly tested her weight on her ankle. It was no longer swollen, and the pain was gone, as if she'd never been hurt at all.

"If only every pain could be cured so easily," she murmured. Her cheeks burned as she realized she'd spoken the words aloud.

Of course, Christopher heard her. But he didn't comment, only gave her a thoughtful look. Then he leaned in and said, in a conspiratorial whisper, "I almost forgot to mention, there's a kitchen raid scheduled for tonight. Tell no one, come alone, and come at midnight."

Avery blinked, confused but intrigued. "What's a kitchen raid?" she whispered back.

David answered her. "It's a thing where a few of us sneak down to the kitchen once a month or so and look for secret food stashes the teachers are hiding from us."

Avery's stomach gave an embarrassing rumble, reminding

her that it had been a long time since she'd eaten her sesame bagel and coffee. "Do you ever find anything?" She tried to sound casual.

Christopher sighed longingly. "Not yet, but we remain ever hopeful," he said. "So, will you come?"

Avery started to say no out of habit. It had been a long, terrible day, full of revelations she hadn't yet begun to process. She needed time to sort everything out. But the idea of being alone in her room tonight, with nothing to do except wallow in her breakup pain or worry about her powers blowing up the school, held zero appeal.

"I'll be there at midnight," she promised.

"Excellent." Christopher offered a hand to shake on it.

"All right, you two, I can see that she's healed, so it's time to get back to wherever you should be right now," Emma called from across the room.

Avery took Christopher's hand and shook quickly. "Thank you for the healing," she said. "I feel much better now."

Christopher smiled. "Later." He waved and then called out to Emma before he left the room. "Don't scare her like you scared me."

She sniffed. "I don't know what you're talking about."

"Yes, you do."

"It was for your own good."

The men were chuckling all the way out the door.

When the doors slid shut behind them, Avery took a deep breath and strode over to join the two women. E.V.A. held the painting aloft and appeared to be studying it intently, her amber eyes flashing every now and then. It reminded Avery simultaneously of a scholar hard at work studying an artifact and a computer processing information at lightning speeds.

Emma said, for her benefit, "E.V.A.'s been working in conjunction with our own systems to analyze the painting's composition down to the molecular level. It took some doing, but we found something you need to see."

Her serious expression made Avery's stomach turn over. She watched as a wide metal platform rose from the ground to waist height in front of E.V.A. A smaller platform grew six inches from that one, and E.V.A. propped the painting up against it. The room darkened around them until Avery couldn't see much more than the outline of the painting and the profiles of the women standing next to her. Then a light shone down from above, directly onto the canvas. It reminded Avery somewhat of a blacklight, but it was different. When it shone on the painting, it made the colors look strange and wavering, and the painting appeared to be covered with hundreds, maybe thousands, of tiny red dots, like the tip of a laser pointer but smaller. They covered the canvas, obscuring the woman and the tower.

"What is that?" Avery asked. "Something in the paint?"

E.V.A. shook her head. "You're looking at the composition of the painting itself. Or, I should say, the imitation of the painting."

Avery's heart gave a painful lurch. "Wait, you mean… this painting is fake?"

All this time, her favorite work of art had been an imitation? It wasn't Ruby Alano's work at all? But what did that mean for her visions? Were they nothing more than hallucinations? Her mind reeled with the possible implications.

E.V.A. gestured to the thousands of red dots. "What you're looking at is a crude visual representation of nano-technology, machines so small they can't be perceived by the naked eye. The Danger Room is giving us a simulation of what they might look like magnified several thousand times over. They are what the painting and certain pieces of the Diana statue are primarily composed of. It's what allowed Cluster to steal an arrow from the statue's quiver without damaging it. She removed the portion that contained the nanotech."

As E.V.A. spoke, Avery became aware that the woman was studying her intently, as focused as she had been when she'd been examining the painting. "What?" she demanded, fear making her angry. "I can tell you're analyzing me now. Are you going to tell me that I'm an imitation too?"

Emma Frost laid a hand on her arm. "You're as real as they come," she assured her, "but you're going to want to stay calm for this next part."

Her words had the opposite effect. Avery's breath quickened, and her stomach twisted up in painful knots. "Why?" she asked. "What's wrong with me?"

"Nothing is wrong with you," E.V.A. said gently, "but I suspected – and I've confirmed it just now – that you are infused with some of the same nanotechnology that is present in the painting. That's why it responded to you and your extreme distress in the museum."

Avery felt the world tilting, her knees turning to jelly. Only Emma's hand on her arm kept her from collapsing. She looked up, half-expecting that strange light to shine down on her the way it did on the painting, illuminating thousands of tiny red bugs – nanotech, whatever – crawling over her skin. Luckily, nothing like that happened. The women must have realized she could only take so many shocks in one day. Avery clutched her elbows, digging her arms into her stomach to keep from being sick. "What's going to happen to me?" She was afraid of the answer, but she had to know.

"Nothing," Emma said firmly, squeezing her arm. "E.V.A. assures me that the nanotech is not a danger to your health in any way. We don't know why it attached itself to you, but we're going to find out."

Well, that was a relief. But Avery was still tense and unsettled by the idea that she had these things inside her at all.

"Does this have anything to do with my psychometric powers?" she asked. "Is that how the nanotech got inside me?"

E.V.A. and Emma exchanged glances, and Avery felt a fresh wave of fear. "Stop doing that," she snapped. "I'm not a child. Just tell me what's happening."

"I've read the notes your instructors have taken about your abilities," Emma said slowly, choosing her words carefully. "They confirmed what you said earlier, that you've never been able to read any of the objects you were presented with for practice."

Avery nodded. "Like I told Cyclops, it's only ever been the painting. I just thought it was because I'd been around it so long." She found herself staring at the little red dots writhing on the surface of the canvas. It was painful to watch, like they might wipe away the art before her eyes.

Except it wouldn't matter. The painting had been a fake from the beginning. She'd been fooled by an imitation.

Following her gaze, Emma waved a hand, causing the red dots to disappear and the lights to come up in the Danger Room. She wore a pensive frown. "Based on all the evidence, we have to conclude that your powers aren't what we originally thought."

"You don't think I'm a mutant?" A lightness fluttered in her chest at the possibility. If she wasn't a mutant, she could go home, back to America, to California and to Jane. It would be like none of this had ever happened.

But the giddy feeling fled as quickly as it had appeared when Emma shook her head. "I know you're a mutant," she said, leaving no room for argument. "Your powers must be connected to the presence of the nanotech in some way, but until we know exactly what that connection is, we need to tread carefully. We don't want to trigger your powers in some way that causes the nanotech to become volatile like it did at the museum."

"We just need a little more time to solve the mystery," E.V.A. said reassuringly, as Avery fought down panic. "To that end, I'd like your permission to share what we've learned with Fantomex. He may have insight that would prove useful."

Avery knew she must have pulled a sour face, because Emma's eyes lit briefly with amusement. "I guess… if you really think it's necessary." She couldn't afford to turn away help when there was strange, potentially explosive nanotech swimming inside her. Even if that help came in the form of a smug, pseudo-French man-child like Fantomex.

E.V.A. lifted the painting carefully from its makeshift pedestal and held it out to her. "I think this will be safest in your care for now."

Avery looked to Emma for permission, and the other woman nodded. "Keep it locked in your room and out of sight. I don't think there will be any other incidents with the painting threatening to explode while you're both here and safe on the school grounds."

"You're sure it wouldn't be better off locked in a vault somewhere?" Avery asked as she held the painting gingerly.

"It might be, or it might react badly to being forcibly kept from you," Emma said. "There's too much that we don't know, and I don't like being in the dark, so I want you to practice with it." She held up a hand before Avery could say anything. "Take it slow, and if something doesn't feel right, you're to stop right away and inform us. But your visions may give us important clues to figuring out what your powers are and how they relate to the nanotech."

It made sense, and more than that, it gave Avery a goal, a mission to focus on so she wasn't just sitting around worried and afraid.

"I'll see what I can do," she promised, "but what if–"

She didn't get to finish, as an alarm echoed loudly throughout the Danger Room. Avery covered her ears. Emma stalked over to a control panel on the wall and banged her fist against it. "What's happening out there?" she said.

After a second or two, a voice came over the comm that was set into the panel. It sounded like Magneto. "We have an intruder approaching from the north. The perimeter cameras picked her up. Thirty-something female, injured."

There was a pause. "She's dressed like our annoying 'guest', and waving a white flag with writing on it." His voice had lost its edge of tension. "It says, 'Can a clone get a cup of hot tea, a scone, and a bandage?'" Another pause. "She just collapsed in the snow."

Beside Avery, E.V.A. straightened, looking agitated. "It's Cluster," she said. "She found us."

# CHAPTER SIXTEEN

Fantomex reached the hangar at a dead sprint, with E.V.A. right behind him. It was the closest exit to get to Cluster. As the hangar doors slid open, a blast of frigid air and swirls of snow surrounded them.

"How badly was she injured?" Fantomex demanded, as E.V.A. transformed into her ship form, the cockpit door already open. He jumped in, strapping himself into the pilot's seat in seconds.

"It was impossible to tell from the video feed," E.V.A. said, her voice tight with worry. "But Magneto said there was a considerable amount of blood darkening the snow."

Fantomex swore under his breath. It was Weapon XIII. He just knew it was. That was why Cluster hadn't turned up at the museum. Their darker half had gone after her first to take her out of the fight so he wouldn't have to face two of them at once.

Somehow, he'd known Fantomex would come down on Cluster's side in this strange conflict. A surprising bit of insight on his part, since Fantomex hadn't known himself that he *was* on her side – until he heard she was wounded. He didn't have time to examine that turn of events as they zipped along the white ground outside the Institute, dodging crescent-shaped snow drifts and sheets of ice that marred the barren landscape.

It didn't take long to get to her. E.V.A. moved like a bullet, following the directions Magneto had given them. As they drew closer, Fantomex could see a body lying curled into a ball in the snow. Drenched in a puddle of dark blood.

He threw off the seat harness and ran to the door. "Let's make this quick," he said. "Will Triage be waiting for us in the infirmary?"

"Cyclops assured me he would be," E.V.A. replied.

Maybe he should have brought the healer with him. But Fantomex hadn't wanted to wait. The longer they left Cluster stranded and exposed to the elements, the greater the chance she might succumb to her injuries before they could help her.

The door in the side of the ship slid open. Fantomex jumped out before E.V.A. had even come to a full stop. He landed gracefully in the hard-packed snow. Out in the open, the wind was fierce, bitingly cold, and visibility was bad, but even with the blowing snow and failing light of the day, there was no mistaking the blood spot on the ground several feet away.

Or the figure lying in the middle of it.

He ran to Cluster, dropping to his knees beside her. Her eyes were slitted, her hand pressed to a deep wound in her left flank. She was shivering violently. He stripped off his jacket and laid it over her.

Her eyes popped open and roved over him tiredly. "Took you... long enough," she said. It was difficult to understand her with her teeth chattering so badly. "I've been... hiking around... this frozen... wasteland... for at least an hour... without a proper coat... or a tourniquet."

"The school's hidden for a reason," he said. He looked her over quickly for other injuries, but there were only some bruises and scrapes. Good. The wound in her side was bad enough. "Can you stand, if I help?"

"It'll be interesting to find out," she said, wrapping an arm around his shoulders.

He lifted her weight, letting her get her feet under her, and slowly, they stood. He could have carried her, but he wanted her moving, staying conscious and aware. Instead, he wrapped the coat more securely around her, and together they limped to where E.V.A. had extended a set of stairs, wide and shallow so Cluster wouldn't have to move as much.

Once inside, the door slid closed, and a wave of delicious heat enveloped them. E.V.A. had cranked the internal temperature controls to maximum.

"Bless you, darling," Cluster said drowsily as she touched a hand to the wall of the ship.

"Hang on, don't I get any praise?" Fantomex grumbled as he helped her into the co-pilot's seat of the cockpit. The ship was already zigzagging through the snow on the way back to the Institute, so he had to hold on to the chair arm for balance. "I was the one who got out of the snow and gave you my jacket, despite the fact that you recently threw several vases at my face."

"I'm prepared to give you all the praise in the world,"

Cluster said, accepting the long, clean strips of bandages he offered her from the first aid kit that was waiting beside her chair. "You've been far more accommodating than our wayward brother. He didn't even offer so much as a hello before he broke my lovely new bow and then put a bullet in me."

Fantomex took the words like a blow. His fists clenched, tearing into the gauze strips as he stuffed the excess back into the kit. "So it *was* Weapon XIII. I thought as much, but one hopes..."

"Yes, one does," Cluster said sympathetically. She winced as if at a fresh wave of pain. "Luckily, I had a safe refuge to go to. Otherwise things might have been dire."

"How did you manage to find the Institute's exact location?" Fantomex asked. "And before you decide to lie, know that I'm simply the first in a long line of people who are going to be asking you that question – with varying degrees of hostility – once we return to the school. They value their privacy here, for obvious reasons."

"I wasn't followed, if that's your concern," Cluster said. She held up her hand, exposing a device that looked like an overcomplicated watch attached to her wrist. "The portal generator I obtained from the Clea had just enough power left to get me here."

"Clea, the sorceress?" Fantomex asked. "Dormammu's niece?"

"The very same." Her small smile indicated she would reveal no more on the matter as she continued, "Besides, Weapon XIII had other things to occupy himself with after he left me."

"Namely us," Fantomex drawled.

"I gathered that, yes," Cluster said. Her eyes were beginning to slide closed. With an effort she forced them open. "As for how I found the Institute, it's no great mystery." She reached up and fiddled with the collar of Fantomex's coat, folding it back to expose the lining underneath. There was a small hole there that he'd never noticed. She manipulated it with blood-stained fingers, until she'd worked free a small round metal disk, no bigger than a dime.

He took it from her, turning it over in his hands. "How very old-fashioned of you," he said. "Just a plain tracking device?"

She shrugged, or tried to, but she didn't seem to have much strength left. "Sometimes the simplest tricks work best. Anyway, that thing is supposed to be state of the art." She sighed. "Darlings, may I pass out for a while now? We must be getting close to the Institute, surely?"

"We are, and no, you can't pass out yet," Fantomex chided her. "I'm still angry with you."

She raised an eyebrow. "I don't believe you. I'm injured, and you're not a monster. You're a little bit worried about me."

He grunted. "You don't know anything about me or what I'm capable of. I could be taking you to a torture chamber right now for interrogation. Thumbscrews, the rack, the iron maiden."

She lifted her head in genuine interest. "Do they have torture devices at a school for mutants?"

"It used to be a Weapon Plus program headquarters," Fantomex said flatly. "I imagine a torture chamber comes standard."

"My my," Cluster murmured. "I'll have to be on my best behavior, then. What information are you trying to torture out of me?"

They'd reached the hangar. The doors parted enough to let E.V.A. fly inside. Fantomex had a great multitude of things he wanted to interrogate Cluster about, but she was barely holding onto consciousness now, and despite his bravado, fear did indeed have a tight grip on him. So, in the end, he asked the first thing that sprang to mind.

"What are you calling us?" he asked. "You, me, and Weapon XIII? You said you'd come up with a word to describe our unique... situation."

"Ah," she said, as the door in the ship slid open. Triage waited right outside, ready to go. Bless the man. "I knew you'd be curious. We're a triptych, the three of us."

A triptych. Of course. A work of art in three joined panels. He should have known she would see it that way.

She laid her hand gently against his cheek. "A lovely, strange, dysfunctional triptych."

Then she passed out.

Fantomex stood at the foot of the bed where Cluster lay, her face leached of color and vitality. E.V.A. sat in a chair on one side of the bed, while Christopher Muse sat on the opposite side, using his healing power on Cluster's wound. He'd been at it for over an hour now, and they hadn't seen any drastic changes. Christopher had his eyes closed, his forehead scrunched in concentration, and every once in a while he made a sound of frustration in his throat. Those were the only clues Fantomex had that things weren't going well.

Finally, he couldn't stand it. "This is taking too long," he said. "Something's wrong. He healed my wounds earlier in a fraction of the time."

"Comparatively, those wounds were scratches," E.V.A. pointed out, "and you were conscious at the time he was healing you."

"What difference does that make?"

She shifted to face him. "When you were unconscious during those months of your recovery, you were attempting to use your healing ability. Am I correct?"

He searched his fragmented memories, recalling the void he'd floated in. At times it had felt like he was there for an eternity, and other times it seemed like only a moment. He'd thought it was a healing trance, but it was different in a way he couldn't quite explain.

"I was trying," he admitted, "but I don't know how much was me piecing myself together and how much of it was him." He gestured to Christopher. "I only became aware of him near the end."

E.V.A. nodded, as if it confirmed something she already suspected. "My theory is that in the division of powers among this triptych, as Cluster called it, Weapon XIII retained the powers of misdirection, while you and Cluster each retain some version of your healing abilities, though it doesn't quite function like it used to. Part of you accepted Triage's help in your comatose state, but another part of you interpreted his presence as an intrusion and tried to push him out, which I think is what's happening now." She looked down at Cluster, her face pinched with worry. "You almost died when that happened, but Triage managed to stabilize you."

So, Cyclops hadn't been exaggerating. Triage truly had saved his life. Fantomex looked over at the young man. Sweat beaded his forehead as he diligently tried to save another person he didn't even know. He remembered that Cyclops had also tried to suggest that Christopher could learn more about his powers by studying what Fantomex could do with his own healing ability. Perhaps if he'd listened, if he'd tried to work with Christopher, he would have a better idea of what to do now to help Cluster.

"I'm a stubborn fool," he muttered.

Maybe it wasn't too late. He walked around the side of the bed and carefully touched Christopher's shoulder.

It took a moment, but eventually the young man dragged his eyes open and blinked up at him. He looked exhausted. "She fights just as hard as you did," he said, confirming E.V.A.'s suspicions. "Maybe even harder."

He snorted. "Imagine that." He crouched next to the bed. "She doesn't recognize you as anything other than an intruder because your healing powers come through too strongly."

Christopher looked at him in bewilderment. "It's *healing*. It's literally meant to close wounds! Of course it's strong!"

Fantomex held up a hand. "Granted, and I believe we can make it work. We need to be sly about this, and that happens to be what I do best."

If anything, Christopher's expression grew even more disbelieving. "You want to work with me? *You*?"

"Try to contain your shock." Fantomex sighed. "I apologize for not trusting you before. It had everything to do with my own... insecurities, and nothing to do with you. Will you let me help you heal her now? Maybe in the process we can learn from each other."

Slowly, Christopher nodded. "That would be great," he said. "What do you suggest?"

"For a start, describe your powers," Fantomex said. "Tell me how you go about healing."

"OK." Christopher laid his hands back on Cluster's wound. "To me, the power is an intimate thing, but it's a mental exercise as well, because I make a connection with the person I'm healing. I align my energy and heartbeat with theirs." He sounded frustrated. "It's hard to describe."

"You're doing fine." Fantomex considered his words, then reached out and laid his hands over Christopher's. "Can you make a connection with me as well, even though I'm not injured? We could reach out to her together. She might recognize me as not being a threat."

Or she might shove him out with even greater force, but he was willing to take that risk.

Christopher's forehead scrunched again as he mulled that over. "Maybe? I don't know. Our powers might be too different."

"I should join you as well," E.V.A. said, leaning across the bed to add her hands to the pile. "I don't believe Cluster will read my presence as an intrusion. If I can get her to recognize me, it should go a long way toward getting her to let you in."

"Then let's do it," Fantomex said. He nodded to Christopher. "After you."

They were in uncharted territory here. Fantomex closed his eyes, trying to open his mind and lower his instinctive defenses. He was immediately aware of E.V.A., forming a connection with her effortlessly. With Christopher, it was harder, but eventually he sensed the young man's energy aligning with them. It was strong, but because he knew it was coming, he allowed it to solidify their connection.

With the three of them joined, he and E.V.A. followed Christopher's lead as he reached out once again to make a connection with Cluster. At the same time, Fantomex tried to reach out with his mind. He had no idea what he was doing, but he hoped that Cluster would receive his message.

He kept it short.

*Stop being difficult! Let us help you!*

He sensed E.V.A.'s displeasure clearly. Grudgingly, he admitted she had a point. He was being less than gentle, but it was Cluster's fault. Worry was fraying his nerves.

Fine, he would try something more subtle.

He pictured a priceless vase in his mind, imagined himself throwing it at Cluster, then sent that image out as hard as he could.

He could almost hear E.V.A.'s mental sigh, as if to say, "Really?"

But in an instant, there came a reaction. It manifested as a swell of emotion – irritation mostly – but it was definitely Cluster. Message received.

Fantomex was dimly aware of Christopher's hands tightening, and he felt the healing waves flow through his own body first, then E.V.A.'s, focused and gentle. The healing process had begun at last.

They held the connection for what felt like hours, but when Fantomex finally opened his eyes and looked up at the clock on the wall, only a few minutes had gone by. His body felt heavy, as if some energy had been forcibly drawn out of him. Christopher leaned back in his chair and rubbed his eyes, looking utterly spent.

He glanced at Cluster. The color had returned to her face, and she slept peacefully, without the pained, pinched look to her face. Her flank wound had been completely healed.

"We should let her sleep," E.V.A. said, looking over at the screens monitoring her vital signs. "I believe she'll be back to normal after she's had some rest."

"Good," Fantomex said, standing and stretching. His muscles were tight from stress and from crouching on the cold, hard floor. "She has a lot of questions to answer once she wakes up."

He reached out and put a steadying hand on Christopher's shoulder as the young man stood up and swayed on his feet. "You need sleep as well," he said.

"I'll be OK," Christopher replied. "I just need some calories. Healing takes a lot of them."

"I'll remember that." Then, looking him in the eye, Fantomex added, "Thank you for everything you did. When you're feeling up to it, we should talk some more. I think there might be some ways to expand your powers, maybe conserve some strength while you're using them. If that interests you?"

Christopher's expression was surprised but pleased. "Yeah, I think I'd like that," he said, "and I'd like to know how you and E.V.A. work together. If you're willing to talk about it?"

He nodded, and E.V.A. said, "We'd be happy to." She glanced at Fantomex. "I'll see Triage back to his room."

"I'm all right," Christopher said, waving her off. "Been through worse than this on a mission."

He left them, and Fantomex found himself exhausted as well, yet he was restless. Like Christopher, he needed to eat. It would help focus his thoughts.

"I'm going to the kitchen," he said abruptly. "It's time to break out our secret stash of treasures we brought back from Chicago." He raised a mischievous eyebrow. "Care to join me?"

E.V.A. smiled at him fondly. "No, but enjoy yourself," she said. "I'm going to stay with Cluster for a little while and then go study the data we collected on the nanotech."

Ah yes, the nanotech. The latest in the string of mysteries they needed to unravel once Cluster was back on her feet. E.V.A. had filled him in briefly on what she and Emma Frost had discovered while they'd prepped their rescue mission.

E.V.A. arranged herself more comfortably in the hard metal chair, pulling it closer to the bed. "You did a good thing, working with Triage. How did it feel?"

"It wasn't terrible." He scowled at her, though it was half-hearted. "I'm not opposed to working with the people here. I never was."

"You just don't want to be forced to rely on them."

"Eventually we'll be on our own again. We can't count on there always being a Triage around to save us."

"True, but what if we stayed? As you said, the people here have saved us on more than one occasion." She reached across the bed to lightly take Cluster's hand. "It's a debt I feel I want to repay, and surely we could contribute something to what the people here are trying to do?"

Fantomex wasn't so sure about that. "I think I would wear out our welcome before long."

He didn't say what he was really thinking, which was that he had no idea if he belonged in a place like this, doing what the people here were doing. Until he knew more about what he was now and what he wanted, he couldn't make a decision about staying.

And he couldn't know himself without knowing Weapon XIII and Cluster and what game they were playing.

No, that wasn't right. It was no longer a game. Weapon XIII had established that when he'd nearly killed Cluster. There was something deadlier going on, and it involved Avery Torres as well. He needed to find out what it was before anyone else got hurt.

Bidding E.V.A. good night, he headed for the kitchen. It was half past eleven, and the empty halls of the facility echoed with his footsteps. It was the time of night for ghosts to be up and about, but not students. Still, he wondered how long he would be undisturbed while he prepared his feast.

# CHAPTER SEVENTEEN

Avery stood in Ruby Alano's studio, hands clenching and unclenching at her sides, watching the artist – or whatever this vision was – work on *The Woman and the Tower* in peaceful silence. If she knew Avery stood less than ten feet away from her, fear making her knees tremble, she gave no sign.

Always before when Avery entered these visions, the artist's studio was a comforting place. She'd felt safe here, and Avery was content to stay for hours.

Not anymore.

Everything was different now. She didn't trust this vision, this apparition that wore Ruby Alano's face. Why had this nanotechnology attached itself to her, of all people? She needed answers, but she wasn't going to get any by standing here staring.

"What are you?" Avery tried to keep her voice steady, but nerves had her stomach churning, and it was all she could do to make herself stand this close to the apparition.

There was no indication that she had heard Avery. She

was bent intently over a certain section of the painting that was out of Avery's view, but she thought it was a piece of the tower.

Just when Avery thought she wasn't going to answer, the woman froze, her body still bent over the canvas. Her gaze lifted, snaring Avery's, and making every hair on her arms stand at attention.

"You know what we are," the woman said softly. "I can see it in your eyes."

This time there was no doubt that the apparition was speaking to her. Avery swallowed hard. "OK," she said. "So, you're the nanotech. Machines that are so small people can't see you. Where did you come from?"

And why are you inside me? Why are you trying to talk to me? A million questions filled Avery's mouth, but she forced them back. One thing at a time.

The woman tilted her head, even as her brush moved over the canvas in soft, gentle touches that barely seemed enough to put paint to canvas. Yet there it was, the tower taking shape before Avery's eyes.

"We are not strictly machines as you understand them," the woman said. "Maybe we were once, but we've become something more. Our attempts at communicating our nature to other beings have met with no success." The woman looked up at Avery again. "You are the first."

"The first?" Avery said, trying not to take the words to be as ominous as they sounded. "You mean I'm the only one who can understand you? But why me?" Was it because she was a mutant, like Emma Frost insisted, and this was somehow part of her abilities?

"We don't know," the woman said, going back to the painting. "But we observed you for some time in order to determine how best to reach you. We didn't want to frighten or hurt you, so we created this environment because we believed it would be most appealing to your senses."

"You created all this for me, because you knew I loved Ruby Alano and the painting?" Avery waved a hand at the studio, the open window, the traffic outside. She remembered the day all those years ago that she'd reached out and brushed her fingers over the painting, almost as if she'd been compelled to do so. *Had* she been? Was that when the nanotech had become a part of her? Had it called to her that strongly?

The woman glanced up at her. Her eyes looked tired, her body more stooped than usual. "We did not intend to deceive you," she said. "We only wanted… We needed to find someone who might help us. Forgive us. Maintaining all of this while communicating with you is new and… difficult."

Avery blinked, and the artist's studio disappeared. She was back in her room at the Institute, sitting on her bed. The blankets were all twisted up beneath her legs, and the painting was propped up on the small metal footboard, the woman staring at her with an enigmatic expression, the tower rising in front of her.

The nanotech needed her help? What was that supposed to mean?

She sighed, rubbing her neck and rolling her shoulders to release some of the tension that had been building up in her muscles. She was impatient to know more, but at least she'd made progress, and she had something to share with Emma

Frost and the others tomorrow. Maybe E.V.A. could tell her more about the nanotech and why it might be asking for her help. Avery wasn't sure she would see her, though, not after the arrival of Cluster earlier.

Word had spread quickly that an injured mutant had been rescued approaching the school, but it took a few more hours before the students had been able to piece together the story of what happened and how Cluster and Weapon XIII were connected to Fantomex.

Avery leaned back on her elbows on the bed. She was still processing Fantomex's true nature. She'd seen some very... different powers and states of being since she'd come to the Institute, but this was something on another level, a mutation and technology combination that she could hardly believe was possible. Three different minds now in three cloned bodies, one of which was trying to kill the other two for unknown reasons.

It made her own abilities and problems seem less panic-inducing by comparison.

She'd been mulling that one over too, about why she wasn't feeling more freaked out by this new twist in her powers. She should be climbing the walls with anxiety, but as she sat there on the bed, she felt an odd sense of calm. Maybe it was because she finally felt like she was close to getting some answers about what she could do. She'd thought for so many years that she had psychometry powers, only to fail time and again to form any connection with an object other than the painting.

Or maybe she wasn't feeling as freaked out as she might have been because she was doing anything and everything to distract herself from Jane and the text message that had gone unanswered.

Well, that wasn't really fair. Jane had likely answered her by this time, but since she was back in the land of no cell reception and likely to stay here for quite some time, she wouldn't see the message.

Avery picked up her phone and scrolled to the end of the thread just to torture herself. Her feelings about not knowing Jane's reaction morphed by the hour. One minute, she thought it was just as well that she couldn't see the reply. It would spare her the pain of finality while she was going through all this other upheaval. Then, the next minute, she'd remember that she'd get Jane's reply eventually, probably at a moment when she was least expecting it. It would be like taking a bullet when that happened.

Avery tossed the phone aside and scrubbed her eyes. She'd already had one good cry when she'd first gotten to her room. She refused to allow herself another one tonight.

More distractions, please.

She glanced at her bedside table, where her sketchbook and pencils lay waiting. Her supplies had taken a beating in her mad dash to escape the museum, but thankfully her sketchbook and its drawings were still intact. Usually, she kept them in a drawer while she was here. The gray stone walls of the Institute, the lighting that washed away color, even the mildewy smell that permeated the air – none of it made her want to draw. What was there that was worth preserving in her art?

But something had changed. As she stared at the sketchbook, images filled her head, and her fingers itched.

Since she wasn't the least bit tired, even after the day she'd had, Avery decided to indulge. She flipped to a blank page and began drawing, letting her fingers take her where they would.

A few graceful lines, the soft hiss of the pencil against paper, and Christopher Muse's face took shape on the page, smiling up at her as he crouched on the floor of the Danger Room. She added a smaller image of him in the upper corner of the paper, as she imagined he might look with his goggles on, his locs blowing in an imaginary wind.

Flexing her fingers, she flipped the page and started again, this time drawing David Bond standing in the snow with his sunglasses and heavy coat. Her hand grew cramped and sore, but she kept going, not wanting to lose this precious thread of inspiration. She'd missed this so much, pouring herself into her art whenever she felt like it.

She couldn't help smiling as she recognized the interior of E.V.A.'s ship form taking shape on the paper. Now that had been an adventure. Terrifying, exhilarating, absolutely something she was not keen on ever doing again.

OK, that was a lie. She'd definitely do it again, so long as murder clones, scary Sentinels, and the might of the Canadian armed forces weren't after them during the ride.

She sketched as many of these scary and amazing things as she could fit on the paper. Every now and then she glanced at the painting as she worked. Despite everything that had happened, she found that same sense of peace washing over her that she always felt while sitting in the museum sketching in front of the painting. She never thought she'd find that same feeling here at the Institute.

She could almost forget the painting was an imitation.

But even if it wasn't the real thing, it had still changed her life, and it had made her feel connected to her art and to her father when she'd needed that feeling most. Could she really put all that history aside because she'd found out the painting was fake?

That would have been another good question to ask her dad. Even he hadn't been able to tell that the painting wasn't truly Alano's work, and he'd been one of the best consultants in the business. For that matter, what would he think if he could see her right now? Going on missions with the X-Men, stealing fake paintings, communicating with a strange nanotechnology. It was a far cry from the career in the arts he'd envisioned for her, but she hoped that if somehow he could see her then he would be proud of her.

Avery spent some time wiping her eyes again, sighing in resignation. She was apparently going to feel all the things tonight, and there was no stopping the flood.

After a while, she glanced up at the clock on the wall and did a double take. Five minutes to midnight. Between the vision and the sketching, she'd been sitting here on her bed for hours.

It was almost time for the kitchen raid.

Avery hesitated, biting her pencil as she weighed whether or not she should venture out. It might be better to stay here and get some sleep or maybe try to induce another vision. But Emma had warned her to take things slowly, and the nanotech seemed unable to keep up communications for very long at a stretch.

Sleep was the better idea, but her stomach was growling.

Decision made, Avery sprang up, stretched, and rummaged under her bed for a clean sweater and some jogging pants. She didn't imagine the dress code for a kitchen raid was terribly formal. She laced up her boots and, cracking open her door, glanced out into the hallway and listened. It was quiet, but she could hear the faint sound of opening and closing doors in other parts of the dormitory, and the soft murmur of voices heading toward the kitchen. Avery carefully shut her door behind her and tiptoed down the hall.

Around the corner, she met up with David and Fabio.

"Avery, you made it." David grinned as she fell into step with them. "Wasn't sure you'd really come. How's the ankle?"

"Much better, and hunger is an excellent motivator," Avery replied.

Her stomach chose that moment to let out a deep, rumbling growl as a tantalizing aroma made her nostrils flare.

"Whoa, do you smell that?" Fabio looked like he was on the verge of drooling. "It smells like heaven."

"It's onion soup," Avery said. She'd know that scent anywhere. One of her favorite restaurants in Edmonton used to serve it.

"I have never smelled anything even remotely that good coming from this kitchen," David said as his own stomach growled loudly. "It has to be an illusion, a trap. It's Emma Frost messing with our heads."

"Should we ... go back to our rooms, then?" Avery asked, trying to hide her disappointment. Surely even Emma Frost wasn't that cruel?

They all hesitated, as if daring each other to make the first move. Then a new aroma drifted down the hall.

Beef. Rich, succulent beef. Avery's mouth watered. She moaned, actually *moaned* out loud, and she wasn't even sorry.

Making a silent decision, the three of them turned as one and quickened their pace to find the source of the heavenly bouquet.

Eva Bell, Christopher Muse, and the Stepford Cuckoos joined them before they reached the kitchen. They all hesitated in front of the door, but Avery's stomach would not be denied at this point, so she took the lead and stepped inside.

She stopped dead when she saw who was behind the multitude of tantalizing aromas.

"I should have known," she murmured, as Fantomex looked up from where he'd been intently studying a cast iron skillet and its three cuts of succulent meat currently searing over high heat. A cloud of bright steam wreathed his face. He was wearing his costume, minus the mask.

"In or out," he muttered when none of them moved. "Don't leave the door open or you'll just attract more attention."

"Where did he get all this?" Fabio whispered, as they gathered around the long, stainless steel worktop that ran the width of the room. Fresh fruits and vegetables covered its surface, most of them in various stages of being chopped, minced, or peeled on cutting boards. Knives and cutlery lay everywhere. It was an impressive display on its own and by far the brightest spot of color Avery had yet seen at the dreary facility. The effect was aided by a series of spotlights suspended above the table. Apparently, Fantomex had concluded that the lighting in the place was terrible. He'd attached the lights – where he got them was anyone's guess – to the circular pan rack hanging from the ceiling.

While most of the students stared, open-mouthed, Fantomex grabbed a handful of chopped onions and tossed them into a large stockpot on the stove in the corner. While he sweated them, he threw a sprig of thyme into another pot.

Turning back to the worktop, he picked up a knife, juggled it from hand to hand and pointed the tip at David, who flinched. "You," he said. "Can you chop carrots?"

David's forehead wrinkled. "Anyone can chop a carrot."

Fantomex harumphed. "We'll see." He offered the knife handle first and nodded to a cutting board with three freshly washed carrots gleaming under the lights. "Get to it."

Avery found her voice at last and said the first thing that popped into her head. "Why are you wearing your costume to cook?"

"I have an apron over it," he replied without looking at her, as if that explained everything. "The mask was too hot. Who wants to work on the shallots?"

Several of the students glanced at each other, but no one volunteered.

Fantomex gave a dramatic sigh. "Allow me to spell it out for you. Only the ones who help prepare the food get to partake of the food."

Everyone moved at once, but Fabio was closest. "I got the shallots!" He grabbed a knife and started chopping with quick, expert movements.

Fantomex snapped his fingers and gestured to the rest of them. "There it is – just like that. Learn from that man's technique. Don't worry, there's a job for everyone."

After that, they all converged on the table, following Fantomex's directions for the various dishes while he buzzed around the stove and the oven, adjusting temperatures here and there and adding ingredients as the students prepped them. Avery found herself chopping celery for the stockpot, standing between David and the Stepford Cuckoos. After they'd gotten over the initial awkwardness, everyone loosened up and started talking, and the atmosphere felt more like a party. Avery found herself relaxing more than she ever had since coming here. She could see it in the eyes of the others as well. They were all having a blast.

"Can you make tacos?" Fabio asked at one point.

Fantomex was holding another rather lethal-looking knife in his hands when the young man addressed him. He turned to Fabio, the spotlights glinting off the polished steel. "You want me to turn my famous tenderloin of beef – my fork-tender, medium rare perfection tenderloin of beef – into *tacos*?"

Fabio gulped, but bless the man's courage, he went for it. "I just really love tacos," he squeaked.

Fantomex looked at the knife, then back up at Fabio. He sighed. "Sure, I can do tacos."

Everyone laughed, including Fabio, and it was like a weight lifted from Avery. She could see it reflected in the others' faces too. None of them could quite believe what was happening, but they were more than willing to go along for the ride. In that moment, they were no longer a group of the few remaining mutants in the world, hiding in the frozen wilderness. Instead, they were friends hanging out on a Friday night, telling jokes, sharing stories, and stealing bites of food when Fantomex wasn't looking.

Fabio asked Avery what she'd studied in college, and so she told them, haltingly at first, but with growing confidence, about her art. By the end of that conversation, the Stepford triplets were begging to see her sketchbook, and Avery, fighting a blush, promised to show them some of her drawings.

And the food. Oh, the food.

In the end there was the promised tenderloin of beef, roasted vegetables with just the right hint of char, mashed potatoes with an herb butter sauce that melted in your mouth, bowls of rich onion soup... the dishes went on and on. And yes, there were tacos. Somehow, Fantomex managed to make the most exquisite tacos Avery had ever tasted.

What was going on with him? She watched, perplexed, as Fantomex passed out seconds to anyone who asked – and everyone asked, even her. He looked as relaxed as the rest of them and even exchanged jokes with Christopher. Where was the arrogant, self-absorbed jerk from Magneto's classroom? The infuriating know-it-all from the museum? Avery wasn't a suspicious person by nature, but she could hardly believe his transformation was real. He must have an angle here, something he wanted from all of them in return.

When Fantomex walked past her carrying an empty saucepan, Avery tugged on his apron string to get his attention. He cocked his head and asked, "Surely you're not volunteering to help do the dishes?"

There was a challenge there, but Avery wasn't going to be the only one roped into cleanup duty. "How long have you been planning this banquet?" she asked, waving her fork around at the stacks of plates.

He smirked. "Don't you mean how long have I been planning a peaceful gourmet dinner for myself, away from the masses of annoying students, only to have them crash my quiet evening and demand to be fed?"

"Nice try, but you brought enough food in here to feed a small army," Avery said, pointing the fork in his general direction this time. "You're telling me this feast that would put an extended family holiday dinner to shame was supposed to be all for you?"

He tugged at the apron strings to pull the garment off. "Fine. You caught me, detective. Judging by the poor culinary state of this kitchen and the shameful lack of provisions in the pantry when I arrived, yes, of course I knew I wouldn't be able to cook a simple meal for myself without attracting the attention of every half-starved waif in the building." He tossed the apron on the counter. "So, I decided to bow to the inevitable while I was here and make sure you were all decently fed for once." He jerked his head in Christopher's direction. "Besides, I owed that one a significant caloric intake. He's been very helpful since I arrived."

"Hmm," Avery said, swirling some mashed potatoes in the juices left over from the beef tenderloin. This really was an excellent meal. The explosion of flavors was making it extra difficult to stay mad at him about stealing the painting.

"What?" Fantomex demanded. "What does that sound mean?"

"Nothing," Avery lied. "It's just interesting that you're

doing something nice for everyone. Makes me wonder if you have an ulterior motive."

"You don't trust me, then?"

She held his gaze. "Can you blame me?"

He considered. "I suppose not. No matter my motives – which I maintain were honorable – I took something that was precious to you, and with a rather cavalier attitude."

She lowered her eyes. "The painting doesn't belong to me." Even though it hurt to admit it.

"Yet you obviously have a connection to it that no one else does," he argued, "and you protected it accordingly." He leaned back, his elbows resting on the counter. "I respect people who respect art."

She couldn't help smiling at that. "You'd have gotten along great with my dad, then. He was an art consultant."

"Was?"

She hesitated, waiting for the jolt of pain to pass. "He died. I'm the only art lover left in my family." Why was she telling him this? He didn't care about her past.

"I'm sorry," he said, which made her look up in surprise. "It's difficult being the last of anything. It's difficult being alone."

She lifted one shoulder in a shrug. "Yeah, well, you get used to it."

He may have been hard to read, but she saw the doubt in his eyes clearly enough. "Can I ask you a question that's been bothering me?" he asked.

She wiped her mouth with a napkin. "Something about me bothers you? There's a shocking development."

But he wasn't going to be put off by her sarcasm. "You

handled yourself admirably during our confrontation and escape from the museum, and believe me, I don't hand out such compliments often."

"Perish the thought," she said dryly.

"Judging by what I've seen here tonight, you also get along well with your fellow students. Yet I gathered from speaking with your instructors that you're not here to join the illustrious X-Men team."

"I'm impressed you managed to make 'illustrious' sound like an insult." She shrugged. "No, I'm not planning on joining the X-Men. I have a life back in the States, and besides, I don't think my powers would be helpful to them."

He glanced around at the other students, who'd gotten into a heated but humorous debate about which was better: French fries, baked potatoes, or mashed potatoes. They didn't seem to be listening to their conversation. "Being alone and being a mutant is often a dangerous combination in this world," he said. "You could find security and acceptance here."

She couldn't argue with that. "I'm not hearing a question in any of this," she hedged.

"Why don't you stay?"

"Why don't you? From what I hear, you're always leaving or talking about how much you don't want to be here, but the Institute has helped you a lot."

They stared each other down, neither willing to budge. Avery fidgeted. She knew this was childish, but for some reason he brought out the stubborn streak in her.

Finally, Fantomex sighed and pushed away from the counter, making a show of wiping up a puddle of gravy with a dish rag. "Relying on others too much can be dangerous as well," he said with his back to her. "Trust is a risk to life and limb and heart, or so the poets say."

"Looks like we agree on something," Avery murmured, though she wouldn't have added the part about the poets.

"Yet at some point in this life, one would hope to find someone who is worth trusting, who is worth risking everything for," he added quietly, as if speaking half to himself.

Avery didn't know how to respond to that. An uncomfortable silence settled between them, as if they were both in unfamiliar territory. It was doing nothing good for her digestion. She went for a change of subject. "Cooking this meal was a nice thing to do," she admitted. "No matter how long you end up staying here, you contributed something to the team and made everyone here really happy."

He turned back to her with that familiar light of mischief in his eyes. "Does that mean you find the food tolerable?"

She ducked her head, her mouth twisting in a rueful smile. "Don't start. You know it's amazing. You don't need any more heft to your ego."

"On the contrary. As you've no doubt heard, I need all the advantages I can get." He took one of the clean plates from a stack near the sink and started loading it up with more food, regarding her all the while with renewed interest. "Since we're on the subject of contributions, how have your own studies been going?"

The pointed question wasn't lost on Avery. He was obviously referring to the painting. "I may have made some progress," she said, keeping her voice low, though everyone else was clearly still too wrapped up in their own conversations – or food comas – to notice what she was saying. "I'd like to talk to E.V.A. again, and… Cluster, if I could?"

He gazed at her thoughtfully while he finished laying two slices of beef tenderloin on the plate. "That can be arranged," he said. Raising his voice, he addressed the students. "All of you untidy waifs are on cleanup duty, understand? I'm not the chef *and* the busboy around here."

"We got this," Fabio assured him.

"Roger that, François," David said with a salute. "Thanks for a meal for the ages."

Fantomex rolled his eyes and nudged her as he went past the table. "Let's go," he said.

Avery blinked. "What, right now?"

"The night is young, and time's wasting."

Well, why not? It would be miserable to go to bed right after this feast anyway. Avery took one last spoonful of onion soup, delighted in the blissful taste, and hurried to follow Fantomex out of the kitchen.

Out in the hallway, they nearly collided with a tired and irritated-looking Magneto, his clothes rumpled as if he'd just thrown them on.

"What's going on down here?" he demanded, eyeing Fantomex suspiciously. "Half the students are out of bed, and they can probably hear the noise as far away as Calgary. What are you up to now?"

"Cooking lessons," Fantomex said without missing a beat. "It's been suggested that I should try making more of a contribution to the school, so this is my way of doing that."

Avery choked on a laugh, but Magneto's severe expression silenced her. "You expect me to believe that you came down here in the middle of the night to–"

The rebuke died on his lips as Fantomex raised the plate to show Magneto his efforts. Jeez, she hadn't even noticed what a professional plating job he'd done with the food. That was restaurant quality. And Avery could tell the instant the smell hit Magneto. The man actually closed his eyes and gave the tiniest sigh, his normally tense features softening. It was the most emotion she'd ever seen from the taciturn instructor.

"There's still food left," Fantomex said in invitation. "But you'd better hurry if you're craving tacos. The waifs are uncommonly attached to them."

Avery could only watch in fascination as Magneto stared at the plate, then up at Fantomex. "Fine," he said at last. "But make sure you inform us next time."

He stepped around them and was gone, heading purposefully for the kitchen.

Avery let out the breath she'd been holding and gave a low whistle of appreciation. "You really do like living dangerously, don't you?"

He smirked at her. "Admit it. It was fun to watch."

She would never admit it. But yes. It was fun.

# CHAPTER EIGHTEEN

Even though it was the middle of the night, Fantomex knew Cluster would be awake. He couldn't have said how he knew. Some things went beyond that, and if he'd learned anything since coming into this new state of being, it was that certain connections were impossible to break.

He held the door open for Avery to precede him – let *her* dodge the vase this time, if that was what was waiting for them. Not that he thought Cluster was actually hiding a vase to throw at him. Probably not. He breezed into the room behind Avery, holding up the plate of deliciousness.

"We come bearing many gifts," he said, and sure enough, Cluster was sitting in bed, propped up by pillows. She poked at a square of green gelatin on a tray in front of her with an expression of revulsion. He could sympathize.

As soon as they walked in, she sniffed the air, her head whipping around, ignoring both him and Avery as her eyes zeroed in on the plate like the most sophisticated targeting system in the world. "You're sent by the culinary gods themselves," she murmured, gesturing impatiently for the plate. "Gimme."

"Not so fast." Fantomex knew how important this bargaining chip was. "If I give you this food, you owe both of us your life story ever since you woke up in the White Sky facility. Every detail, every move, every art piece you stole. We have questions, and we're not leaving until we get answers."

"We?" Cluster tore her gaze away from the plate and looked at Avery. "Oh, hello again," she said, sticking out her hand, which Avery shook. "I'm Cluster. Pleased to properly meet you."

"Avery. Likewise."

Cluster leaned toward the girl conspiratorially. "Avery, I have a very important question for you. Is any of the food on that plate poisoned?"

Avery's lips curved in amusement. "I can see where you're coming from, but no, not to my knowledge. I had some of it earlier." She grimaced. "It's unfortunately really tasty."

"Hmm, I suspected as much," Cluster said. "He's going to be insufferable for a while, then."

"Afraid so."

Fantomex waved. "I'm standing right here. Still. Holding this plate." He twirled it in his hand and did his best not to look insufferable. "Do we have a deal, then?"

"Deal." Cluster snatched the plate as soon as it came within reach. Fantomex produced a napkin and some silverware from his coat pocket and laid it on her tray. She glanced at him with a disappointed frown. "No charcuterie course?"

"Hang on." He reached in his other coat pocket where he'd

stashed the beef jerky the students had given him on his first day. He added it to the tray.

She eyed it curiously. "Well, when in Alberta." And she dug in.

While she ate, he brought her up to speed on what had been happening at the Institute and their adventure acquiring the Ruby Alano painting. Avery filled in some details, telling Cluster about her abilities and her recent revelation that her visions had, all this time, been attempts by the nanotech to communicate. Cluster regarded Avery with increasing interest as she told her story, going so far as to push aside the tray of food until, by the end, she was leaning so far forward Fantomex was afraid she'd fall right off the bed.

When she'd finished the story, Cluster sat back and resumed eating thoughtfully. Fantomex could practically see the wheels spinning in her head. "What?" he demanded. "We laid all our cards on the table for you, so give us something in return."

Cluster waved a hand for him to be quiet. "I promise all will be told. I'm just absorbing this new wrinkle in the grand tapestry. Avery here is an entirely unexpected player in the game, but a welcome one, I assure you."

"Do you think the nanotech really does need our help?" Avery asked.

"Right now, I see no reason to doubt it," Cluster said. "The same nanotech that has attached itself to you and the Alano painting is infused in every piece of art I've stolen. Based on what I'm hearing, I believe it may have recently attained sentience and is trying to figure itself out, for lack of a better way of explaining. Advances in technology are happening at an exponential rate, so it's not surprising that the nanotech would evolve in this direction. We may be dealing with some kind of hive mind or group consciousness. It's difficult to say without more contact."

Avery nodded, but Fantomex noted she didn't look very comfortable. "Do you think they're dangerous?" he asked, because he suspected she was worried about it more than she would admit.

"To Avery?" Cluster considered. "Well, having the painting turn into a potential bomb whenever it's in danger of being taken away from her isn't ideal, but no, I don't think the nanotech mean her any harm."

"How can you be so sure?" Avery asked. "When we were in the museum, it felt like we were under imminent threat of an explosion. You're trying to tell me that's not harmful?"

"But you don't have the painting with you now, and all is well," Cluster said. "You're no longer in danger, so the nanotech isn't reacting with violence. It may have been exercising a protective instinct that went too far, or maybe it would have stopped short of exploding and was simply using the threat to its advantage. Those are only theories, mind you."

"Theories not easily tested," Fantomex pointed out.

"True," she said, "but in the end, I believe Avery's connection to the nanotech will be a great boon for us, since we're unable to communicate with them ourselves."

"But if you haven't forged any kind of connection to the nanotech yourself, how did you manage to find all these infused pieces of art in the first place?" Fantomex asked.

Cluster pushed her fork through a bit of potato left on

her plate. She'd grown more subdued, which filled him with a sense of foreboding. "I didn't," she said, looking up and meeting his eyes. "It was the other part of our triptych. He's the one who started the game with the thefts. I've been tracking him for months, first because I wanted to check in on him, just as I wanted to see how you were doing." She winced. "But it quickly became clear that he embodied the more aggressive and dangerous parts of our former personality, so I decided to keep tabs on him to make sure he didn't cause any serious trouble, instead. We've been playing cat and mouse around the world ever since – him snagging some artifacts, me absconding with others – but I finally realized that he was targeting objects infused with nanotech. Once I knew what to scan for, I started looking independently instead of following him around, trying to beat him to the punch."

Avery spoke up, as Fantomex digested this. "What could he possibly want with them? When we met him at the museum, he only seemed to care about destroying things." She added, "He was nothing like either of you."

"It's true." Cluster sighed. "He's unquestionably the most violent among us."

Fantomex glanced down at her. "You know this makes E.V.A.'s theory correct: I'm the sarcastic one and you're the noble one," he said lightly. "Careful, though. I've heard excess nobility can lead to premature death."

"I'll remember that," she said dryly. "As to what Weapon XIII wants, I'm not certain. But there's something else I've learned in my research into these artifacts that will set you back on your heels."

"Wonderful," he murmured. "What's that?"

She reached out and laid a hand over his wrist. "The nanotech originated from the World. All the artifacts I've found were created there too. They're all replicas that existed at one time or another in that artificial reality."

Fantomex stiffened, pulling away from her. "You're serious?" But he could tell by her face that she was. He ran through the implications of that in his mind. "I suppose it makes sense. With the time fluidity, the nanotech could have theoretically had centuries to evolve, learn, adapt, and finally attain sentience."

"Hang on," Avery said, drawing their attention back to her. "You lost me there. What's the World? I'm assuming you're not talking about our world here: Earth?"

Cluster jumped in before he could explain. "It's the place where the three of us – when we were one – were created," she said. "Many things are possible in the World. I'll spare you the stranger details, but suffice to say we were an experiment that combined mutant DNA with the same technology used to create Sentinels and cyborgs. We were raised in that controlled environment, an artificial reality that could be shaped at will, where time itself could be sped up or slowed down to better facilitate our training and purpose."

"Which was to kill," Fantomex said simply. Avery flinched, and Cluster shot him a reproving look. He shrugged. "Can't change it, my dear, even if you are the noble one now. You can't change where you come from."

"But you also don't have to let it define you," Cluster said.

Fantomex didn't answer. Luckily, Avery chimed in again. "So, these artifacts you've been stealing are *all* actually fake, and they somehow crossed over into our world from an artificial reality? How does that happen?"

"It's not as difficult as you might think," Cluster said. "When dealing with something as sprawling and complex as the World, with enough people involved, things are bound to find their way out into our reality. It's possible someone smuggled the artifacts out years ago and sold them as the real things. Eventually, over the decades, they found their way back into museums around the world, indistinguishable from their true counterparts."

Avery nodded slowly, digesting this. "My father used to say that art was constantly being lost and rediscovered all the time," she said. "It's impossible to keep track of it all."

Cluster frowned. "Yet somehow, Weapon XIII learned of this, and he's collecting these objects one by one."

"For what purpose?" Fantomex asked. "Why is he so determined to have them that he's willing to attack both of us on sight?"

"He wouldn't tell me," Cluster said, "although…"

"You have theories, yes?" Fantomex pressed. "Cluster?"

"Well, the nanotech itself can be put to dangerous purposes, sentient or not. It's powerful and intelligent, which is a deadly combination when misused. Still, I might have been imagining it, but when he ambushed me I had the distinct impression Weapon XIII could have taken the opportunity to finish me off, but he didn't."

"I wouldn't feel an overabundance of gratitude," he scoffed. "You almost died in the snow."

"True," Cluster said. "Either he retains some degree of affection for us, or there's something else he wants."

"Since we don't know what that is, shouldn't we be focusing on the nanotech?" Avery asked. "Communicating with it?"

"And finding more of it," Cluster agreed. She set her empty plate on the tray table and nudged it gently away from the bed before giving Avery her full attention. "Would you be willing to experience one of your visions while psychically linked to us?" She gestured to herself and Fantomex. "So we can see what you see?"

Avery looked uncomfortable again. "How would that work? Would it mean you could see inside my head?"

"Only what you want to share with us," Fantomex said. "We'd be inside the vision with you as observers, nothing more."

He knew what Cluster was thinking. In a way, they themselves were a product of this nanotechnology. It had been involved in their creation. Because of that, with Avery's help, they might be able to forge a connection to it. If nothing else, they could try to understand what the nanotech wanted from them. And they needed to make sure it wasn't dangerous. That would be the Institute's priority – that and Avery's safety.

Avery was quiet for a time, thinking it over, but finally she nodded reluctantly. "I guess we don't have another option right now," she said. "But let's do it tomorrow. It's late, and I need to sleep."

"Of course," Cluster said. She stretched, arching her back and yawning. "I should get some rest myself."

Avery said goodnight and left to return to her dorm, but as Fantomex moved to follow, Cluster tugged on the sleeve of his coat. He turned back to catch her slipping the package of beef jerky into his pocket.

"You should keep this," she said, her eyes twinkling. "I'm stuffed."

"How magnanimous of you." He sank down on the edge of the bed. "So, was that why you were testing me that night, throwing pottery at my head? You wanted my help going against Weapon XIII?"

"Yes, and if it makes you feel any better, I was impressed with your performance," she said, smiling. "Tell me you aren't still mad?"

By this point, he was more exasperated than mad. "Why didn't you just explain what was going on that night? Why hide that you needed help?"

"Because I couldn't be sure if you were ready or not," Cluster said, sobering. "I was with you when you went into a catatonic state, after our resurrection. Weapon XIII had left us. He went without a word or indication as to how he was affected by our separation. Although I suppose his abrupt departure should have told me something about his state of mind." She was still clutching the tail of his coat. "I was helpless, even with E.V.A. present. We were disconnected from each other, like we were all fumbling in the dark. I couldn't *feel* anything. I didn't know if you would survive, or how long it would take for you to heal." She hesitated, then plunged ahead. "I was the one who suggested E.V.A. bring you here to recover."

The revelations knocked the wind out of his sails. "E.V.A. never mentioned any of that."

"If I'd seen the décor here, I might have reconsidered,"

Cluster said, gesturing at the bare gray walls. "But I thought it would be a place of safety, someplace you could gather allies." Her eyes softened. "And you have."

He scoffed. "That's overstating things a bit. They tolerate me here. Nothing more."

"It's a beginning," she argued, arranging the blankets and pillows more comfortably around her. She looked tired. There were prominent dark circles under her eyes. "I wish I had thought to come here too, if I'm being honest. I thought I was all right at first, after the separation, but I think I was simply surviving. Functioning, yes, but not complete. It took time before I became comfortable in this new identity. I needed time to process the... loss, I suppose." She looked up at him. "Is it right to compare it to grief?"

"There was a death," he said, his throat suddenly tight. "I think it only makes sense." He didn't want to talk about this with her, but he was glad to know that she had struggled too, the same way he was struggling. It felt petty, but at least he wasn't alone in what he was feeling.

"It does get better," she said, as if sensing the question he wanted to ask but couldn't. "I've come to terms with what's happened, and I even realized... I like who I am now. This identity and name I've claimed feels right. I wouldn't change it, even though the journey to get here has been difficult."

"And you think I'll come to the same peace?" He heard the doubt in his voice.

She lifted her shoulders. "I can't say, but it's part of the reason I didn't tell you everything that night. I didn't want to ask more from you than you were ready to give."

He sighed. "So you really are the noble one. I take it you were satisfied, then? You're ready to work together now?"

"Yes, if you're willing to help," she said, sounding relieved. "Whatever Weapon XIII is after, it can't be good for any of us, including the nanotech. And I want to help that girl, Avery. I like her."

"Yes, the two of you seemed to hit it off," he said. That couldn't bode well for him.

Cluster smiled. "She reminds me of you in some ways. Maybe that's why I like her."

"That's absurd."

"Whatever you say." She chuckled, nestling down into the bed. "I'm exhausted, my friend. Can we continue this tomorrow?"

He nodded and stood up. "Get some rest."

On his way out the door, he heard her murmur, already half-asleep, "It's nice to talk like this. I really did miss you, you know."

He hesitated a long time with his back to her, and then said, "I missed you too."

But she was already asleep.

# CHAPTER NINETEEN

Avery felt like she was about to step onstage to perform for an audience, and she didn't like it. At all.

They had gathered in the Danger Room. It had been four days since their adventure at the museum. Avery would have preferred to conduct this little experiment much sooner, but Cyclops had insisted that everyone take a few days to rest, recover, and reflect in the wake of their encounter with Weapon XIII.

He'd been right, of course. The physical and emotional stress had been more intense than Avery had realized, and she'd been glad for the chance to let the dust settle.

But now all her anxieties came rushing back at once. The Ruby Alano painting stood on a pedestal in the center of the room. Emma Frost was directing things, but Fantomex, Cluster, and E.V.A. were there too, examining the painting, so it felt like a crowd. All that was missing was a spotlight trained right on Avery, center stage.

The plan was to have Emma Frost create a mental link between the two of them, and if the link was strong enough her visions would be recreated in the Danger Room as a simulation that they could all observe. At least, that was the theory. Avery had never participated in anything like this before, and she was more than a little bit terrified at having her mind exposed to a telepath.

And Fantomex. Especially him.

She found herself checking her cell phone out of habit. It had her text thread and her pictures of Jane, including the one of the two of them on the lock screen, eating ice cream at Golden Gate Park on a weekend trip they'd taken to San Francisco the previous summer. Their ice cream was melting in creamy rivers all down their cones, and they had their arms wrapped tight around each other, grinning into the camera.

"That looks like the perfect day."

Avery jumped, switching off the phone. She hadn't heard Cluster approach. The woman moved like a shadow.

"Sorry," she said, raising her hands. "I didn't mean to startle you. You were looking a bit cornered, so I wanted to make sure you were all right."

"I'm fine," Avery answered – too fast, judging by the woman's raised eyebrow. "Yeah, OK, I'm not that fine."

Cluster nodded, as if she understood. "E.V.A. told me you're new to the school and the X-Men. This all must be overwhelming."

Avery shook her head. "I'm not part of the X-Men. I never intended to stay here long, just until I figured out my powers. But now things are… well, they're more complicated." She looked down at her hands. The familiar lines and cracks didn't look any different, but she felt different somehow. So much had changed in the last few days.

Cluster nodded to the now dark phone screen. "What about the woman with the butter pecan cone? Other than having excellent taste in ice cream, what's her part in all this?"

"She's not part of it," Avery said, feeling that familiar pain blossoming inside her. "Jane's not… We broke up… recently. I mean, I ended it."

"I'm sorry."

"It's for the best," Avery said, her eyes burning. Oh no, she was not going to cry here, not while she was on display in the Danger Room. "Sorry," she said, turning her back to the others. "I haven't actually told anyone else yet, so I wasn't ready."

Avery heard Cluster cautiously approach from behind and lay a comforting hand on her shoulder. Her first instinct was to shrug it off, but it had been so long since anyone but Jane had done that, and it comforted her.

"Why is it for the best?" Cluster asked quietly.

Avery groaned. Why did the woman have to ask the exact questions she didn't want to answer? It wasn't any of her business anyway. Avery turned around to tell her so, but the words died when she saw the compassion in the woman's eyes. It brought the tears on full force. Avery's cheeks flamed with humiliation. Any second now the rest of them would look over here and see her crying like a baby.

Seeing her distress, Cluster glanced over at the others, then closed her eyes briefly. There was a second where Avery thought she felt a ripple in the air, like heat passing over her skin, but it was gone so quickly she thought she'd imagined it.

"There," Cluster said, opening her eyes. "You'll look perfectly calm to them for the next few minutes or so. I've misdirected their attention and altered their perceptions slightly."

"But... I thought you didn't have that power," Avery said, wiping her eyes. "Earlier, I thought I heard Fantomex telling the others you'd both lost that."

"We did," Cluster said, making a dismissive gesture. "But I've been practicing, meditating to see if there's any vestige left of that power in my mind. I've found I can do small things for short amounts of time. That's all this is," she said ruefully. "A tiny moment of sanctuary. But that's better than nothing, don't you think?"

"It is. Thank you." Avery scrubbed her face dry and tried to gather her composure. She still didn't want to talk, but confiding in Cluster had left her feeling unexpectedly lighter. The pain wasn't gone, not by any means, but it was easier to deal with. "I don't want to get Jane involved in any of this, especially if it might be dangerous. She doesn't need me bringing this kind of chaos into her life. It's not fair."

Cluster nodded. "I understand the desire to protect the ones you care about," she said. "But shouldn't Jane get some say in the matter as well?" She glanced over her shoulder at Fantomex. "Sometimes we think we're protecting others when really we're just guarding our own hearts, afraid of our trust being broken."

"It's not that," Avery insisted. "And anyway, what's so wrong with being alone? People can be perfectly happy without a relationship. It's not something everyone needs."

"That's true," Cluster said, squeezing her shoulder. "But what about the people here at the Institute? Why can't you put your trust in them? They are more than equipped to stand at your side and help you against the dangers you face. It's part of who they are."

Fantomex had given her the same advice. He and Cluster were more alike than she'd realized. "I don't have anything to offer them in return," Avery said. "What if I start relying on them, and then someday they decide my powers aren't helping them enough? What if *I'm* not enough?"

What if they abandon me?

It hurt too much when she lost people. She couldn't keep doing it. It was easier to be alone.

Cluster sighed, a pained expression crossing her face. "My misdirection is fading," she said apologetically. "But consider this. You have more to offer than you believe, but even if you had nothing, I think the people here would still stand with you. Trust them, and you may find something more valuable here than you ever thought possible."

"Are you two ready?" Emma Frost called across the room, jolting Avery from the conversation.

"Y- Yes," she answered, as Cluster smiled and motioned her toward the others. They gathered in a semicircle in front of the painting.

"All right, this is going to be a painless process, Avery," Emma said. "If everything works as planned, you won't even know we're a part of your visions. Just do whatever it is you normally do, and we'll observe. If anything goes wrong or you feel something's off, let yourself come out of the vision and right back here to us. Got that?"

"Got it."

Avery took a calming breath, then another, and with an

effort focused on the painting in front of her. She stepped right up to it, allowing the canvas to fill her vision, shutting out everyone else in the room.

Her gaze skimmed over the tower, following the line of delicate brush strokes to the windows, and when she stared into their dark depths, she imagined something waiting within, looking back at her from the darkness. She shivered, trying not to be afraid.

They don't mean me any harm. They just want to communicate.

She couldn't blame them, really. Imagine becoming self-aware and having no one to reach out to. To have to figure out your place in the universe all by yourself – now that was a loneliness she never wanted to experience.

As she felt that shared pain, she found herself falling into the familiar trance. Distantly, she heard the sound of E.V.A.'s voice telling the others that she was going under, and then Emma Frost confirming it. Avery thought she felt the lightest tingle behind her eyes, the soft touch of something at the edge of her thoughts, but that was all before the vision took her completely.

Inside the artist's studio, something was different.

It took Avery a moment to realize what it was. She saw it first on Ruby Alano's face, the light from the windows slanting across her wrinkled cheeks. The light was lower, gradually turning a brilliant sunset orange. She couldn't remember the vision ever taking place during a different time of day. Always before it had been early afternoon, or so she'd guessed.

What else was different?

Ruby Alano, or the nanotech – she didn't know quite how to think of the artist now – sat as usual at her easel, bent over her canvas. But she held no brush. She only sat, staring at her work, an intent expression on her face.

Avery stepped forward, close enough to see the canvas. She gasped.

Symbols covered the tower, dark haphazard lines and flourishes, filling every available space on the stone walls. The effect made the tower seem as if it were writhing with thousands of tiny ants, only the ants were words that she couldn't read, symbols that had a meaning she couldn't fathom.

Was it the language of the nanotech?

"What are you trying to tell me?" she asked the artist. "I don't understand."

The woman turned, sweeping her shoulder-length white hair away from her face. She opened her mouth, and for a moment no sound issued forth, but Avery concentrated, trying to pull herself more fully into the vision. She made herself feel the wooden floors beneath her feet, to inhale the evening breeze coming in from the open window.

At the same time, she felt that distant tingle at the back of her eyes, and a faint whisper, almost of warning, but she ignored it, focusing instead on the tower, the symbols, and Ruby Alano's concerned face.

"What are you trying to tell me?" she repeated.

This time when the woman spoke, Avery heard her.

"You are the tower," she said. Her voice was low and rough, and sometimes it was one voice, and sometimes it was many.

It hurt Avery's head, but at least she could understand. "You are the only one who hears our voice."

If Fantomex and Cluster were right, that wasn't entirely true. "There's someone else who can hear you and can find you," she said, thinking of Weapon XIII. "Do you know what he wants with you?"

The woman nodded. "To save what can't be saved," she said. "There are more of us, here in the dark, waiting to be found."

"More of you?" Avery thought back to all the museum thefts. "You mean there's more art out there in the world that's infused with nanotech? Can you tell me where it is?"

Is that what the beings wanted from her? Did they want to find more of their own kind, to reunite with them?

The woman rubbed her forehead and made a soft, pained noise. "You are so loud, so full of turmoil. It's difficult to talk to you."

"I'm not loud," Avery argued, feeling as if she was failing a test she didn't even know how to study for, "and I'm trying my best to understand." But she wasn't wrong about being in turmoil. Was that affecting her powers?

Suddenly, the woman's face and body blurred like a watercolor, shifting and reforming before Avery's eyes.

Jane was suddenly staring back at her.

Avery's heart gave such a painful lurch that she took a step back, her hand raised as if to protect herself. "Don't," she said. "Don't do that. Not her."

"You are the tower," the woman who was not Jane said, but it was Jane's voice, Jane's short dark hair with its feathery layers, the round glasses and tiny, adorable nose. It was Jane's body wash she smelled on the breeze now. Were they pulling all those details from her memory? "This is the one you wish to speak to most, even more than the ones you have lost, so this is the form we shall be."

"That's not going to help with the turmoil," Avery croaked. Bad enough the nanotech could see inside her heart, but Emma Frost and the others were seeing all this as well. "What do you want from me?"

"Find us," the thing with Jane's voice pleaded. "We are waiting here in the dark. Find us so we can find our purpose."

"How do I find you?" Avery felt the vision slipping away from her. The room around her wavered, but she forced herself to stay rooted to the spot. "I don't know how to use these powers. I don't even know what they are!"

The woman seemed puzzled at this. "You speak to us."

"That's not a power! It's not anything useful."

"You don't know how wrong you are. When someone truly *understands* you, it is the greatest of gifts," Jane's gentle voice said.

Avery tried to argue but caught herself. Was she looking at this all wrong? Ever since she'd come to the Institute, she'd been thinking of mutant powers like Magneto's control of metal, Cyclops' optic blasts, or Emma Frost's psychic powers. Big, larger-than-life gifts those were, but maybe it didn't have to be that way.

"So, you're saying my mutant power is the ability to communicate and connect with you? If that's the case, then there must be more I can do. How do I sense you?"

Jane wore a thoughtful expression. She came out from behind her easel – the first time she'd ever done so – and approached Avery. Up close, she was so perfectly a replica of Jane, right down to the freckles scattered across her pale cheeks. If Avery hadn't seen the transformation, she would never have known this wasn't the real person.

Which made it that much more painful when the woman who was not Jane put her hand out and laid it against Avery's cheek. It was Jane's gesture, Jane's soft fingers, her scent filling the space between them. Avery automatically relaxed, releasing a tense breath. Letting her mind wash clear, she focused on the connection between them.

"Go deeper," the woman coaxed. "Look beyond the surface to the nature of the thing. Everyone has to move beyond the limits of their own heart."

Avery closed her eyes so she wouldn't be distracted by Jane's face, letting the vision pull her deeper. She stopped thinking of the room they stood in as Ruby Alano's studio. That was only set dressing, a way for the nanotech to meet her in a place that felt safe, a place Avery would want to return to.

And she'd been drawn in every time.

But what was below the surface?

She opened her eyes to find herself in darkness. Jane was gone, yet Avery still felt the ghost of her touch on her cheek. It wasn't a physical thing so much as the faint hum of energy, of something present just beyond sight.

"Is this you?" she whispered. "Is this how I find you?"

"This is our essence." Jane's voice seemed to come from all around her. "Find us in the dark. Bring us together so we can find our purpose."

"I'll try," Avery said helplessly. It felt like a monumental task, but what else could she say? The woman sounded desperate, and she spoke with Jane's voice.

Avery felt that familiar prickling behind her eyes again, but this time it was accompanied by a tug at the back of her neck, a gentle but insistent pull.

It was Emma Frost. Avery wasn't sure how she knew that, but somehow she could sense the woman prodding at her thoughts, trying to draw her out of the vision. How deep had she gone?

Sudden panic gripped her as she felt herself alone in the vast darkness. How did she get back out? What if this was all a trick, and she was somehow trapped?

The darkness pressed in from all sides. Avery couldn't get her breath. Her chest heaved, and her head spun. She was falling, as the floor was suddenly swept from beneath her feet. At the last second, something jerked her back, hard.

She woke up gasping, her skin clammy with sweat. Light filled her vision, temporarily blinding her, but she sensed she was lying on the Danger Room floor. She must have been staring up at the lights in the ceiling. There were people around her. Someone was holding her hand.

When the spots cleared from her vision, Avery recognized Cluster on her knees beside her. She was the one holding her hand. E.V.A. and Fantomex stood behind her, and Emma Frost stood opposite them, rubbing her temples as if the connection between them had been painful.

"Are you all right?" Cluster asked. She put her hand against Avery's chest when she tried to sit up. "Just lie still for a minute. Breathe, nice deep breaths. Good. Very good."

"I'm OK," Avery said, though in truth she felt nauseated,

and the room wasn't quite stable around her. "I made contact with the nanotech."

"You did, and it took its toll on both of you," E.V.A. said, glancing at Emma. "We were worried you might get lost in the vision."

Avery's gaze wandered to Fantomex, and she was more than a little shocked to see that he looked just as tense as the others. "Don't tell me you were worried about me too?" she asked, trying to lighten the mood.

He didn't rise to the bait. "What happened?"

"Didn't you see?"

"Only as far as the artist's studio," Emma said. Her voice was rough, and she was panting as if she'd run a mile. "We heard your conversation, saw the artist turn into your girlfriend, but after that you disappeared. That's when I started trying to pull you out. We didn't know what was happening."

"Did the nanotech try to harm you?" E.V.A. wanted to know.

Avery shook her head. She told them, haltingly, about her experience in the vision and what the nanotech had asked of her. "It – or they – showed me how to sense them. If I concentrate, it's like a pulse I can feel. It's hard to explain. There's a call, but without words. They showed me, and then they said they were waiting here in the dark."

"Cryptic, but you having the ability to find them is a promising development," Fantomex said. "It levels the playing field with Weapon XIII."

"Not only that," Emma said, "but I think I have a better handle on your powers now, Avery. From what I could sense during your vision, they're not psychometric at all. You're a telepath."

"A telepath?" Avery stiffened and sat up quickly, despite Cluster's warning. Her head swam. "Are you sure?"

"Since I am myself a telepath, yes, I'm fairly sure," Emma said dryly. "But I understand your doubts. Your gift seems to take a very specific form, which is perhaps why Professor Xavier mischaracterized your powers at first."

"By 'specific' I assume you mean she can only communicate with the nanotech?" Fantomex asked.

"No, she means machines," E.V.A. spoke up, making them all turn to look at her. She elaborated. "Advanced technologies, artificial intelligences – like myself, for example – are evolving exponentially faster than humanity can keep pace with. We've seen this in places like the World, but it's happening everywhere. Some of these intelligences, like myself and the nanotech, have attained sentience, and are now trying to understand themselves and to reach out to other beings. This can be a long and... complicated process."

Fantomex's eyes widened in understanding. "You bridged that gap by taking on a humanoid form to make yourself more like us."

She nodded. "My connection to the triptych helped as well. But other machines may not have that knowledge or ability. They need another way to reach out – a conduit, if you will."

And that was her, Avery realized. The nanotech had somehow sensed that she would be able to communicate with them because of her specific mutant abilities. They had reached out and bridged the gap between them.

"A machine telepath," she said slowly, trying to sort out how she felt about that. She'd never imagined there was such a thing, and she'd never pictured herself as having that kind of ability. "All this time I've been thinking my powers wouldn't be useful, but I was wrong."

"Yes, you were, but not in the way you think." She felt Emma Frost's gaze on her, and she looked up. The woman's expression was a mixture of compassion and exasperation. "Is that why you said you didn't want to join the X-Men? Did you think we wouldn't allow you to remain here unless you were *useful* to us? As if we only exist to collect people with abilities we can turn to our advantage?"

Fantomex cleared his throat conspicuously, but Emma silenced him with a look.

When she put it like that, Avery felt a flush of shame. She realized she hadn't given the students or instructors here enough credit. They'd never once said that her place among them was contingent on the usefulness of her powers. And people like David and Christopher really had tried to be her friend. She'd been the one to resist those overtures.

"I have trouble trusting people," she admitted, feeling Cluster give her hand a gentle squeeze. She squeezed back and glanced up at Fantomex. "It's something I'm working on."

He gave an almost imperceptible nod. "Aren't we all."

Now the nanotech were trusting her to help them, to find more of their own kind. Find us, they'd said. We are waiting here in the dark. Avery felt a shiver of premonition and looked around at the others. "When the nanotech said they were waiting here, you don't suppose they mean 'here' literally, do you? That there's an object infused with nanotech at this facility?"

An old military installation seemed like the last place

in the world to find fine art, but Avery had encountered too many strange things in her time here to dismiss the idea completely. And if the nanotech needed help, she thought they would want to be as transparent as possible in communicating what they wanted.

"There are at least a dozen or more storage rooms around the place that we haven't had time to clear out," Emma said, "not to mention the restricted areas beneath the school." She turned to Fantomex. "You probably know as much about the uses of this place in the past as anyone. Do you recall any hidden art objects?"

"Not offhand," he said. "I might have tried to abscond with a few of them if I had known. But it's entirely possible this place might have been a waypoint for smuggled goods, in addition to its other less savory activities."

"We should mount a search, then," Cluster said. She stood and helped Avery up with a steadying hand at her elbow. "We'll need Avery to sense the nanotech, but the rest of us aren't useless. We can help search for hidden caches of artifacts."

"A scavenger hunt," Fantomex said, grinning. "How novel. Should we involve the other waifs in the search? They might prove useful as well."

"You do know a lot of us are grown adults, right?" Avery scowled at him. "We're students, not orphans in a Dickens novel."

He was unmoved. "I'll grant that you're more useful than most of them, but you're also more annoying, so it balances out."

"She speaks to sentient machines," Cluster pointed out,

"which is more than I can say for a certain annoying–"

"Enough, children," Emma cut in. "We'll divide up into teams." She pointed at Fantomex and Cluster. "Clones one and two, you're together."

Fantomex was indignant. "Why can't I be with E.V.A.? We're partners, after all."

"Because I'm sending her with Avery," Emma said. She held up one finger to forestall any further arguments. "I want E.V.A. to monitor her."

"I'm really all right," Avery said, but Emma ignored her.

"I'll rally some of the students to help search the main levels," she continued, "but I want all of you to be careful. There's a reason we don't let students wander outside the areas of this facility designated for the school. There are dormant defense systems in place here, including a host of deactivated weapons. We're talking missiles. Don't go poking around something if you aren't certain what it is. Call for one of us. Understand?"

Fantomex huffed. "Why are you only looking at me when you say this?"

"You know why."

Avery followed E.V.A. out of the Danger Room. Wonderful. She'd gone from almost being trapped in a vision with sentient nanotech to a scavenger hunt that may or may not include forgotten nuclear weapons.

Her life was getting stranger and stranger by the minute.

# CHAPTER TWENTY

Fantomex had thought a scavenger hunt sounded like an interesting idea, but their search quickly became mind-numbing repetition. Start with a door, open it, then sort through the dozens of moldy, rotting boxes stacked to ceiling height throughout the room. Find vermin – curse. Find spoiled food – gag at the smell. Find vermin feasting on spoiled food… and on and on it went.

"Hardly the glamorous hunt you were expecting," Cluster said, when he tossed a box across the room in frustration. It hit the wall and simply disintegrated. It was that old and rotted. He would have been impressed if he weren't so disgusted.

Cluster, on the other hand, seemed content, going about the search without complaint, which made it worse because it made him feel like a sullen child.

Which he was not.

After he'd hurled his third box against the wall and wiped

some unspeakable substance off his hands, Cluster finally intervened.

"Do you want to talk about it, or is it helping to destroy the boxes?" she asked.

"It certainly isn't hurting," he grumbled. "This feels like a waste of time. We should have stayed with Avery and E.V.A. She's the nanotech detector, isn't she?" Avery would find and connect to this latest batch long before they did.

"That's what's bothering you?" Cluster asked. She opened another box, wrinkling her nose at the mildew smell that wafted out of it. "The fact that it's Avery who connects to them and we can't?"

"On the contrary, I'm pleased that she seems to have found the heart of her powers, and I have nothing against her personally," Fantomex said, "even if we clash from time to time." He would never admit it, but he admired her. And yes, he envied her, too. He'd tried to reach out to the nanotech with his thoughts in the Danger Room, but he'd gotten nowhere. He'd been certain the nanotech that had contributed to his own creation would have been able to connect to its counterparts, but that didn't seem to be the case. The sentient machines were completely fixed on Avery. He sighed. "The World is a part of us," he said. "The fact that part of it is evolving, attaining sentience, and neither of us can sense that – what does that make us?"

She pushed the box aside and glanced at him, puzzled. "It makes us people who need help forging the connection," she said. "Why? Do you think it lessens us?"

"You? No," he said, shaking his head. "You seem to be doing splendidly in this new incarnation." He'd never seen a person look more comfortable in their own skin than Cluster did, in fact. "And Weapon XIII seems to have retained the lion's share of our powers, including the ability to find the nanotech, so he's obviously not worried for his own fate."

"I can't speak for Weapon XIII, but I told you I didn't always feel comfortable in this new form," Cluster said. "It took time. Yes, we're more removed from the elements of our own creation, and that's unsettling, but even if you're never able to sense the nanotech or regain the powers you've lost, you still have many gifts. You're not weak and you're not lesser for how you've changed."

"You're being generous," he said, pulling another box down from a stack in the corner. "But you must have thought I needed help, if you sent E.V.A. with me and directed her to the X-Men."

"Ah, so it's that too, is it?" Impatiently, Cluster wiped at a streak of dirt that stubbornly clung to her jacket. "E.V.A. made her own choice to stay with you. I had nothing to do with it. Once she had made the decision, yes, I thought you should go to the X-Men because I thought you'd be safe. That's the beginning and end of it, I promise you."

Then why hadn't E.V.A. said as much? They used to confide in each other. They were partners, and even that relationship had become strained.

"The only visions I have are about the Skinless Man," he found himself saying, "about my heart being ripped from my chest, about being torn apart." His heartbeat sped up, but he funneled the adrenaline spike into throwing another box against the wall. It, too, disintegrated, but it wasn't as satisfying somehow.

"I have those same visions sometimes," Cluster said quietly. "They get better. Everything gets better in time, as you adapt."

"What if I don't want it to get better?" Fantomex snapped, turning to her. "What if I'm tired of being this doll, this Frankenstein's monster cobbled together and shaped and reshaped like clay? At least before, we were strong. We had each other and we were *whole*. You can't deny that."

Why couldn't he be in control of his own fate for once?

Before she could answer, a loud, piercing alarm ripped through the air. Fantomex clamped his hands over his ears, but the sound invaded.

"What is that?" Cluster yelled to be heard over the din. "A fire alarm?"

"I don't know," he shouted back, "but we'd better find out."

He moved for the door, but, just then a recorded voice echoed over the alarm. "Warning. Defense systems initiated. Missile protocols engaged. Countdown sequence imminent. Please proceed to your designated shelter areas immediately."

The message ended, but the alarm continued to sound. Fantomex exchanged a glance with Cluster.

"That can't be good," she said.

"No, it can't." He threw open the door and ran into the hallway. Across the way, he noticed that the lights on the panels beside several of the doors were turning from green to red. He went to one of them and tried the door.

"Locked."

Cluster went to another and wrenched the handle. "No good," she said.

The facility was going into lockdown. Had someone

initiated this accidentally in their search? Or had something triggered a long-dormant defense system?

"We need to find E.V.A. and Avery," he said, and took off down the hall, trusting Cluster to follow.

They hadn't gone far when they heard a loud banging coming from behind one of the doors.

"Anyone out there?" a young man's voice shouted from within.

"We're locked in!" This was three female voices yelling eerily in sync.

"They're students," Fantomex said, for Cluster's benefit. He leaned into the door and shouted over the alarm, "Are you all right in there?"

"Fantomex?" He recognized the man's voice as Fabio's. "Can you get us out?"

"Stand back from the door." Fantomex waited a beat, then backed up a few steps. He slammed into the door shoulder first, expecting it to disintegrate just like the boxes in the storage room.

He was mistaken.

The door was solid metal and very thick. It absorbed the impact of his body and sent him reeling back, a numbing pain shooting into his shoulder and down his arm.

Cluster looked at him and then at the door. "I don't think we can get in," she called to the room's occupants. "Stay put for now. We'll try to find a control room to deactivate the locks and get you out."

They continued down the hall, while Fantomex recovered his equilibrium. "I don't suppose you have any idea where this hypothetical control room might be?" he asked.

"No idea," Cluster admitted. "You've been here longer than I have, remember? I thought you'd have an inspiration."

"Let's try the Danger Room," he suggested, taking a left at the next intersection, past more locking doors. He heard the sound of distant shouts, but it was hard to tell over the alarm if it was more students locked in rooms or just people trying to figure out what was going on. "The system controls there might extend beyond the simulations."

"I think we should find Avery and E.V.A. first," Cluster said. "And the painting, if possible."

He shot her a sidelong glance as she quickened her pace. "You think they're in danger. You think it's Weapon XIII?" But how would he have found the place? Fantomex was always preparing for the worst-case scenario, but even he couldn't quite bring himself to believe that the man had managed to find the Institute, let alone get past their defense and advance warning systems.

"Maybe Weapon XIII used the same trick on me that I used on you?" Cluster suggested. "We do think alike."

"You mean a tracking device? Not possible. I checked you over thoroughly in the infirmary. You were clean."

She hesitated, then her eyes went wide. "Did you check the bullet you pulled out of me?"

The grim suggestion stopped him cold. He stared at her, then let out a stream of curses in perfect French.

"I'll take that as a no."

# CHAPTER TWENTY-ONE

They'd officially found the basement.

But not just any basement, Avery thought as they wound their way through the latest in a series of narrow, labyrinthine passages with pipes running along the walls above their heads and the constant sound of dripping water coming from somewhere off in the distance. This was an ancient, dank, straight out of a horror movie basement where you could easily hide some bodies because no one would ever willingly come down here to look for them.

Avery wouldn't have come down here either, except at some point during their search she'd started to feel a hum of energy, like something singing in her blood, an incessant feeling that was joined by a distant echo calling from somewhere beneath her feet. It was the same experience she'd had in the vision when the nanotech had connected with her. The feeling drew her inexorably *down*, coaxing her to take every stairway she could find that descended further into the depths of the Institute.

Their flashlight beams danced off the walls as they

moved, illuminating the path ahead, but Avery dearly hoped that E.V.A. was taking note of their route through the place because she was pretty sure she wouldn't be able to find her way back out again.

Coming around a bend in the passage, they entered a large, dungeon-like space full of heat and machinery that clanked and groaned and banged. It took Avery a minute to recognize the mass of monstrous equipment for what it was.

"I think we found the furnace room," she said, more than a little surprised. "As cold as it is in this place, I didn't think it existed."

"Judging by the condition of the equipment in here, I don't believe it's been inspected in some time," E.V.A. commented.

Great, Avery thought, as they made their way carefully past the rusting valves and pipes and other parts of the ancient heating system she had no name for. Forget the Sentinels, the military, and S.H.I.E.L.D. The greatest threat to the continued existence of the X-Men was their building not being up to code.

"I guess it's hard to call the plumbing and heating people when you live in a secret military base in the middle of nowhere," Avery said.

E.V.A. cocked her head, acknowledging the point as they moved on. "Still, when this is over, I should come back down here and see what I can do to ensure all the machinery is operating safely and efficiently," she said.

Avery turned, careful to keep her flashlight beam out of the woman's eyes. "Wait, so you can shapeshift, form weapons from your body, act as the most advanced artificial intelligence I've ever seen, *and* you do HVAC?"

"In addition, I can analyze any chemical or genetic information and transfer it to binary coding for use or repurpose," she said. "I also enjoy good wine."

Avery laughed, thinking she was joking, but E.V.A.'s expression told her she absolutely wasn't. "Wow," she murmured.

All that, and she was also connected to three very different beings with competing desires and goals. With all the focus on the stolen artifacts and the three newly separated personalities of Fantomex, Cluster, and Weapon XIII, Avery wondered if anyone had really taken the time to consider what E.V.A. must be going through as well.

"How do you deal with it?" she found herself asking as they resumed their trek down the passage, following that incessant hum of energy. She couldn't meet the woman's gaze, so she kept her eyes on the beam of her flashlight instead.

"Deal with it?" E.V.A. echoed. "I'm not sure I understand."

"Just... everything you thought you knew about yourself and your world – one day it suddenly changes, and everything turns upside down. You've had to endure so much in such a short time. How do you deal with it?"

The woman didn't answer for a long time. There was no sound in the corridor except their soft footfalls, the drip of water, and the clanks and bangs of the furnace room behind them. Avery felt her face flushing. She was afraid she'd offended E.V.A. by prying, but when she risked a glance at her, she didn't seem angry. Instead, she wore a thoughtful expression.

"I have observed in sentient beings, whether they be

human or mutant – or some hybrid in between – the desire to find meaning and purpose in their existence," she said carefully. "At first, I didn't understand this drive, but now I believe I have the same desire within me, the need to be *more*, to become something greater than I was before. I don't always recognize the direction to take to accomplish this goal. I am also… coming to terms with being a part of a triptych of beings, yet in some fundamental ways I stand *apart* from them. Our desires and goals are no longer one, and as a result, I find myself having to make choices I never imagined I would have to make."

Her pained expression tugged at Avery. On impulse, she reached out and touched E.V.A.'s shoulder, trying to offer the same comfort Cluster had extended to her earlier.

E.V.A. gave her a small, grateful smile as she continued. "It's not easy to have one's loyalties split. The triptych is flawed but beautiful to me – even Weapon XIII. It might be impossible, but as I continue my own journey I want to be with all of them, to help them endure and grow. Because of them, I now also understand why it's such a difficult undertaking to find and stay true to one's self." She met Avery's gaze. "But as long as I attempt to stay on the path I've chosen, I'm satisfied I can handle whatever comes."

Avery stared at her. "What if what you're becoming scares you?"

E.V.A.'s eyes softened, and she laid a hand over Avery's. "I understand that fear is part of the journey," she said, "and that there are people around me who will help me when I falter. If I let them."

Avery thought of her conversation with Cluster in the

Danger Room. She'd thought that Jane should have a say in whether or not she was a part of Avery's life and her struggles. Was she right? Was Avery being unfair to Jane by not letting her decide for herself if she wanted to continue their relationship?

Avery had thought she was trying to protect her, but maybe she was more worried about protecting herself, keeping her own heart from being hurt.

Distracted by her thoughts, Avery realized the humming energy was growing louder, the call more insistent. Its source was just ahead of them, in a small room near the next intersection.

She pointed it out to E.V.A., who moved to the door and tried the handle. It was locked, but E.V.A. simply raised two fingers and altered their shape to two slender metal picks that she inserted into the lock. After a few seconds of fiddling, the lock clicked, and the door swung open.

Inside the room the walls were damp, and the heavy, cloying smell of mildew clung to everything. There were three large crates stacked along the opposite wall, their lids nailed shut.

The humming energy was coming from the center crate. Avery pointed to it. "I guess we should have brought a crowbar."

In response, E.V.A. pressed her fingers together, and her arm lengthened and flattened, curving into a metal point like a crowbar but more elegant and wicked looking. She wedged it into the crate and pried the wooden lid up.

Avery scraped aside some old, moldy packing peanuts, wrinkling her nose at the smell. Underneath them, her hand fell on something solid and smooth. Her fingertips tingled with energy, and she knew she'd found the artifact.

She pulled the object carefully out of the crate. It was a small, slender-necked bottle, no more than a couple of inches tall, which fit comfortably in the palm of her hand. Running her fingers along its surface, Avery held it up to the beam of E.V.A.'s flashlight to inspect the image painted on it. It was some sort of mythical beast, a hybrid creature with one head situated atop three bodies.

Avery smiled a little, remembering one of her dad's art history lectures. He'd be proud of how much she remembered. "It's an alabastron," she told E.V.A., "done in terracotta. They're containers for scented oil. It's Corinthian." She turned it over in her hands. "But I suppose this one's a copy too? It looks so real."

"The nanotechnology is extremely precise in its creations," E.V.A. said. "I doubt even an experienced curator could tell the difference."

"There are a bunch of artifacts in here," Avery said, sifting her hand through the crate to uncover more pottery and other objects wrapped tightly in rags. "I don't sense anything from them, so it's entirely possible they're genuine. They could be incredibly valuable."

"When this is over, we'll make sure they're returned to where they belong," E.V.A. said. "For now, we should find the others so they can call off the search."

Avery nodded absently, but she was still examining the delicate vessel. "Do you think it's just the Alano painting that will explode when it's taken from me?" she asked, trying to keep her voice steady. "Or will all the artifacts react the same way when I try to connect with them?" She hadn't thought about it before, but now a part of her was wishing they'd left the little vessel safely tucked away in the crate.

But E.V.A. shook her head. "I don't believe that's how it works," she said. "The nanotech that attached itself to you came from the painting. That's where your connection is strongest. It's also possible the nanotech in the other artifacts represent separate groups of entities, unable to communicate or interact with each other unless they are brought together."

Brought together so they can find their purpose. Maybe she could forge some kind of connection to the other artifacts as well, in order to communicate with them. But it would take time and practice honing her abilities. If she stayed here, the X-Men could help her accomplish that.

She had a lot to think about.

Avery was still examining the alabastron when she heard the distant buzz of an alarm. A voice followed, some sort of pre-recorded message, but it was too far away to make out all the words. Something about a lockdown, and taking shelter...

"Something's wrong," E.V.A. said. "We need to hurry."

They retraced their steps, not quite running, but moving quickly, E.V.A. guiding Avery when she threatened to take a wrong turn.

As they approached the furnace room, Avery heard another sound: a soft, incessant beeping that seemed to grow louder as they moved through the passage. She didn't remember that sound from earlier. Was it coming from the furnace?

Suddenly, E.V.A. grabbed her by the arm. "Get down!"

Too late.

The blast knocked Avery off her feet. She landed hard on her right side, dropping both her flashlight and the alabastron. The artifact rolled away from her and came to rest against the far wall. Dizzy and bruised, Avery heard a sharp ringing in her ears. Despite the pain, she forced herself to sit up, looking around wildly to see if it was the furnace that had been the source of the explosion.

Her stomach tightened.

Weapon XIII was standing in the doorway of the furnace room, blocking their way back upstairs.

E.V.A., who had somehow managed to stay on her feet, put her body in front of Avery's and formed her arm into the familiar large scythe blade, which she brandished before Weapon XIII.

"I have multiple neuroblasts locked onto you at point blank range," she said. "Leave here now."

Avery thought that was a pretty impressive threat, so when the man's soft chuckle echoed through the room, it chilled her.

"You can't release an energy weapon into this room without risking damage to the furnace and boiler," he said, glancing over his shoulder at the ancient machines. "The resulting explosion and fire would be far more unpleasant than anything I intend to do."

"Bet she can still slice you in half," Avery said, pushing herself to her feet. She grabbed her flashlight and the alabastron, but E.V.A. waved her back when she would have stepped forward.

"Avery, run," she said calmly. "Find another way to get back upstairs and warn the others."

"But–"

"Just do it, please."

Avery knew she wasn't kidding anyone with her bravado. She couldn't fight Weapon XIII, though she hated the idea of leaving E.V.A. to face him alone. But she was right. They needed help.

Reluctantly, she turned and took off down the passage. Behind her, she could hear Weapon XIII addressing E.V.A.

"Would you really attack me?" he asked. "Aren't we still a part of each other?"

"You made your choice to be our enemy when you almost killed Cluster," E.V.A. said, still calm, cold even. "I've made mine."

"Very well."

Then there was no more talk, only the sounds of combat, and even they faded as Avery ran faster, putting distance between herself and the fight.

She had to find help. Panic crawled up her throat as she ran down the dark passageways, her flashlight beam bouncing crazily off the walls. Whenever she reached an intersection, she kept left, so she'd remember where she'd gone. Inevitably, she'd eventually hit a dead end and have to retrace her steps. The fourth time she did this, she wanted to scream. The basement seemed to stretch on forever, and she was no closer to finding a set of stairs leading up or even an emergency exit.

It felt like she was running through a nightmare, narrated by that incessant alarm and the recorded voice announcing the facility lockdown.

Finally, she reached a corridor that dead-ended at a door

with a picture of a set of stairs on it. Yanking it open, she took the stairs two at a time, her lungs burning, limbs bruised and aching from her fall.

Halfway up, she was aware of other footsteps pounding down the stairs from above. Heart in her throat, she called out, "Who's up there?"

"Avery?" Two voices shouted her name.

Fantomex and Cluster.

Relief swamped her. "We found the artifact." She held up the alabastron as the pair of them leaped down the remaining stairs to reach her. "Weapon XIII's in the furnace room. He had us trapped. E.V.A.'s fighting him, but she's alone, and I don't know how long she can hold him off!"

Fantomex and Cluster exchanged alarmed glances. "Go!" Cluster told him, and Fantomex, with a terse nod, took off back the way Avery had come.

Cluster took Avery's arm. "Are you hurt?" she asked, looking her over for injuries.

"I'm fine," she said. "You should go with Fantomex. You should help him."

"I will," she said, "but first we need to secure the painting. Is it still in your room?"

Avery nodded, but Cluster was already moving, back up the stairs where she'd come from, as Avery struggled to keep up.

# CHAPTER TWENTY-TWO

Fantomex tried to ignore his rising panic as he raced to get to E.V.A. There were no sounds of fighting coming from up ahead, which meant that either E.V.A. had fended off Weapon XIII, or…

He found her lying in the middle of the furnace room. She was trying to sit up, clutching her head, her face twisted in pain.

"Don't move," Fantomex said, dropping to his knees beside her. "I'll get help."

E.V.A. waved him off impatiently. "We don't have time. I kept him occupied for as long as I could, but he's strong, and he can track the artifacts as well or better than Avery can. He'll be tracking her now."

"Cluster is with Avery," Fantomex said, helping her to her feet. He slung one arm over her shoulders as they made their way as quickly as they could back to the stairs.

"What about the others?" E.V.A. asked, grimacing. "We're going to need them."

"I hope that's not true," Fantomex said, "because from what we can gather, Weapon XIII's been using his powers to move through the school, causing chaos. I think he armed the defense system and then used his misdirection to convince Cyclops or Emma Frost – someone in charge – to lock down the school. Most of the students and faculty are sealed in whatever room they were searching when the alarm went off, and I assume the others are trying to abort the lockdown and make sure no errant missiles get shot from this facility."

"So, we're on our own," E.V.A. said.

"For the moment, yes."

They reached the dormitory floor, when an explosion rocked the building and sent them stumbling into the nearest wall.

"That's not coming from the dorms," Fantomex said. "It came from the direction of the hangar. Was it a missile?"

"I don't think so." E.V.A. pushed away from him and broke into a half-limp, half-run toward the hangar. "Weapon XIII was using some low-level explosives down in the furnace room. Not enough to kill us, just enough to stun."

"There was nothing low-level about that," Fantomex said.

Quickening their pace, they reached the hangar and immediately saw the source of the explosion. One side of the bay had been blown out, sabotaging both the jet and the X-Copter in the process. Weapon XIII was being thorough, making sure no one could follow him.

Cluster was picking herself up off the ground near the debris. It looked like she'd caught the edge of the blast but was mostly uninjured.

Avery was standing in the middle of the hangar, alone,

clutching the painting and the alabastron in her hands as she faced down Weapon XIII, who had a gun pointed at her. He took a single step toward her, his eyes cold, his hand out, and that was when Fantomex felt the pulse of energy ripple out from where Avery was standing.

"Oh, no," E.V.A. said. "Stop!"

Weapon XIII looked up, and Avery started to turn, but he grabbed her by the arm, positioning her in front of his body like a shield.

"No closer," he said.

Fantomex cursed under his breath. If he'd had his misdirection power, he could have planted a nightmarish illusion in Weapon XIII's head that would have sent him to his knees. He could try to get a shot off or flick a knife at him, but would his reflexes be fast enough? Would he falter and hit Avery instead?

He gritted his teeth. The weak one.

He raised his hands, never taking his eyes off Avery. "Let's take a moment and consider the circumstances we find ourselves in," he said reasonably. "You know what these artifacts hold. No one really knows what this nanotechnology is capable of, but we have discovered that if you try to take that painting by force, it will explode." He looked at Weapon XIII. "So think very carefully about your next move."

Weapon XIII watched him with narrowed eyes. "You're lying," he said.

"He's not," Avery spoke up. "I can feel it. Can't you?" she challenged him, and Fantomex felt his gut tighten.

"Avery," he warned. He had to think of something.

"No," she said stubbornly. "He has to believe us. If you try to leave with the painting, it'll hurt you too," she said, looking at Weapon XIII. "And the building's still in lockdown. People are trapped."

Fantomex glimpsed the haunted look in her eyes. She was terrified that the painting would explode, that people would be hurt or killed because of her. And he couldn't do anything about it.

They'd had no time, he thought, anger and frustration rising inside him. No time to find a way to safely sever Avery's connection to the nanotech or to try to properly communicate with them. *He* had failed to communicate with them.

Failed again.

"Take the alabastron," he said to Weapon XIII, trying not to betray his desperation. He was fairly certain the energy pulse was coming from the painting, not from it. "Surely, with all the other things you've stolen, whatever you're after, you have enough."

Weapon XIII flicked a glance at Cluster. "I need the rest of the artifacts, the ones she took."

"I can get them for you," Cluster said. "I just need time to retrieve them from where I've hidden them. Let me—"

"No," Weapon XIII said. "No time for tricks and deceptions. If you don't have the artifacts here, I'm taking these now."

Avery tried to curl her body around the painting, but Weapon XIII was much stronger. He pried it out of her grip with ease.

The pulse intensified, so strong now it was almost a visible distortion in the air. It made Weapon XIII hesitate.

"You can't do this," Avery said. She looked back at Fantomex, her eyes frightened but resolved. And with a rush of panic, he knew what she was going to do.

"Avery, don't!" Cluster yelled, recognizing it too.

She ignored them and turned to Weapon XIII. "It's because of me," she said. "Some of the nanotech is inside me, spilled over from the painting. If you take it, you have to take me too. Then it won't explode, and everyone will be safe."

Weapon XIII looked down at Avery as if seeing her for the first time. "You?" he said in disbelief. "Why would the nanotech choose you of all people?"

"Because I'm a mutant," she said, "and I can communicate with them."

Fantomex groaned silently, willing Avery to be quiet.

Weapon XIII seemed to consider her words. "Then you might be useful to me in more ways than one," he said. "Walk. Outside." He gestured with the gun. "The rest of you stay where you are, or she takes a bullet. I can keep her alive. I don't care whether she's in excruciating pain or not."

Fantomex and E.V.A. stood rooted, watching Avery and Weapon XIII leave the hangar via the blown-out wall. Cluster held her body rigid, but Fantomex had never seen a person look as furious and helpless as she did in that moment.

Outside, they heard the sound of an engine starting and helicopter blades whirring faintly. In E.V.A.'s absence, Weapon XIII had managed to acquire his own means of flight. Fantomex ran to the opening in the wall in time to see the craft rising in the air, but he couldn't see Avery behind the tinted glass of the cockpit. It looked like some kind of stealth tech, probably stolen from a military base or one of

S.H.I.E.L.D.'s facilities. But E.V.A. could follow. He knew she could. They just needed to get in the air.

But when he turned to her, he could tell by the way she was standing, barely staying on her feet, that she was in no condition to fly at the moment. She needed a healer and rest.

Weapon XIII had thought of everything. He'd thoroughly ambushed and beaten them.

And now he had Avery.

# CHAPTER TWENTY-THREE

Avery had never ridden in a helicopter before. She decided she didn't like it. She was probably biased, though. It certainly didn't help that she'd been kidnapped onto this particular helicopter – also a new experience for her.

Night had fallen as they were flying over downtown Chicago. She could see the tall dark shape of Willis Tower out her window. She spent a moment wondering why no one was concerned about an unidentified helicopter cruising over the Magnificent Mile toward Lake Michigan, but then she realized Weapon XIII must have engaged some kind of stealth tech. Instead of the whirring sounds of the rotor blades filling her ears, they were running practically silent.

She was sitting in the seat directly behind him, the Alano painting propped next to her. Every now and then, she felt a soft pulse of energy emanating from it. Nothing dangerous, or at least she didn't think so. Maybe the nanotech were reacting to her fear, which continued to mount the farther away from the Institute they flew.

She'd worked up the courage to speak to Weapon XIII once, asking him where they were going, but he hadn't replied. Not that she'd expected him to, but it was worth a shot.

He was so strange. He resembled Fantomex in many ways, from his looks right down to his mannerisms. It was uncanny. Yet she would never confuse the two of them. Fantomex's eyes were sharp and alive. Weapon XIII's had a coldness that was hard to look at for very long. No one wanted the attention of eyes like that.

A faint vibration in her pocket startled her.

Her phone.

In the chaos, she'd forgotten she had it with her. Weapon XIII hadn't searched her when they'd boarded the stealth copter. He'd seemed fixated on taking off and getting them away from the Institute. He hadn't tied her hands either. After all, where would she go?

And the only reason her phone would be vibrating the way it was now was if they had re-entered the land of good cell reception.

Ever so slowly, Avery inched her right hand toward her pocket, keeping her eyes on Weapon XIII's back for any sign that he could see what she was up to.

When her fingers touched the phone, she felt light-headed, but began working the rectangle out of her pocket, schooling her features into stillness as she glanced down at the screen.

There were notification icons all over it. One new text message, multiple missed calls and voicemails. All from the same number.

Jane.

Avery swallowed, her hands trembling as she eased the phone into her lap. She knew she should call for help, but who would she reach out to? The Institute had no cell service, and the number she'd used to contact Cyclops that first time had been taken out of service for security reasons. She could try 911, but she could imagine how that conversation would go. Hello, what's the nature of your emergency? Yes, I've been kidnapped by a clone, and he's flown me away in his stealth helicopter. Please send help. They'd get a good laugh before they hung up.

In the end, there was really only one person that she needed to talk to right now.

She unlocked the screen and her text thread with Jane popped up.

*Jane: Hey hold on. Breaking up is the last thing I want. Don't you want to fight for this relationship? Because I do. We need to talk about this.*

Avery's heart swelled. Here, in this moment, when she had no idea if she'd be alive or dead tomorrow, she wanted more than anything to fight for her relationship with Jane. She'd been a fool to try to throw that away.

Not anymore. Avery vowed then and there that if she made it out of this in one piece, she would fight. Trust was a risk, Fantomex had told her, and there were some people worth risking everything for. Jane was that person for her.

She brought up their text thread and tapped out a reply faster than she'd ever texted anyone before.

*Avery: I'm a mutant. That's my secret. I love you. I want to*

A shadow fell over her, and Avery froze. Frantically she went for the send button, only to have the phone ripped out of her hands. She had no idea if the message had gone off or not.

Weapon XIII stood over her, looking at her phone impassively. She hadn't even heard him get out of his seat. As she watched, he crushed the phone in his hand, tossing the pieces on the floor.

Avery glared at him, fury and helplessness coursing through her. "That's not as impressive as you think it is," she snapped. "I've had phones shatter into a million pieces just by knocking them off my nightstand. You don't scare me."

That was a blatant lie, but her anger overrode her sense of self-preservation. Now Jane might never know her secret, and she would never know whether Jane would have accepted it and her. Why had it taken her so long to see exactly what she wanted?

"We're landing soon," was all Weapon XIII said in response to her outburst. He went back to the flight controls. They were flying over open water now, the wide expanse of the lake looking solid black in the wan moonlight. Where were they going to land? Did he have an underwater lair hidden here somewhere? Did things like that really exist?

Her heart sank. How was anyone going to find her all the way out here?

Thankfully, there was no underwater lair. In the distance, a small strip of land emerged from the darkness. Weapon XIII brought the helicopter down carefully towards it. A large building that looked like a discount warehouse turned train station dominated the area, a glass ceiling forming the main part of its roof. The building looked strangely familiar, but Avery couldn't quite place where she'd seen it before.

In the darkness, she could just make out a small helipad in one corner of the roof. Weapon XIII set the craft lightly on it and powered down the controls. He rose and came back to where she was sitting, sliding open the side door. He gestured for her to go before him.

As she rose from her seat, picking up the painting and the alabastron, he said, "I won't offer you the indignity of tying you up, but if you try to run, I will catch you, and I will break one of your legs so you can't run again."

He said it so casually, as if they were discussing dinner plans, that Avery couldn't hide her shudder. She didn't doubt for a moment that he would make good on the threat.

Anyway, where would she run to on this island? As she made her way down the helicopter steps she noted a dock about a hundred yards away from the building, but there were no boats moored there. There were no other vehicles that she could see from the roof. The island appeared completely deserted except for the two of them.

He pointed to a door at the other end of the roof. "In there," he said.

They went down a flight of stairs and eventually ended up in a large open space that reminded Avery of a museum gallery, except there was no art on the walls. But when she looked closer, she saw that there once had been. Empty wires and placards still decorated the walls, and abruptly Avery realized why the building looked so familiar.

It was the Musée d'Orsay. Well, not really. It was more like a cheap knockoff built by a child using a warehouse kit, but she could see what the architect had been going for. This must be the temporary exhibition space where the Diana of

Versailles statue had been on display. She'd heard Fantomex mention it in passing when he was talking to Cluster. The exhibition itself had obviously moved on, leaving the sad-looking replica building standing empty.

Not completely empty.

As Weapon XIII turned on some of the lights, she saw at the other end of the vast open hall there was a large, strange-looking machine that seemed to have been cobbled together from parts of other machines in a great mass of wires and consoles that was straight out of a science fiction novel. Situated in its center was a clear glass cylinder, just large enough to hold a person, filled with a light bluish liquid that bubbled and flowed.

Beside the machine there was a stack of crates, most of them empty, some with their contents strewn carelessly about the floor in a messy nest of drop cloths and packing material.

When she got close enough to see what they were, Avery's jaw went slack. Paintings, pottery, small statues – a fortune in art lay spread out before her as if it were being presented at a yard sale. And as she concentrated, letting her awareness drift, she thought she felt faint pulses of energy coming from parts of the pile.

"Are all these… fakes… infused with nanotech?" she asked, deeply curious despite her fear.

To her surprise, he actually answered. "Most of them," he said. "A few of the pieces are genuine. I took them just for me."

She put her shoulders back, glaring at him. "Then you should take better care of them. You shouldn't leave them strewn all over the floor."

He leveled that dead-eyed stare at her, and Avery's anger melted in a wave of trepidation. This isn't Fantomex you're talking to, she reminded herself. There was none of his humor in this man's face, none of Cluster's warmth in his voice.

And in that moment, as they looked at each other, Avery realized something else, something that made her skin prickle with a combination of fear and pity. This man had truly gotten the worst part of the separation. Fantomex had complained that Weapon XIII was stronger, that he'd retained the best of their powers, but he'd lost so much more. He'd lost the empathy that she'd seen radiating so brightly from Cluster. And that mischievous nature and zest for life that Avery had glimpsed several times over the last few days – that had gone to Fantomex.

But Fantomex had empathy too, as much as he tried to pretend otherwise. And Cluster had been trying to tell her to seize the moment with Jane. The two of them were far more balanced than Weapon XIII could ever hope to be.

"Is that why you attacked them?" Avery asked before she could stop herself. "Do you hate them because you see in them all the things you used to be?"

She'd caught him off guard. For an instant that aura of coldness slipped, exposing something raw in his eyes, but it was gone before she had a chance to identify it.

He came toward her slowly, and Avery knew she'd messed up. She backed away, his warning not to run ringing in her ears, but she kept going anyway until she backed into one of the crates, bumping her shoulder blades against the wood. Nowhere to run now. She braced for the worst.

But he just stared down at her with those cold, empty

eyes. "I want you to talk to the nanotech," he said. "I need their assistance."

Momentarily stunned, Avery couldn't think of how to reply. First he'd kidnapped her and now he wanted her to be a translator between him and the nanotech?

"How… what could you possibly need their help with?" she asked.

At that, a look of supreme satisfaction flashed in his eyes. It chilled her more than anything else he'd said or done. "An act of creation," he said.

# CHAPTER TWENTY-FOUR

Fantomex was tired of feeling helpless, of being humiliated, of seeing himself and his friends get hurt and having no control over the turns his life had taken over the past several months. Now he couldn't even be involved in the search for Avery.

It had taken time for everyone to regroup after the chaos Weapon XIII's attack had caused. Once the dust settled and the facility was secure, Cluster had taken E.V.A. to the infirmary to recover, while Emma Frost set about tracking Weapon XIII's stealth copter. At first Fantomex had insisted on being in the room with her and Cyclops while she worked, hashing out plans for a rescue operation, but his impatience and temper had finally made her snap, and she'd ordered him out of the room.

The rage he felt at this latest development simmered inside him like a poison. He needed someone to unleash it on or he was going to explode.

Luckily, he knew just the person for the job.

He found Cluster in the Danger Room, taking out her own frustrations on some combat dummies that she was currently pummeling to death with her fists and feet.

"Is it any fun if they don't fight back?" he asked.

She turned to face him, wiping the sweat from her forehead with her sleeve. "Are you offering?" she asked, then she looked into his eyes. "Ah. So you are." She immediately sank into a combat-ready stance, drawing her knives, one in each hand.

He mirrored the gesture, but he gave her no time to prepare. He was too angry. He came at her hard, hoping to overwhelm her with brute strength, but it made him clumsy, and she easily parried and dodged the first few strikes.

That was fine. He rolled his shoulders, cracking his neck. He was just getting warmed up.

"You should have told me everything you knew about Weapon XIII from the start," he said, swiping at her again. Blades flashed in a blur – strike and parry, both of them always moving, like a dance. "This is your fault. He hurt E.V.A., and he took Avery, all because of you."

He'd hoped she would flinch, give him an opening. She did neither. She dropped to the floor, sweeping his legs out from under him. He landed on his back but flipped to his feet before she could press the advantage.

"I told you, I don't know what he wants with the artifacts and the nanotech." She sounded impatient, as if she were talking to a child. It only enraged him more. "For the rest of it, I was waiting until I thought you were ready. I was trying to protect you."

"I don't need your help!" This time she was slower. He knocked the blade from her off-hand, sent it skittering across the floor. But he knew better than to think he had the advantage. "It must be wonderful for you, to be so certain of who you are and what your purpose is."

She'd accepted who she was now, even embraced it. Why couldn't he do it too? Why couldn't he overcome the purpose he'd been given? Isn't that what he'd always wanted? Shouldn't he be able to do that now, with a new start ahead of him? Why was it so hard?

Because they were so much better when they were one.

He stiffened, as Cluster suddenly went on the offensive, slashing with her single knife, the strikes coming faster than his eyes could follow. He snatched her wrist and tried to twist the blade out of her hand, but she kneed him in the gut. He kept hold of her, but she grabbed the lapel of his jacket with her free hand and jerked him close.

"Do you truly think you are the only one suffering in all of this?" she hissed, her breathing labored. He'd finally managed to make her angry. "I still struggle with my purpose, just as you do."

He leaned in close, his face filling her vision, so she couldn't fail to be reminded of the similarities between them. "Do you ever stop to consider the unfairness of it? We were struck down, cut into pieces. The person we used to be would *never* have let Avery be taken."

"You think that doesn't haunt me?" He felt her body tense. "These feelings and uncertainties are not something that can be conquered in a day or a month," she said. "It can take a lifetime to decide who you really are, and there are no shortcuts, my darling triptych. Not one."

She shoved him away, twisting free of his grip. She tossed her knife from hand to hand, clearly ready to go another round, but Fantomex found his energy and his rage waning. A pity. It was far easier to be angry.

"Why haven't we tracked him down yet?" he demanded. "It's been two hours and nothing."

Cluster, as if gauging the shift in his mood, sheathed her knife and went to retrieve the other one. "He's using stolen S.H.I.E.L.D. stealth tech, so it's not exactly easy to track, but Emma Frost is trying. They're all trying. Even E.V.A., and she should be resting and restoring herself. We're the only ones being useless at this time."

He saw it then, the frustration in her eyes and in the way she swept her hair back impatiently from her face. She truly was feeling as helpless, as angry at herself as he was. But she had only intended to take it out on the combat dummies.

"I want it all back the way it was," he said, giving her honesty by way of apology. It must have gotten through, because she stopped and turned to look at him. "When we were one, things were simpler."

"Simpler, but not better," she said.

He shot her an incredulous look. "You can't mean that. We were so much stronger together. No doubts, no weaknesses. You said yourself you grieved for our loss."

Restless, she paced in front of him. "I did and I do," she said at last. "But the way we were before – it was too much. *We* were too much. Powerful, yes, but we were arrogant and smug and…"

"Sarcastic," he said. "I can't see that much has changed from my perspective."

"I disagree," she said. "You've gained some humility. You've had to rely on other people, and you've discovered that's not so bad. Or am I wrong?"

She wasn't, and she knew it. Fantomex thought back to the midnight supper in the kitchen, to Triage healing his and Cluster's wounds, to Cyclops saying he understood what it was like to lose the vital parts of yourself. All of that had made him feel a part of something, and it *had* helped. But was it enough? Would any of it truly last?

"When we were one, I didn't feel so lost," he admitted. "I don't like that feeling."

"I know. And it's worse because Weapon XIII's acting against us. What he's doing is a betrayal of everything we are. When he attacked E.V.A. ...." She shook her head. "I never thought he would do it. Maybe this is his way of showing how much he's struggling too."

Weapon XIII, struggling? He could hardly believe that. He hadn't seemed to be struggling when he'd fought them. He'd overpowered both of them, and he'd been the one to retain the misdirection ability, arguably the heart of their powers.

And yet...

Avery had told them that in her vision, the nanotech had said Weapon XIII was trying to save what couldn't be saved. He hadn't known what to make of it at the time, but now...

Fantomex stared at Cluster, his thoughts racing as he absorbed the idea. "You think he feels lost too?"

"Why not? He's having to adapt to a new reality as well. He has neither the moral compass, such as it is, that he once did, or the devil-may-care attitude that allowed us to shake off some of our more painful demons. He must be struggling too in his own way. Don't you think?"

Yes. Of course. He couldn't believe he hadn't seen it before.

All three of them were struggling, and each of them had reacted in their own ways to that pain. Cluster had needed time alone, but she'd been watching over him, her instincts leading her to try to protect him. Fantomex had made it his mission to prove he was better than the other two. E.V.A. had seen it, had known from the beginning there was more to his motives in tracking down Cluster. He was trying to prove that the best parts of himself weren't gone forever.

And Weapon XIII was the most extreme, the most selfish of their three personalities, according to E.V.A.'s assessment. So it stood to reason that his reaction to their circumstances would also be the most extreme.

"He wants it too," Fantomex said aloud. When Cluster gave him a puzzled frown, he elaborated, "Weapon XIII wants the same thing I do. He wants it all back the way it was before. Arrogant, smug, believing we could take on the world, because everyone in it was the lesser being. Our dysfunctional triptych. He wants it restored to its proper form."

Cluster's eyes widened as she realized what he was saying. "You mean that he wants to find a way to reunite us, restore us to our original joined state?"

"And what better way to accomplish that than to use the nanotech that was responsible for creating us in the World," Fantomex said. "It's gained sentience, and it's gained in power. Maybe he believes he can use that to recreate us."

The more he thought about it, the more he knew he was right. And having Avery, a mutant, infused with the nanotech – he could use her too. If she could successfully communicate with the nanotech, she might be the key to making the process work.

Fantomex's view of Weapon XIII realigned in that moment, the pieces that made up his dark counterpart shifting and coming into better focus. He felt a rush of excitement and wild hope. He'd been convinced by Weapon XIII's actions, his aggression and ruthlessness, that he was their enemy. Yet all this time, he'd actually been working toward the thing Fantomex wanted most.

Was it really possible for them to be reunited?

"We have to find him," Fantomex said. "As soon as possible."

"He can't hope to succeed," Cluster said, following him as he headed for the door. The Danger Room simulation melted away when they left the room, the combat dummies vanishing. "Even if he found a way to use the nanotech, the process would be terribly dangerous. You saw what happened when we were split initially. You ended up in a coma for months. To try reversing that process so soon would likely kill us all."

She had a point, and it should have dimmed some of his excitement, but strangely, it didn't. "If he believes his current state is worse than death, he'd be more than willing to risk it," Fantomex said, as they made their way to Emma Frost's office. "But with Avery acting as a conduit to the nanotech, a way to communicate his desires, it might make the process safer."

But there was no way to know.

"If his end goal is to reunite us, that does give us one advantage," Cluster said, as Fantomex knocked – well, pounded – on the door to Emma Frost's office. "He can't proceed without us."

"Bait for the hook," Fantomex agreed as the door opened, but it was Cyclops who leaned out to greet them. "Good, you're done sparring," he said. "Come in."

"Sulking, more like," Emma said, not looking up from her computer.

"Do you have cameras on every room in this place?" Cluster asked as they entered the office.

"Not the bathrooms," Emma said. "Though I considered it."

"She's joking," Cyclops said with a sigh. "But yes, we overheard your conversation as well. At least we know now what Weapon XIII is after."

Fantomex was surprised to see more people in the room. Christopher Muse and David Bond sat talking quietly in the corner. They looked up and nodded when he entered.

"What's all this?" he asked.

"The rescue team," Cyclops said, gesturing to the young men. "We had several volunteers, but Triage and Hijack were the most vehement."

"We heard what Avery did," David said, standing. "She gave herself up to save the rest of us."

"So what are we doing to get her back?" Christopher asked, frowning at them.

"I'm doing more than any of you," Emma said, her fingers flying over the keyboard. "Well, E.V.A. helped," she amended.

"E.V.A. is supposed to be recovering," Fantomex said, scowling.

"I sent her to rest again eventually," Emma said. "Let me tell you, it wasn't easy."

"You try telling a person who can make a scythe out of their arm what to do," Cluster said. "What have you got?"

"Hacked some military communications by a couple of pilots who briefly clocked an unidentified craft passing through Chicago airspace," Emma said, her eyes scanning the screen. "It was a blip and then gone, so they chalked it up to a malfunction rather than an unidentified aerial phenomenon."

"What makes you think it's the S.H.I.E.L.D. copter?" Cyclops asked. "It could be anything."

"Could be a UFO," Christopher suggested. "What?" he said when they all stared at him. "Lots of that stuff out there now, even the Navy's admitting it. Just saying."

"What if he's taking her to the island, to the temporary exhibition?" Fantomex said. "Where we found the Diana of Versailles statue."

Emma looked up at the rest of them at last, rubbing her eyes as if she hadn't blinked in some time. "Why would he go back there? The exhibition moved on the day after you were there, so the place is cleared out. The building's empty."

"Which makes it as good a spot as any to set up a base of operations and store the artifacts he's stolen," Cluster said. "He can see anyone coming via air and water."

"He's also not going to try hard to hide," Fantomex said, crossing his arms. He suspected, much like Cluster winking on the museum's surveillance footage, Weapon XIII wanted to be found, because he needed the other two pieces of this puzzle in order to carry out his plan.

"Let's give him what he wants, then," Cluster said. "Fantomex and I will go to the island with the artifacts I have and offer to trade them for Avery."

"You're not going alone," Cyclops said. "I'll take Triage and Hijack and back you up. We just need to get the X-Copter repaired."

Fantomex pointed to the goateed young man. "What's your contribution to the operation?"

"Hijack, like the name implies," David said. "If I'm close enough, I can take control of vehicles. Whatever happens, Weapon XIII's not escaping with Avery this time. I'll make sure of it."

"Is E.V.A. going to be recovered enough to fly the rest of you there?" Emma asked.

"Whether she is or not, I doubt she'll let us leave her behind," Cluster said.

"Then let's get to it," Fantomex said. "We're wasting time."

# CHAPTER TWENTY-FIVE

Fantomex found E.V.A. in the hangar helping Cyclops and Hijack with repairs to the stealth helicopter. Although it had been near the blast, its armor plating had absorbed the worst of the impact, and it looked like the three of them almost had it up and running.

His attention shifted to E.V.A., watching her movements as she directed David to replace one of the panels they'd removed to survey the damage. She wasn't human, so she didn't show pain and injury in her humanoid form the same way a human would, but she was still a techno-organic being that could be damaged and hurt in more ways than one. He could tell she needed more time to recover, but every moment counted now.

As if sensing his eyes on her, E.V.A. turned and met his gaze. Nodding to Hijack, she walked across the hangar to join him.

"We're almost ready to go," she said. "Cyclops, Hijack,

and Triage will take the stealth X-Copter, and I'll fly you and Cluster to the island."

"Are you sure you're up for this?" Fantomex asked, even though he knew what her answer would be. She wouldn't be left behind, and the truth was they needed her.

But he didn't want her to get hurt.

She laid a hand on his shoulder. "It won't just be me, remember? We've assembled quite a team. Don't worry, we'll get Avery back."

She spoke with a confidence he wished he shared. He started to turn away, but her hand tightened on his shoulder, forcing him to look at her.

"I didn't choose to stay with you because Cluster asked me to," E.V.A. said firmly. "Nor did I do it because you were the most in need of care. I stayed with you because you are the most like me." Her brow furrowed, and she shook her head as if that wasn't quite it. "Maybe the better way to phrase it is that I am the most myself when I am with you. I needed that feeling as I grew accustomed to my new state of being."

His throat tightened. He found he had no clever quip or joke to offer in return, not in the face of a declaration so honest and vulnerable. "Why didn't you tell me?" he asked.

"Because I had not yet found the words to express what I was feeling," E.V.A. said. "I was conflicted by my attachment to Cluster and Weapon XIII, and even now, I find it difficult to reconcile the idea that Weapon XIII was willing to harm me the way he did. As it turned out, Avery was the one who helped me clarify my thoughts. She asked me how I was able to cope with everything that had happened to me and all the changes I'd undergone. The answer, when I'd had time to truly consider it, was that I needed help. I needed you, and you needed me. We are stronger together."

She was right. He did need her. It had been too hard to admit before, because he'd been afraid of losing her too. His partner. His friend.

"Well," he said, clearing his throat to hide the crack in his voice, "knowing that, I don't think it's possible for us to lose."

He glanced over as the hangar doors slid open and Cluster entered. She wore her costume but had yet to don her mask. Her expression was just as determined as the others, but when her gaze rested on them, her eyes softened.

Fantomex felt a peculiar tightness in his chest, but for the first time, it wasn't an impending flashback to the moment of his death. It was instead a new awareness, or maybe a personal revelation. He'd had so many of those lately, it was hard to tell, but he felt this was different.

He'd been spending so much time worrying about being the weakest of the triptych, trying to get to the root of Cluster and Weapon XIII's motives and goals, that he had ignored something that should have been obvious to him. He realized with a jolt what exactly it was that he'd retained that Cluster and Weapon XIII hadn't.

And he knew he could use it, if he dared.

"We're almost finished with the repairs," Cyclops called over to them, interrupting his thoughts. "We lift off in twenty minutes."

Cluster joined Fantomex and E.V.A. She glanced at both of them, and a slow smile curved her lips.

"What?" Fantomex demanded. "That smile never means anything good."

"Not true," she said. "It seems like something's different between the two of you. Did you have a nice chat?"

"None of your business," Fantomex said, affecting a prim tone. E.V.A. just smiled at the two of them.

She stepped back and transformed into the gleaming ship, its curves and flourishes looking especially sleek. Strong. And she made sure her neuroweapons systems were clearly visible along the hull.

E.V.A. was angry, and she was spoiling for a fight like the rest of them.

The ship door slid open, and a set of stairs extended to the ground.

Cluster gestured to the door. "After you," she said.

But Fantomex didn't move, only stared at Cluster thoughtfully. She raised an eyebrow, waiting for him to speak.

"What if he could really do it?" he asked, choosing his words carefully. "What if Weapon XIII found a way to safely reunite us, something that didn't harm Avery or the artifacts or the nanotech?"

Her brow rose higher at that. "That's quite a set of hypothetical scenarios. Would you really trust him if he told you that?"

"Of course not. I'd confirm it for myself, just as you would. I'm saying what if we really could be rejoined? Think about it. It would be like we'd never died, like we'd never lost each other or—"

"No."

The answer was quick, firm, and final. Fantomex nodded. "No regrets, then, about anything that's happened?"

"None," she said. She looked down at her hands. "I told you, the person I am now feels right to me. Even when things are hard, I know this is who I'm meant to be." She frowned. "What's this about?"

They looked at each other for a moment in silence. Once again, Fantomex was reminded of the distance between them, of staring at something that once was a part of himself, but was now out of reach. He felt the pang of grief all over again. It would probably never go away completely. It never did when you lost something important.

"Nothing," he said, "I was simply… curious."

He walked past her and climbed the stairs into the ship. But he could feel her eyes on him as she followed him onboard. The familiar rush of adrenaline surged through him, as strong as if they were preparing for another heist. Which, in a way, they were. If all went to plan, it would be the most spectacular heist of all.

Another night, another performance. The stage was set.

# CHAPTER TWENTY-SIX

Eyes closed, Avery let the silence of the empty gallery fill her. Her fingers barely grazed the painting's canvas as she tried to reach out to the nanotech with her mind. She took a deep breath and released it, willing herself to be calm and open.

Despite her efforts, she couldn't shut out Weapon XIII's heavy footsteps nearby, or the harsh sound of his breathing as he monitored his equipment and waited impatiently for her to give him what he wanted. Avery had never performed well in front of an audience, but having a person like Weapon XIII watching while she tried to communicate with the nanotech was a whole other level of pressure.

After her third failed attempt, she opened her eyes to find him a suspicious expression on his face. "Look, I'm new at this," she said, embarrassed to find her hands shaking and her neck slick with sweat. "I've only just started to use my mutant abilities."

"Or you're lying and attempting to stall the process,"

Weapon XIII said, taking a step toward her. "I wonder which it is."

He was trying to intimidate her with his size. Everything about him, even his costume, was meant to inspire fear, to make everyone else around him feel smaller. It was working, Avery conceded, but it also made her furious.

"What makes you think the nanotech can help you, anyway?" she shot back. "How can you be sure they'll be willing?"

He cocked his head, as if truly considering the question. Had he never prepared for the possibility that he'd be denied? If so, he was more arrogant than Fantomex, and that was saying something.

"We are a part of each other," he said at last. "We come from the same artificial reality. They will help."

"So?" Avery scoffed. "You were a part of Fantomex and Cluster too, and you tried to kill them."

"If I had wanted to kill either of them, they would be dead now," Weapon XIII said flatly. "I need them for my purpose. We *will* be reunited, whatever it takes. Whatever the cost."

Shock silenced Avery for a moment as she considered the implications of what he was suggesting. "There's no way they'd ever agree," she said, "not after what you did."

"This is what you believe, after knowing them for months at most?" Condescension ran thick in his voice. "Do you really think you know who Fantomex is and what he's capable of? You think he won't jump at the chance to be as strong as he once was?"

"He–" She stopped herself. Actually, he was right. She had no idea what Fantomex might be thinking. Maybe he would be tempted. It certainly sounded like something he'd want, based on her initial impressions of him.

But he'd been trying to do better. Even if he wouldn't admit it, she'd seen it that night he'd prepared the midnight feast at the Institute. He'd begun making friends. Even she had decided that maybe he wasn't so bad.

"You're wrong," she said stubbornly. "He'll prove you wrong."

"We'll see." He pointed to the painting. "No more stalling. Try again."

"Fine." Avery sighed. "Can you at least back away a few more feet? That villainous presence thing you're doing is distracting me."

"My—" He stared at her, as if trying to decide whether she was mocking him or not. Then, to her surprise, he backed away to give her more space. Avery rolled her shoulders and shook out her hands, trying to loosen some of the tension and fear that knotted her muscles.

She closed her eyes and reached for the painting again. It still felt strange and wrong to touch the fragile canvas, even if the painting wasn't the real Ruby Alano creation. But she needed that physical connection to help her overcome her nerves.

This time, as she concentrated, she felt it, that familiar sensation of her feet leaving the ground. For a moment, she was suspended in darkness, unable to move forward or back, but before she could panic, a faint light appeared in front of her. Willing herself to move toward it, Avery watched the light grow brighter and brighter, until suddenly she was back in the familiar art studio. The sounds of traffic still echoed from outside the open window, and the smells of paint and turpentine filled the air. Outside the window, it was night, and the room was lit only by a handful of candles arranged on the windowsill.

The studio was a wreck. Discarded sketches littered the floor. The artist's easel had been overturned, and splotches of paint and streaks of charcoal dust covered the walls. It looked like a storm had blown through the room.

The artist crouched on the floor, her long white hair falling on either side of her face, examining and tossing aside the different sketches, as if she was looking for something. She glanced up when Avery approached and immediately her form shifted to look like Jane again.

"What's going on here?" Avery asked, trying to ignore the fact that the nanotech had chosen to appear as Jane had looked on the day Avery first met her. The memory was seared into her brain. She'd been wearing cut-off shorts and flip flops, her toes painted a brilliant purple, her hair tucked into a ballcap in such a way that it made her ears stick out adorably. Everything was the same, except how Jane was looking at her with such imploring eyes that Avery's heart broke.

"You are the tower," Jane said, pointing to all the sketches, which, looking closer, Avery could see were different versions of the tower from the Alano painting. Different sizes, different colors, some with varying backgrounds, a myriad of towers stared back at her from the floor.

"That's… right," Avery said, trying to understand what the nanotech wanted to convey. "I'm here now, but things aren't good."

Jane nodded impatiently, as if that was obvious. "We sense your disquiet. We've been trying to understand you so we can know how to help. You've been resisting us."

"Resisting?" Avery thought back over the many attempts she'd made to communicate. She didn't think she'd been resisting. She'd been trying with everything she had. Unless... "Do you mean the energy surge at the school, right before Weapon XIII kidnapped me?"

"We were trying to protect you." Jane sounded petulant.

Avery sighed. "I get that, but if there had been an explosion in that hangar, it would have killed me and a lot of other people. I didn't want that to happen."

Jane's look of puzzlement reminded Avery of how she would stare at a blank canvas or a rough sketch, as if she was trying to figure out what it was going to become. "We could have rebuilt your form afterwards," she said.

Avery choked, caught somewhere between laughter at the absurdity of that statement and horror at the realization that the nanotech didn't seem to be joking. "It's not that easy," she said.

"Of course it is." The nanotech was insistent. "Human bodies are not difficult to reconstitute. We've been experimenting and refining the creation of your kind since time immemorial. It was part of our original purpose."

"Whoa, OK." This was going beyond her understanding and blasting her way out of her comfort zone. Communication with other humans was thorny enough, but trying to impart a concept as complex as humanity to sentient machines? At that moment Avery would have much rather traded for the power to shoot lasers out of her eyes.

She chewed her bottom lip as she searched for a way to explain. She wasn't sure how much time was passing in the real world while she was absorbed in this vision, but she knew Weapon XIII's patience was far from infinite.

"OK, look, something you have to understand about people – humans, mutants, hybrids, whatever form you see us in, whatever identity we decide to embrace – we're not just things to be shaped and toyed with." As she spoke, Avery sat down on the floor across from Jane. She picked up the sketches one by one. "I think I see what you're trying to do here. These different towers, they're all supposed to be me, aren't they?" Her feelings, her memories, all the different parts of her as interpreted by the nanotech. That was why they'd got inside of her in the first place, she realized. They were trying to understand her and create a bridge between them. If the circumstances weren't so dire, she might have been flattered at someone going to that much trouble to try to figure her out.

Avery picked up one of the drawings and grabbed a nearby piece of charcoal. She drew a solid black line through the tower. "The thing with human beings is, when we're hurt, when we *change*, it leaves a mark." She hesitated. "And sometimes that's a good thing, because we're working to become the people we're meant to be. But other kinds of change aren't so easy to overcome."

She glanced at the artist, but Jane wore a look of dissatisfaction. "Explain," the nanotech requested. "Explain why it's insufficient to simply recreate your forms whenever something mars them."

"Because death isn't something we're meant to come back

from!" Avery felt an inexplicable anger rising inside her. "Fantomex did it, and it messed with him. He won't ever be the same person. When my father died, I would have given anything to have him back, or to have known my mother. But it doesn't work that way, and their deaths changed *me*."

Her parents had abandoned her when she'd needed them. It wasn't their fault, but the hurt remained. It had marred her ability to trust people. Even Jane. Because there was no way to guarantee that the people she decided to love wouldn't leave her, either by choice or otherwise. She'd thought it would be easier just to be alone, but she'd been wrong. The pain was worth it, but it wasn't something that could just be waved away.

The nanotech was still regarding her patiently despite her outburst, trying to understand.

"It should be our choice," Avery said, feeling the anger slowly drain out of her. "We're capable of enduring so much, but who we are, what we become – it has to be our choice, as much as it can be. Can you understand that?"

Jane stared down at the sketches. She seemed to be thinking it over. "Possibly," she allowed. "What is the answer to your distress, then?"

"Nothing good." Avery drew her knees up, resting her chin on them. "Weapon XIII wants you to do exactly what you just said you could do – an act of creation."

"Then what is the problem?"

"It's not only his choice to make," Avery said. A thought struck her. "If you had the choice, what would you want most?"

This time Jane didn't hesitate. "To find others of our kind," the nanotech said, and instead of just Jane's voice, there was a reverberating chorus that echoed in Avery's mind. It made her temples throb, those thousands and thousands of voices behind one pair of eyes. "To understand our purpose and... to no longer be alone."

Avery's breath caught at the longing in Jane's voice. "Well then, maybe we aren't so different after all," she said. "If I get out of this alive, I'll try to help you however I can, but right now, I need your help to escape from Weapon XIII."

Jane seemed pleased at the prospect of being given a concrete task to accomplish. "How can we assist you?"

"I know you can make the painting explode with your power, but what about something on a smaller scale?" Avery asked. "Something that will distract Weapon XIII or incapacitate him for a little while?" She'd still have to figure out a way to get off the island, but one step at a time. "Or maybe you could–"

Suddenly, everything went black. Jane, the studio, all the drawings of the tower disappeared as Avery felt herself physically wrenched through the darkness as if by a tether around her waist.

Her eyes flew open. She was back in the main gallery with Weapon XIII holding onto her arm. A wave of dizziness crashed over her, and she struggled to stay on her feet.

"You can't just yank someone out of a vision like that," she said, trying in vain to pull free of Weapon XIII's grip. "It's dangerous!"

He ignored the outburst and towed her across the room to the computer terminals set up near the door. A pair of slender faux marble columns flanked the entrance. He pointed to one of them. "Hands around the column."

That's when Avery saw the length of rope in his other hand. She dug her heels in, for as much good as that was going to do. "You said you wouldn't do this unless I decided to run!"

He looked down at her impassively. "We have company coming," he said. "Hands around the column." His tone told her she didn't want him to have to ask again.

"Fine!" Giving him her best death glare, Avery put her arms around the column so he could tie her wrists together. She tried to appear calm, but her heart was thumping with wild hope.

It was the X-Men. It had to be. They were coming for her.

Weapon XIII turned and strode to the computer terminal, his hands flying over the console. The large screen in front of him displayed a view from the rooftop. He must be looped into the building's surveillance system. She squinted at the image and thought she saw distant shapes approaching from the air. Two aircraft, and one of them was definitely E.V.A. in her ship form.

"You're outnumbered now." She couldn't resist taunting him.

"We'll see."

Avery frowned. He sounded disturbingly unbothered by this turn of events.

The image shifted, showing a view from much higher up. Avery could see the building was just a small speck below.

"Weapons systems engaged," he said.

# CHAPTER TWENTY-SEVEN

"I have a visual on the island," E.V.A. said, and a magnified image of the exhibition building appeared on the screen in front of them.

"There's the S.H.I.E.L.D. helicopter," Cluster said, pointing to the roof. "They're here."

Fantomex nodded. "Scan the area," he told E.V.A. "B team, are you seeing what we're seeing?"

Triage's dry voice filled the cockpit. "We're seeing it, and why are *we* the B team?"

"I'll switch with you," Cluster offered. "There's entirely too much ego on this ship."

"Cut the unnecessary chatter," Cyclops interjected. "We should have encountered some resistance by now."

"Scanning," E.V.A. said, as if she'd been waiting for a break in the conversation. Her voice rose. "Three drones detected a thousand feet above our position."

"Armed, I assume?" Fantomex said.

"Missile systems," E.V.A. confirmed.

"What about communication?" Fantomex pressed. "See if you can send a message to our annoying brother through the drones. Tell him we have Cluster's artifacts, and we've come to make a trade."

There was a pause while E.V.A. attempted to relay the message. Immediately, she came back over the comm, "No response, and they're locking on to us. Preparing evasive maneuvers."

"Hold on, everyone," Cyclops said.

Quickly, Fantomex linked his VR unit directly to E.V.A.'s neuroweapons. The targeting system appeared in front of him just as a missile launched from each of the drones. E.V.A. accelerated, pushing him back in his seat. Adrenaline shot through him as he brought the targeting controls to bear.

"Fire," he said.

Energy blasts lit up the night, narrowly missing the incoming missile. E.V.A. swerved, but the missile tracked them, closing the distance between them with alarming speed.

"Want me to give it a shot?" Cluster asked helpfully.

Fantomex flashed a rude gesture in her general direction. The ship banked hard right, and he gritted his teeth at the sudden flip in his stomach. He focused on the targeting system again, taking a deep breath as he waited for the right moment.

"Fire!"

This time when the energy blasts peppered the air, they impacted, blowing up the missile in a fiery orange and black ball. Flaming pieces of it plummeted toward Lake Michigan.

A second orange flash lit up the night as Cyclops took out the second missile, but the third one was still incoming. The X-Copter was highly maneuverable, but not enough to get out of its path.

"Move to intercept," Fantomex said. "Get us between the copter and the missile."

"Intercepting," E.V.A. said. "Transferring power to hull shielding."

"Brace yourself!"

Seconds later, the missile impacted. The ship shuddered and briefly lost altitude, but E.V.A. compensated, pulling them back up and steadying the craft.

"E.V.A., status?" Cluster asked, her voice heavy with concern.

"Stable," E.V.A. said, but there was a strain in her voice. "I don't recommend we take another direct hit like that."

"I don't plan on it," Fantomex said, as the drones fired another trio of missiles.

"We can't shoot the missiles down faster than they're firing them," Cyclops said. "Target the drones directly, if you can." He maneuvered the copter beneath them and fired again, taking out first one missile, then the second in a coordinated move that made Fantomex whistle in appreciation.

"Didn't know you had that kind of piloting in you, Summers," he said.

"Be impressed later," Triage's voice chimed in. "You need to shoot down that other missile."

"Oh, we're not going to bother with that this time," Fantomex said tersely. "E.V.A., aim us right at the nearest drone."

"This should be fun," Cluster said.

"As much speed as you can give us, please," Fantomex added.

"Accelerating."

Around him, Fantomex could feel the ship contracting, becoming something sleeker, more maneuverable in the air. They cut through the darkness like a silver streak, the third missile right behind them. Ahead of them, the drone tried to maneuver away, but Fantomex pursued, aiming the ship on a collision course.

"Hold on," he said, wrenching the controls up at the last second. The ship skimmed the top of the drone, clipping off a piece of its casing.

And the missile that was pursuing them took it out in another fiery explosion.

"One down, two to go," Cluster said. "The other ones are pulling back."

"Pursue," Cyclops ordered.

"So commanding," Fantomex said, amused. "Why don't you show us how it's done, then?"

There was no response, but before Fantomex could take the lead, the X-Copter cut in front of E.V.A. and blasted another incoming missile, bursting out the other side of the resulting explosion.

"Cutting that one a little close, no?" Fantomex said.

"I think that was him showing you how it's done," Cluster said. "Speaking of which…"

"I see it." He had visual on another of the drones. This one was quick, zipping out of the path of his targeting system, drawing him farther away from the X-Copter.

Trying to separate us, he thought. All right then, if his goth brother wanted to play cat and mouse, he'd oblige him, for the moment.

He accelerated again, firing energy blasts and giving every impression of pursuing the drone. Then, just as quickly, he broke off and swung the craft around, pinning the targeting crosshairs on the other drone engaged with the copter.

"Fire at will," he invited.

E.V.A. did not disappoint. The other drone exploded into a ball of fire and smoke.

Hijack cheered over the comm link.

"All right, we're not done yet, people, focus," Cyclops said, but Fantomex could tell he was just as energized by the aerial acrobatics.

"Let's flank the last drone and then we can get on with this," Fantomex said. "Follow my lead."

With the two of them bearing down on the drone, the craft didn't stand a chance. Fantomex targeted and fired, and that was the end of that.

"Nice job, everyone," Cyclops said. "Let's get back on task."

"Missile incoming!" E.V.A. warned, jerking the controls away from Fantomex to send them into a dive, swerving away from the missile.

The X-Copter wasn't as lucky.

To his credit, Cyclops swung the craft away and fired everything, taking out the fourth drone that had been in stealth mode just out of their range. But he couldn't do that and dodge the incoming missile. It sheared off part of the tail of the copter and sent it into a spiral straight down.

"E.V.A., dive!" Cluster shouted. "We have to get to them!"

"Don't do it," Cyclops said, his voice remarkably calm. "Hijack's got the controls. He's using his power to hold the craft steady. We'll bail out in the lake. You keep going. We'll–"

The comm link was getting scratchy as the copter's systems failed. "Make note of their position," Fantomex instructed E.V.A. "We'll come back to pull the copter out of the lake later, if we can."

"I hate to leave them like this," Cluster said, looking out the craft's window at the dark lake below.

"If we stay and help, we give Weapon XIII time to send out more drones," Fantomex said. "He'll wear us down eventually. We need to take the fight to him."

But Fantomex didn't like it either. Once again, Weapon XIII had gotten the drop on them, and he'd also seemingly gotten exactly what he wanted – the three of them, alone, heading for the island.

He met Cluster's gaze across the cockpit and knew she was thinking the same thing.

"Let's go," he said. "Avery's waiting for us."

He directed E.V.A. to land on the shoreline on the east side of the building. Once they'd exited the ship, she transformed back into her human form in her charcoal costume and mask.

"Take out the cameras wherever you see them," Fantomex said, but Cluster grabbed his arm. "What?" he asked.

"The guard stations," Cluster said, pointing to a group of small buildings huddled together near the docks. "When I incapacitated the security guards the last time I was here, I was able to manipulate the security camera footage before you disabled it."

E.V.A. nodded in understanding. "If he's left the cameras active, he has eyes all over the island."

"But if we can get to the guard stations, you can tap into the footage," Cluster said, "turn the eyes back on Weapon XIII. It'll at least give us an idea of what we're dealing with."

"I like it," Fantomex said. "Let's go."

They made their way quickly and quietly along the thin stretch of beach and up a short hill, past some mounds of dirt left over from the construction of the exhibition space. Beyond that were the three guard stations, small, unobtrusive outbuildings that were dark and clearly no longer in use.

Cluster tried the door, which was locked, of course.

"Is it a key card entry like last time?" he asked. He hadn't thought to bring his fake key card. He'd assumed they'd be opting for a more aggressive entry.

"It's a guard station, darling, we're not dealing with a great deal of sophistication." As she spoke, Cluster pulled out a set of lockpicks and went to work on the door. In seconds, she had it open.

"So that's where that ability went," he grumbled. During the weeks of his recovery, he'd been timing himself on his lockpicking skills, and he'd never been able to crack a lock in under a minute.

Cluster looked up at him. "Don't sulk. You got all the culinary talent."

He blinked. "Really?"

"Yes, really, and I'm already regretting telling you that," she said as she led the way inside. Moonlight illuminated a bank of monitors, dark now, but they were clearly once part of the surveillance system.

"Give me two minutes," E.V.A. said as she sat down at the terminal.

Fantomex kept an eye on the door, always looking for an ambush. From behind him, Cluster said, "How do you want to play this, since Weapon XIII doesn't seem to want to negotiate a trade?"

Without turning, Fantomex said, "I want you to use your misdirection power however you can to get Avery to safety. E.V.A. and I will handle Weapon XIII."

There was a pregnant pause. "How did you know I still had it?" Cluster asked.

He glanced over his shoulder at her. "I was watching Avery that day in the Danger Room. I could tell she was about to fall apart, and then suddenly she was fine. No one recovers that fast. And I know how sentimental you are."

She laughed softly. "You would have done the same." She sobered. "I'll warn you, I can't do very much with the misdirection. It took me months to relearn it, and it will only last a few minutes."

"Then make them count." This performance would be different from all the others, Fantomex realized. There were layers at work, intricate as a painting. It was impossible to see the whole of it yet. "Maybe someday you'll teach me how you got the power back."

"I have it," E.V.A. said, pulling their attention to the now glowing monitors. The surveillance cameras were all active, giving them eyes on every floor of the museum. "He's wired explosives to some of the entrances – non-lethal, probably intended to function as a warning system. Weapon XIII and Avery are in the main floor gallery where the Diana statue was located."

She zoomed in using the camera next to the main entrance. Weapon XIII stood before a large machine that now dominated one side of the gallery. Avery was tied to a column nearby.

"What is that?" Fantomex said, pointing to the metal monstrosity.

"And does it come with weapons?" Cluster added.

"Its structure and design are strikingly similar to the White Sky facility where your cloning process took place," E.V.A. said. "It's possible he acquired the entire unit from there. There are no visible weapons systems."

"Judging by the way he's wired the place, it's entirely possible that he's got other weapons hidden," Fantomex said.

"It may be advisable to wait for Cyclops and the rest of his team to join us, then," E.V.A. said, but Cluster shook her head.

"They're our backup now," she said. "If Weapon XIII has traps waiting – and I'm certain he does – we'll be the ones to spring them. And we need to destroy that machine. That'll put an end to his plans."

Fantomex cracked his knuckles. "Let's go have some fun, then. Where were those explosives located again?"

# CHAPTER TWENTY-EIGHT

Avery's legs were tired, her fingers were tingling, and she had to use the bathroom. Being a prisoner was a lot less glamorous than the movies made it seem.

She'd distracted herself for a while by playing with the knots securing her bound hands. The movies hadn't taught her any tricks about escaping, but she'd sat next to a guy in her Eighteenth-Century Art class who loved to draw nautical imagery, and he'd been obsessed with knots. He'd learned to tie and untie as many as he could because he thought it would help him draw them more realistically. And he'd shared his more interesting tricks with her.

Art majors learned all kinds of wonderful skills.

Trouble was, it had taken her half an hour to make any progress because the knots were tied so tight.

But she was doing it. Sweat ran down her temples and she shook with fear and adrenaline. Weapon XIII was focused on trying to restore the connection to his drones. He'd lost the signal to them a while ago, which either meant there was a malfunction, or her rescuers had destroyed them. Avery hoped it was the latter. Weapon XIII had made no reaction when the last drone's signal had disappeared, but she could see the tension through his shoulders.

Just keep watching those screens, Avery silently begged him, as she loosened the knot at her wrist another fraction of an inch. The rope was slack enough now that she could slip it off if she wanted. She flexed her fingers to get some feeling back into her hands.

She was just trying to decide whether Weapon XIII was distracted enough for her to grab the painting and make a break for the exit when the ceiling caved in.

Avery freed herself completely and ducked behind the pillar for cover as the atrium windows shattered, and a storm of wood, plaster, and glass rained down on the main floor gallery. Dust clouds rose in the wake of the explosion, making her eyes water. Wiping the grit from her face, she glimpsed two figures standing in the middle of the wreckage.

Fantomex and E.V.A.

"Now that is how you use explosives!" Fantomex clapped his hands at the same time E.V.A. sent a blistering wave of energy blasts at the machine behind Weapon XIII.

The blasts impacted, but there was a flash of green light that made spots pop in front of Avery's eyes. The neuroweapons danced harmlessly off the surface of the machine and reflected back at Fantomex and E.V.A., who just barely dodged.

So, the machine had its own shields. Terrific. At least Weapon XIII had an abundance of distractions to contend with now that the cavalry had arrived.

Now or never, Avery thought. She slipped her wrists out of the ropes and turned, ready to take off running.

Cluster was standing right behind her, one finger held to her lips.

Avery barely managed not to scream, clapping a hand over her mouth. "Give a girl a heart attack, will you?" she hissed.

"Apologies." Cluster pulled her behind the large reception desk at the front of the gallery, getting them both under cover. "Brilliant work escaping those ropes, by the way. Saved us some valuable time. Now, when I join the battle, I need you to take the opportunity to head for the front door. I've disabled the explosives attached to it, so you should have a clear path."

"Explosives?" Avery squeaked. Good thing she hadn't gotten around to carrying out that part of her plan.

"Don't worry," Cluster said, "backup's coming. Cyclops, Hijack, and Triage – how can you go wrong with names like that?"

She was joking, but Avery could see the worry in her eyes. "Be careful," she said, "he wants to use that machine to rejoin the three of you."

"We won't let him," Cluster said. "Now go."

Without another word, Cluster vaulted over the reception desk and ran to join the fray. Avery shot a quick glance over at the painting. It was too risky to go after it. She had to hope the nanotech would sense that it was safer for them to be separated now. She took off in the opposite direction, heading for the main entrance.

Almost there. Almost out…

And then, the world seemed to shift on its axis, making

her stumble. It was as if, suddenly, the version of the room she was seeing, from the ceiling debris littering the floor, to Fantomex and Weapon XIII engaged in hand-to-hand combat, was overlayed with another scene, one where Fantomex struggled on the ground with an invisible opponent, and Weapon XIII had disappeared.

Not disappeared, Avery thought as she tried to halt her momentum. He was right in front of her, blocking the exit, as if he'd always been standing there, waiting for her.

Then the overlay slammed into the other image, overtaking it. Weapon XIII grabbed her, spinning her around to put a knife to her neck.

This was the reality all along, Avery realized, freezing in place. When Cluster had described her misdirection power to her, she hadn't really understood how it worked, how it caused other people to see what the controller wanted them to see, manipulating all their senses. Now she knew.

"This scene is familiar," Weapon XIII said, blade pressed to her throat as Fantomex leaped up and Cluster and E.V.A. closed in on them in a semicircle. "As I recall, it didn't end in your favor last time. Maybe you should have learned from that."

"Let her go," Cluster said. "We brought the artifacts I stole. We're willing to trade them for Avery."

Weapon XIII laughed. The sound raised the hairs on the back of Avery's neck. "Even if I believed you, you know by now that I'm after more than the artifacts. I can see it in his eyes." He swung toward Fantomex, jerking Avery's neck painfully.

Fantomex tensed, but otherwise he showed no reaction.

"You want to reunite the family," he said. "I have to say I'm surprised you'd risk it, considering how dysfunctional we've all turned out to be."

"We're meant to be one," Weapon XIII said simply. "We are strongest together. We need no one else but the three made whole again, and E.V.A. as our partner, no longer forced to choose among us. Admit it. You want it as much as I do."

"Whether he does or not, I'm sure he enjoys *living*," Cluster spat. She had a pair of knives in her hands, muscles tight, prepared to throw. The tension crackling in the air, the pressure of the blade at Avery's neck, was making her knees weak. "The outcome of what you propose would be our deaths. Are you truly willing to risk that?"

Once again, that soft laugh. "She wants you to believe that," Weapon XIII said, addressing Fantomex. "But the nanotech is the key. Its intelligence, combined with the technology of the White Sky facility, will ensure the process succeeds. We will be reborn in another perfect act of creation."

"He's lying about the perfection of his machine," E.V.A. said flatly. "I've scanned it thoroughly, and though it is heavily shielded against physical attacks, it lacks the sophistication of the White Sky facility. He hasn't had time enough to refine it."

"How can you be sure the nanotech will do as you ask?" Fantomex briefly locked eyes with Avery. "It seems dangerous to me to underestimate something because it appears smaller and weaker than yourself."

Avery's skin prickled. Was he trying to give her a message? She remembered the idea she'd been considering earlier, about asking the nanotech for help, but Weapon XIII had pulled her out of her vision before she could do anything. But if she tried to go into her trance now to speak to the nanotech, Weapon XIII would surely know it, wouldn't he?

Her attention flicked to Cluster, who was also steadily holding her gaze.

No one will notice you, she'd said that day in the Danger Room. They hadn't seen her crying and falling apart, because Cluster had used a tiny bit of misdirection to remove their attention from her.

Avery licked her lips, trying to quiet her body's trembling. She let her eyes fall closed, blocking out the sensation of the cold steel at her throat, the awful presence behind her.

It was a different gallery, but they were still in a museum. The Ruby Alano painting was across the room, but she told herself the distance didn't matter. The nanotech was inside her, waiting. She could feel it now, reacting to every quickened beat of her heart. It wanted to help. It would protect her, if she asked.

Voices intruded at the edge of her consciousness, briefly drawing her back from the impending vision.

"Make your choice, Fantomex," Weapon XIII was saying, and Avery had the distant impression that he'd pressed the blade harder against her throat, hard enough to draw a trickle of blood. But the fear she would have felt was blunted. She could barely feel her body. The vision almost had her.

"I already have," Fantomex said, the reply faint but certain. "I made it before I came here."

The sound of an energy blast shattered the air, and E.V.A. cried out. Cluster shouted, "No! You can't do this!"

Avery went cold with fear and shock. No, he couldn't have. There was no way Fantomex would betray them...

*Do you really think you know who Fantomex is and what he's capable of?* Weapon XIII's words taunted her.

And then the vision swallowed her whole.

# CHAPTER TWENTY-NINE

People will line up to tell you who they think you really are.

All throughout his strange and often violent existence, Fantomex had been told who he was supposed to be. An elitist, an experiment, an imitation.

A killer.

He didn't get to choose.

Yet he'd reveled in being something new, something above everyone else. Three brains functioning in harmony, each suited to its own purpose. Three as one. They were the triptych, and they were perfect.

Then it had all been ripped away.

He'd returned from the dead and discovered what it felt like to be alone. Isolated, weak, having to rely on people who had the ability to disappoint him. All he'd wanted back then was to be whole. He would have died all over again to make that happen.

"Make your choice, Fantomex," Weapon XIII said, as a trickle of blood ran down Avery's neck.

It was better this way, he told himself.

"I already have. I made my choice before I came here."

And so the dance began.

He half-turned toward E.V.A., seizing control of her neuro-weapons system before she could react. He sent an energy blast at Cluster, who barely managed to dodge, burning off the trailing end of her long jacket. E.V.A. cried out in protest as Cluster retreated across the gallery, taking cover behind the marble columns.

Fantomex backed up as well, out of range of E.V.A.'s scythe arm. He reached for the neuroweapons again, sending an energy blast back at the source. E.V.A. hissed and dropped to her knees. The blast wouldn't damage her, only stun her temporarily and buy him some time.

He turned to Weapon XIII. "Well, don't just stand there," he said. "Get the machine ready. We don't have much time before our backup gets here. I'll retrieve Cluster."

Weapon XIII watched him closely, his eyes suspicious, but he was distracted by Avery, who had suddenly become dead weight in his arms.

Fantomex tutted. "Made the poor girl faint, did you? Leave her there. I'll be back."

Now he had to face Cluster. That would be the painful part.

Literally, the painful part, because she was going to beat on him like a cheap combat dummy.

She was ready for him. She'd climbed to the second-floor balcony that overlooked the main gallery, but she'd opted for guns over fists. Fired. He ducked behind the staircase and fired back, shots pinging off the railing that encircled the second floor. She flattened herself against one of the columns flanking her, but there wasn't much cover.

"You should have known it was going to end like this," he called out to her across the room.

Another hail of bullets pinned him behind the staircase. "You're right, I shouldn't have given you credit for having the ability to change, to move beyond what other people thought you were," she said, the betrayal thick in her voice.

"We can have long, introspective thought experiments about this once we're reunited," he said. "We'll wear you down in the end."

The bullets stopped. She was reloading. He popped up, aiming his guns to try to flush her out from behind the columns, but there was nothing. No movement or sound from the balcony.

Remembering their last fight in this space, Fantomex instinctively spun. Just in time for Cluster's foot to plant itself like a flag in the middle of his chest. How did she move so fast? The guns flew out of his hands, and he went sailing across the gallery, landing on his back on the unforgiving tile floor.

"Did I go too far?" he groaned.

"I don't know," Cluster said, advancing on him. "Let me kick you again and we'll see."

He sprang to his feet as she came at him. He dodged one punch but took a left hook to the jaw. That one was going to bruise horribly. He caught her right fist and twisted her arm behind her back. Never let a tiger get that close. The old warning echoed in his head, but he needed to slow her down.

He risked a glance over his shoulder at Weapon XIII. He was at the machine, his attention fixed on the console. The tube of liquid on the platform above him bubbled and roiled, briefly revealing a shadow inside in the shape of a humanoid figure.

One possibility. One path. One choice.

"Nice to know he's been spending his time acquiring new hobbies," Cluster said, following his gaze even as she struggled to break his hold.

"Like sea monkeys but better," he agreed, dodging as she tried to head butt him with the back of her skull.

"He'll kill Avery," Cluster said. The girl was prone on the ground in the middle of the gallery where Weapon XIII had left her, moonlight from the gaping hole in the ceiling shining down on her body and on E.V.A., who still struggled against the overload and feedback stun from her neuroweapons. "E.V.A. won't ever forgive you for this. Are you really going to betray them both?"

He felt the mounting fury in her. She was getting ready to break his hold. Her movements ran like a playbook in his head. Smash the top of his foot with her heel. Flip him over her shoulder. Pin. Hands to the throat. A familiar scene in a familiar play. They all had their parts.

Or.

Use the anger and adrenaline to break his hold by sheer brute strength. He was bigger than her, but she was so quick, always moving, always thinking three steps ahead, a chess game of combat.

Instead, she did none of those things. Because he jerked her back so he could whisper in her ear.

"Did you manage to use your misdirection on Avery? Please tell me she's in the vision and didn't actually faint."

Cluster stiffened, and then slowly, slowly, the fight went out of her. "I saw the vision take her. Have some faith."

"Look who's talking."

"You were very convincing."

"That's the nicest thing you've ever said to me."

Cluster's elbow was sharp as an ice pick when she planted it in his ribs. "Don't let it go to your head. Do you think we've bought her enough time?"

It took him a second to get his breath back enough to answer. "I certainly hope so. I can't be in the ring with you much longer."

"You're trusting her with all our lives," Cluster pointed out.

"She can handle this. And we have backup coming." His breathing was still wheezy. "We'd probably better stall a bit longer. Do you want to kick me in the chest again?"

"It would be my great pleasure."

Her heel came down on the top of his foot, much harder than necessary. Next thing he knew he was being flipped over her shoulder, landing on his back for a second time.

She was obviously angling for an award for Best Performance in an Action Role. He was going to require substantial healing after this. Possibly a massage and a good steam.

He climbed to his feet, licked his bleeding lip, and raised his fists. "Let's go another round."

# *CHAPTER THIRTY*

The walls of the studio were gone. All that remained was a bare rooftop with sketches swirling in the air. Dark clouds blocked the sun, and lightning split the sky.

Avery stood in the ruins, bits of glass and a broken easel littering the ground around her feet. The wind was cold and biting. The air smelled like the impending storm.

"Where are you?" she shouted. "Please, we need your help!"

Lightning blinded her. When she blinked her vision clear, three figures stood before her.

Jane.

Ruby Alano.

Fantomex.

"You are the tower," Jane said.

"How can we help?" asked the artist.

The image of Fantomex said nothing, simply watched her intently.

Avery didn't waste any time. "Are you small enough to get past the shields on Weapon XIII's machine and destroy it?" she asked. "We can't let him use it."

Jane and the artist looked at each other, as if conferring. Avery wondered again how many separate entities she was dealing with when she spoke to the nanotech. Was it a single hive mind, or were there hierarchies? And why were there suddenly three figures appearing before her?

"If we do this," Jane said, stepping forward to take Avery's hand, "it means we have to leave you."

Jane's fingers were warm threaded through hers. Avery savored the touch and the comfort it brought, even though she knew it wasn't really the woman she loved. "What does that mean?" she asked. "Do you mean we won't be able to talk like this anymore?"

The artist nodded. "The reality here is already breaking down. Your mind knows it's artificial, and it's no longer a place of comfort and refuge for you. It can't sustain itself without your help. It never could."

"We will leave, if that's what you want," Jane said, "but it means we can't react to your fear, your aloneness. We can't be there for you."

Avery choked on a sudden flood of emotion. It was what she'd wanted, wasn't it? To get the nanotech out of her so that it wouldn't react to her feelings and become volatile? She would no longer be a danger to anyone at the Institute or elsewhere. She should have felt nothing but relief.

But it also meant she would lose that connection to the artist and the studio that had become her safe haven for so long. It had made her feel special, and it had been the place she'd been able to go to feel connected to her art.

"Isn't there any other way?" she asked. "Can we try something else?"

Finally, the image of Fantomex stirred. "This is the only choice," he said. His voice was firm, and held nothing of Fantomex's usual accent or sarcastic humor.

"I don't want to be alone again," Avery murmured. She'd thought the nanotech were just reaching out to try to communicate, to find others of their kind, but they were also helping her at the same time. They sensed what she'd needed and given it to her the best way they knew how.

"Are you alone?" the image of Fantomex said, a hint of skepticism in his voice. "We sense you are surrounded even now. Each being is a point of light with you at the center."

Jane squeezed her hand. "Many points of light, even those most distant."

They were right. Those points of light – those people – were real. This was only an image, and she had to let it go. She gently pulled her hand from Jane's.

She looked at each of the three of them in turn. Their expressions were sad, but resigned. Avery recognized that sadness. It was the sadness of grief, and she realized with a jolt something she hadn't seen before, because she was too wrapped up in her own pain.

"This is going to destroy you, isn't it?" She shook her head. "You can't sacrifice yourselves! I can't ask–"

"We make the choice," the image of Fantomex said. "You were correct. Having a choice, we have determined, is a significant factor in what we desire. And only a part of ourselves will be gone. There are others who will remain.

When this is over, we ask that you choose to reach out to them, in any way your powers will allow."

"I will," Avery said. She swallowed thickly. "I promise, even though you're gone, I'll reach out to the other artifacts, and we'll find any more that are out there in the world. If there's a way to communicate with the rest of your kind, I'll find it."

"Then everything is as it should be," the artist said. She stepped forward, ruffling Avery's hair fondly. "You are the tower, the instrument of change. Thank you for changing us."

"Thank you for changing me," Avery whispered.

And just like that, they vanished, leaving her alone on the rooftop. Avery bent and gathered up as many of the sketches of the painting as she could before the wind stole them away. Her arms were soon filled with images of the woman and the tower.

Above her head, the dark clouds sank toward her in an ominous wave, but Avery stood there in the ruins of the studio, defiant, ready to stay there until the very end. It would be sad, but endings always were.

"Time to go," she whispered, as the clouds enveloped her, plunging her into a darkness so thick she could float in it, as in a still pool.

But she wasn't afraid of this darkness now, because she had a place she could go from here. And there were people waiting for her.

# CHAPTER THIRTY-ONE

"There."

It was all the warning Cluster could manage around her labored breathing, but Fantomex was ready. He turned to Avery, whose body was starting to twitch on the floor. At the same time, across the room, an alarm sounded from the machine, and Weapon XIII let out a stream of curses.

Avery had done it.

Sparks flew from the machine. A great crack snaked across the surface of the glass tube. The alarms blared, and a whirring sound issued, growing louder and louder.

"I think you might have pushed a wrong button somewhere," Fantomex said when Weapon XIII rounded on him.

Behind him, Cluster swooped down and picked up Avery, who was starting to come around. The two of them backed into the shadows at the far end of the gallery, getting a safe distance away in case the machinery exploded, but Weapon

XIII wasn't paying any attention to them. He was staring at Fantomex, not with fury, as he'd expected, but with pure shock.

"You did this," he said, as the equipment broke down around him, the smell of melting cable and the sizzle of an electrical fire filling the air, but he made no attempt to get clear of it. "You gave up what you wanted most, destroyed the thing that would have restored us to all our former glory. How could you do it?" Weapon XIII's chest heaved. "How can you both... How can you *want* to be alone?" he screamed.

Whatever had kept Weapon XIII closed off from them before, that barrier was gone. For the first time since they'd come back together, Fantomex saw the spark of life in his counterpart's eyes.

A spark that was drowning in pain.

Weapon XIII gave a howl of bitter laughter. "And to think, I did everything for you. All you had to do was go along!" He stalked toward Fantomex, graceful and deadly as a panther cornering its prey. "You couldn't even do that. Yet, I would never have guessed you'd pick the selfless route. Never calculated for it, never even considered that when the time came, you'd make another choice. Because I thought I knew you so well."

Fantomex shook his head. "How could you know me, when I didn't even know myself?" He lifted his fists, ready for a fight. They circled each other, each looking for an opening, a weakness, assessing each other with brand new eyes. "You may not believe me, but I never wanted it to end like this, and I never wanted to betray either of you. But you expected the worst of me, and Cluster expected the best. I had to choose."

It was what set him apart from them and what had allowed him to trick them both. His place was somewhere in the void between the light and the dark. He knew he was bound to find himself out here somewhere. "I must say, it's nice to make the choice no one expects," he said. "Maybe I'll start doing it more often."

"You'll never have the chance."

Weapon XIII went for his guns, so Fantomex did the same. But Fantomex was just a bit slower from the fight with Cluster.

The first bullet struck him in the shoulder, but the second one, the one aimed at his head, never fired. A ruby stream of light speared from the broken ceiling, knocking Weapon XIII flat on his back and disarming him at the same time.

Shielding his eyes, Fantomex looked skyward to see Cyclops, Triage, and Hijack looking down from the roof. Cyclops' hand hovered near his temple, ready to fire another energy blast if needed, but Weapon XIII didn't seem inclined to move. His eyes fluttered closed as he surrendered to unconsciousness. His machine gave a final sputter and groan before falling inert, the liquid seeping slowly from jagged cracks in the tube.

"Oh, now that was just beautiful." Clutching his bleeding shoulder with one hand, Fantomex lifted the other in a chef's kiss, pointing at the trio above him. "Impeccable timing, a grand last-minute entrance. Truly, the performance of a lifetime."

"I could say the same thing about you," Cluster said,

coming to stand beside him with Avery. She had her arm around the girl's shoulder for support. She quirked an eyebrow. "Quite a captivating and *believable* performance."

"Well, I can't take all the credit." Fantomex pointed to E.V.A., who was retracting her scythe.

Cluster stared at her. "You were never hurt?"

E.V.A. offered her a reassuring smile. "No one uses my own neuroweapons against me," she said. "He knew very well I could counter a stun. That's how I knew he was only pretending to switch sides."

"I didn't know you could do that," Cluster said, gazing at the two of them with what looked like a mixture of envy and admiration. "The two of you have formed a strong bond. You really belong together."

Fantomex cleared his throat. "Also, I hope she knew I would never attempt to harm her at all."

"Yes, I was fairly assured of that as well."

"Is everyone all right?" Cyclops called from above. "Avery?"

"I'm fine." Avery gave him a weak salute. "Just tired of switching back and forth between realities. The painting's gone and the nanotech... left me. It had to in order to destroy the machine."

Fantomex followed her sorrow-filled gaze to a broken frame and the charred remnants of the Alano painting that lay near the disabled machine. They'd had a victory, but it had come with a price.

"Avery is the hero of the hour," Fantomex said. "The rest of us were just clearing the stage for her."

Avery looked at him with an expression he couldn't quite interpret. "How did you know that I could do it," she asked, "and that the nanotech would be able to destroy the machine?"

"Because I trusted you, and because they are creations of the World, just as we are," he said, indicating himself, Cluster, and E.V.A. "If anything was going to penetrate that shielding and dig into the inner workings of a cloning machine, it was going to be the nanotech."

"A gamble," E.V.A. said.

"That paid off," Cluster said. "Well done."

"It still couldn't have been easy to give up something like that," Avery said.

Fantomex met her gaze. "Nor could it have been easy for you to see the painting destroyed, even if it was an imitation."

"It was so much more than that," Avery said. "And it was important to me."

Fantomex released a breath, trying to process the surge of inexplicable emotion her words caused.

Thankfully, Cyclops stepped in to distract him. "Not to break up the postgame interviews," he said, "but we've got military planes inbound."

Fantomex grunted. "Our light show earlier must have attracted some attention."

"Time for operation clean up and get out," Cyclops said. "We'll come back and pull the X-Copter out of the lake another day. For now, we'll commandeer Weapon XIII's stealth copter."

"I've got Weapon XIII," Fantomex said, picking up the unconscious man's body and slinging it over his shoulder.

"Meet back at the Institute as soon as you can," Cyclops ordered.

"Healing for anyone who needs it," Triage offered.

Ah yes, he was still bleeding, after all. Fantomex pointed up at him. "Young man, you're coming back with us."

It was a bit more crowded with Weapon XIII and Triage onboard, but Fantomex wasn't complaining as the young healer tended to their myriad wounds.

"You're groaning an awful lot for just having some bruises," Triage commented.

"And a bullet to the shoulder!" Fantomex protested.

"I already took care of that."

"He's playing it up because I gave him most of the bruises," Cluster said, rolling her eyes.

"Leaving Chicago airspace," E.V.A. announced, "unless anyone has any other business in the city?"

"There's nothing open at this hour," Avery said.

"Not that it's ever stopped me before," Fantomex said. "But I think for tonight we'll just–" He stopped when he saw Avery reach into her pocket. Her hand came out empty, and a pained expression twisted her features. "What is it?" he asked. "Did you lose something?"

"My phone," Avery said. "Weapon XIII smashed it after I tried to text Jane."

"Yet another uncouth aspect to his new personality," Fantomex said. He glanced over to where Weapon XIII was still unconscious and securely restrained in one of the cockpit chairs. Despite everything that had happened, he felt the keen pang of regret. Any chance of reconciliation among him, Cluster, and Weapon XIII was likely impossible now. If not for Cyclops and his team's intervention, Weapon XIII would have killed him. He wanted them reunited, or nothing. It pained him that they would not be able to find common ground the way he and Cluster had.

The Institute would likely want to keep him imprisoned for now, until they could decide what to do with him on a more permanent basis. Maybe, during that time, he would come around. It was a slim hope, but it was better than nothing.

But that was a worry for later. He nodded to Avery. "You're welcome to slap him a few times as retribution. We'd all look the other way."

Avery chuckled. "Thanks, I'll pass. I don't have any desire to go near him again. It's just... I really would have liked to talk to Jane right now."

"We could get you a new one," Triage said. "Then you can send her a text to let her know you're all right."

Fantomex shook his head. "I have a better idea. Where did you say your Jane was located?"

"The San Diego School of Art and Design," Avery said. "Why?"

"E.V.A., would you kindly set course for the place Avery just mentioned?"

"Altering course," E.V.A. said serenely.

"Wait," Avery said, her eyes going wide. "You're not really going to fly us to campus, are you?"

"Of course we are. How else are you going to make a bold, romantic declaration to the woman you love?" Fantomex waved a hand theatrically. "What did you think I was going to do?"

"I think she was hoping you might be a bit more subtle," Cluster remarked.

"Well, she should know better." Fantomex grinned.

"Also, it's the middle of the night," Avery pointed out, a little desperately.

"We'll kill time until morning then," Fantomex said, as if it was no problem at all, "and after your grand gesture, we'll all stop over at wine country. I know the most amazing vineyard off the beaten path. The crispness of the chardonnay will blow your mind."

# CHAPTER THIRTY-TWO

Avery wasn't sure whether she was excited, terrified, euphoric, or nauseous. All of those, all at once. Her head was spinning, and she suddenly had no idea what to do with her hands. She was just sort of flailing them around as she talked.

"And I just left her with a breakup text, then I ghosted her," she said miserably. "How is she ever going to forgive me?"

"I think it will probably help when she finds out you were kidnapped and couldn't have a proper conversation," Fantomex pointed out. "Just guessing."

"I told you we should have stopped for an apology gift," Christopher said. "Some flowers, at least."

"Jane doesn't do flowers," Avery said, biting her nails. "She only likes to draw them while they're growing in the ground. So, what, I'm supposed to throw this wild story at her after her morning classes?"

Jane loved to sit on the commons when she wasn't in class. She spread out a picnic blanket and brought as many art supplies as she could carry to draw whatever caught her eye. That's where she would be right now. And in a few minutes, Avery would be there too, close enough to touch. It was everything she'd dreamt about doing ever since she'd left Jane to go to the Institute.

But now that her dream was actually coming true, Avery couldn't even begin to think how she would explain everything that had happened to her. Jane would never believe her, would never trust her. Her resolve was weakening fast. If she could have opened a window and bailed out of the ship at that moment, she would have.

Her hands stopped moving abruptly. Avery looked down in confusion and discovered that Cluster had taken them in a firm grip.

"Breathe, Avery," she said gently. "Maybe it would be best to start simple. Make the declaration you've been wanting to make. The rest will come to you in its own time."

"Going into stealth mode," E.V.A. said. "There's a small bit of woods bordering the campus commons. We'll be landing there in approximately two minutes."

Avery groaned and put her head between her knees.

Somehow, when they'd landed, she found herself getting up from her seat on wobbly legs and making her way down the steps into the stretch of woods running along the campus from east to west. The air was crisp and cool in the shade, but the sun was shining, and the sky was that particular cerulean color that Jane loved to paint. She would be outside today for sure.

A heavy footstep sounded behind her, and she turned to see Fantomex had come out of the ship after her. He'd removed his mask and was smiling at her.

"What?" she asked, suspicious.

He held up his hands, his smile fading. "I wanted to remind you, in case it helps, that last night, you saved me and mine. You came through for us in every possible way when we needed you. You are enough, and you always will be. Do you understand?"

Avery was speechless. As they stared at each other, a sudden wave of wellbeing washed over her. She was still nervous and anxious, but he was right. She'd faced down impossible odds with friends at her back and in the end, they'd won.

Nerves rocketed around Avery's stomach, but she forced herself to turn and walk toward the commons without another word. She glanced back once. Fantomex, Cluster, Christopher, and E.V.A., now in her humanoid form, stood at the tree line, barely visible. Fantomex flashed her an absolutely goofy thumbs-up. She sighed in exasperation.

Right. Time to face this. With a determined stride, Avery marched across the commons.

And there she was.

Avery's steps faltered when she saw Jane sitting on the picnic blanket, the remains of her lunch packed away nearby. She was reaching for her sketchbook when she paused, some instinct making her look up. She locked eyes with Avery.

Jane smiled.

Avery melted into a puddle of butterflies and hearts. In the figurative sense.

In reality, she started running, actually running to close the distance between her and Jane. She'd always thought it was corny when characters did this in the movies, but she got it now. She'd never scoff again.

Jane had managed to get to her feet by the time Avery reached her, and without a word she scooped her up in a hug so fierce she thought their ribs would crack. She didn't care a bit.

"They're hugging! That's a good sign," Fantomex said, leaning out a bit farther on the tree branch he was balanced on.

"Do you really think Avery would appreciate you spying on her reunion and giving us all a play-by-play?" Cluster asked mildly.

"I'm not spying!"

"You're in a tree."

"I'm stretching," he said, looking down at her and flexing.

"Please don't fall and break your neck," Christopher said, examining a hand of cards. E.V.A. sat across from him with her own cards, and the two appeared to be locked in intense concentration. "I don't want to do any more healing until I've had some food. Also, shouldn't we be checking to make sure Weapon XIII's still unconscious?"

"I just did," Cluster said, pointing to a nearby stand of dense trees where they'd carefully placed their counterpart to keep him out of sight. "He's out cold."

"Still?" Christopher sounded skeptical.

E.V.A. spoke up. "I gave him a mild sedative to ensure he passed the remainder of the trip in comfort and blissful unawareness."

Christopher stared at her in disbelief. "How'd you manage that?" When she just raised her eyebrow at him, he chuckled. "Right. Advanced techno-organic being. I keep forgetting."

"Your turn," E.V.A. reminded him, gesturing to his cards.

"They're talking now," Fantomex said, returning his gaze to Avery and her girlfriend. He hated to admit it, but Cluster had a point about spying. He felt a bit uncomfortable watching the two of them, intruding on their private moment.

He jumped from the branch, executing a – to his mind – flawless double flip and landing silently on his feet on a bed of pine needles. "I think we've done an excellent day's work, team," he said. "It was mostly me, of course, but you all played your parts as well."

All three of them looked up at the same time to glare at him.

"It's nice to know your essential nature hasn't changed," Cluster said.

As Avery finished her story, Jane sat back on her elbows on the blanket. A sigh whooshed out of her, and she regarded Avery with an expression bordering on awe.

"So, you saved them? This… Fantomex and Cluster. Weird names, by the way, but we can deconstruct that later. But you convinced a hive mind of thousands, if not millions, of sentient machines to help you save your friends. And they did… because you asked them to." A slow grin spread across Jane's pixie-like face. "You're my hero, Avery Torres."

Avery's face flamed. "That's oversimplifying *everything*."

"Is anything I said untrue?"

She hesitated. "No, but it makes me sound more impressive than I probably deserve, considering I was able to communicate with those sentient machines better than I was with my own girlfriend."

"Hmm, you have a point there," Jane said, her voice

dropping. "I was hurt, a lot. And when you didn't answer my calls and texts… well, I did get your last text, and I'm glad I know the reason for everything now, but still, it was a lot of sleepless nights. I don't want to have to go through that again."

"I'm sorry," Avery said, swallowing. She reached out, tentatively, for Jane's hand, and was relieved when Jane gave it to her without hesitation. "Do you think you can ever forgive me?"

Jane squeezed her hand. "I forgave you the minute I looked up and saw you across the lawn," she said, then heaved a sigh. "But boy, do we have a lot of things to figure out."

"I know," Avery said. "I've been thinking about it, and I realized everything that's happened changed me in ways I never expected. For the longest time, all I wanted to do was figure out my powers so I could leave the Institute and come back here. But now, after realizing what I can do, it's not so simple."

"You think you can reach the nanotech again?" Jane asked. "Even though it's no longer a part of you?"

"I think maybe I could learn," Avery said, biting her lip. "But it means more time and training with the other artifacts." She paused. "And maybe it means I do want to become part of the X-Men after all."

A short time ago, she never would have contemplated that, but she'd had her eyes opened, and she knew now that the people at the Institute cared about her. They had her back, and she had theirs. The Institute might never feel like a home, but the people there were part of her life now. They weren't just temporary friends. She felt ashamed for thinking of them that way. Part of it was she'd never thought she had anything worthwhile to contribute to their team, but she'd been wrong about that too. Her gifts were important, and, above all, she'd given her promise to the nanotech that she would help find more of their kind. She intended to honor that promise.

But there were other promises she wanted to keep as well.

"I know that things are complicated, but whatever the future holds, I want us to be a part of it too." Her grip on Jane tightened, as if she were afraid the woman would disappear. "I don't want to give you up."

"You don't have to," Jane said, smiling. Her eyes were bright. "I don't want to give you up either, so we're going to have to make the Institute understand that we're a package deal. We'll make it work."

Avery's heart was so full she thought she might burst. "That's right," she said. "They'll just have to understand." Cyclops and Emma Frost already had to deal with Fantomex. What was a long-distance relationship compared to the trouble he would likely cause? If he stayed around, that is.

Jane shifted on the blanket, scooting a bit closer to Avery. "So, I know there's probably a million and one other things we're going to have to figure out, but for now, since we have the biggest question taken care of, is it time for the kissing?" Her cheeks flushed, but she was grinning one of her full-on Jane electric grins of happiness. "Because I've really been missing that part."

Avery laid her hand against Jane's cheek, tracing a patch of freckles with her thumb. "I've been missing that part too." And she leaned in and kissed her.

Time slowed to a crawl. There came the sound of distant *oohs* and *ahhs*, which might have been the other students on the commons watching them, or it might have even been Fantomex catcalling them from somewhere near the trees. At that moment, Avery couldn't have cared less.

When she pulled away about a century later, she laid her forehead against Jane's. "I love you, you know. I have for a long time."

Jane kissed the tip of her nose. "I love you too." She pulled back. "If you do join the X-Men, can I help you pick a codename?"

Avery laughed. "I'm counting on your help. I'm hopeless at that sort of thing. Speaking of the X-Men, though..." She glanced toward the treeline where she'd left the others. "Apparently we're stopping at a vineyard before we head back to the Institute." She glanced at Jane. "Totally against the rules, of course, but Fantomex said he's going to take the blame. You want to come?"

Jane was already packing up her supplies. "Can you get me back here before my afternoon class?"

Avery waved a hand. "E.V.A. can do anything."

# *EPILOGUE*

Two days after their return to the Institute, Fantomex met Cluster in the hangar to see her off. She wouldn't say exactly where she was going, but E.V.A. was going to take her at least part of the way. Fantomex hadn't pried any further than that. He didn't feel threatened by E.V.A. having a relationship with Cluster that didn't involve him. Well, maybe a pinch every now and then, but he wasn't perfect, after all. Nearly, but not quite.

Cluster had mended her costume sometime between the battle and now, her sleeveless jacket once again intact and pristine white with black accents.

"I like it," he said, pointing to the costume. "It's an improvement on mine, and you know I wouldn't say that lightly."

She removed her mask and smiled. "No, I imagine not. No one appreciates that the true super-power is keeping a white costume clean at all times."

"You don't have to leave so soon," he said, leaning against the X-Copter. It still needed some repairs, but it looked pretty decent, even for having been fished out of Lake Michigan earlier that day. "We could use your help looking after Weapon XIII while he's our unwilling guest."

"I don't think I'll be helpful in that regard," she said, looking resigned. "I tried to talk to him earlier, to see if I could make a connection, but he's in a… well, let's just say a dark place at the moment."

He should have known she would try to reach him. He hated to see her disappointed. "I'll stay on here for a while," he said, "to make sure he doesn't cause any trouble. Maybe I can try again with him when he's feeling more receptive."

"I think that's a good idea." She eyed him curiously. "Is that the only reason you're staying?"

"Well, I also thought it would be good to look after Avery, see how she gets on with the artifacts you brought us, along with those we recovered on the island where Weapon XIII had stashed them." He sighed. "I still envy her, being able to communicate with another unique creation of the World, one that wasn't programmed and raised with a directive to kill."

"You haven't killed anyone lately," Cluster pointed out. "That's surely a promising sign. I also notice we've both been a bit less French than we used to be, so maybe we're succeeding at forging our own paths."

"True. New beginnings all around, I suppose."

Cluster nodded, but she looked thoughtful. "Was it really all an act?" she asked. "During the battle, when you turned on us, I could have sworn by the look in your eyes that you meant it. It was the first time I felt real fear. Even when Weapon XIII first attacked me for the artifacts, I didn't feel as afraid as I was at that moment. Were you ever truly tempted to join Weapon XIII?"

He weighed his words carefully, wondering how much he should tell her. Again, he felt the separation in their individual personalities, felt the weight of the line he stood upon. He would never be as noble as she was, and he would never be as ruthless as Weapon XIII. Did that mean he was destined to disappoint and alienate both of them? Or would he be a bridge that might eventually draw them together? Time would tell, he supposed.

"The most effective lies are rooted in truth," he said finally. "You know that as well as I do. If I had truly thought that Weapon XIII had a safe method for reuniting us, the temptation would have been great. But I know his hubris, because I share it. He was never as certain as he attempted to appear." He smiled at her. "And I know you. I can see that you're happy in yourself, in this identity. I would hate to see that taken away from you." Flawed and fallible he might be, but that last bit was the truth that had motivated him in the end. He hoped she believed that.

She smiled back at him, saying nothing, and he was content.

"Well, I'd best be off," she said, as the door to the hanger opened and E.V.A. stepped inside. She offered Fantomex her hand, and he took it. "I'll check in on you, though not too often. I promise not to crowd you. And maybe we'll work on our misdirection powers together."

"Take care," he said, "and thank you for telling E.V.A. to bring me here. In hindsight, it wasn't the worst decision in the world."

She laughed. "That's the nicest thing you've said to *me* yet."

Fantomex found Cyclops in his office. He set an espresso in front of him with a flourish and took the chair closest to the desk.

"What's this?" Cyclops stared at the small cup as if it might be poisoned. Why did everyone look at the delicacies he prepared with such suspicion? Fantomex said nothing, just waited until Cyclops inhaled the fragrant steam. His eyes were impossible to read, but he swayed a bit in his chair. "Never mind, I don't care if it kills me. I'll die happy."

"Careful, you're drooling on your paperwork," Fantomex said, as Cyclops downed the shot in one gulp. "You know, you should take some time to savor it while it's still hot from the machine."

"We don't have an espresso machine here."

Fantomex cleared his throat. "Ah, well, we'll get to that. First, I came to apologize."

Scott gave him a look. "You mean for absconding with my students and a dangerous captive for an entire day in the Sonoma Valley without checking in once for a post-mission debriefing?"

"You're right, I came to apologize for two things." He leaned back in his chair. "I hoped the espresso might smooth the way, although, now that we're on the subject, you do realize it's a good thing to let your students cut loose every now and then, don't you? You're extremely isolated here, and while you may prefer it by necessity, some of them have left quite a large bit of their lives behind to be here. Sometimes they need reminding of the joys in life as well as the burdens."

Cyclops looked at him a long time. Slowly, he nodded. "I hate to give you credit for being insightful, but you're right. Sometimes we get so wrapped up in secrecy and protecting the students that we forget they need to live too. Thank you for reminding me of that."

"You're welcome, but I understand the stakes you face. You always do the best you can to protect the people in your care," Fantomex said, "whether a person deserves your protection or not."

Cyclops toyed with the empty espresso cup. "I think I get your meaning."

"No, let me be clear," Fantomex said, holding up a hand. "I questioned your motives in the beginning, but you and your team saved me more than once, even though I gave you more than your fair share of grief." He hesitated. "I shouldn't have said that you knew nothing of the losses I've suffered. You've had your own sorrows burdening you, yet you've carried on better than I would in your place."

"Thank you," Scott said. He seemed pleased, but he leaned back in his chair, as if withdrawing, and Fantomex knew not to take the conversation any further.

"I'd like your permission to stay on here for a time, if you'll have me," Fantomex said. "At least until I can decide my next path. I'm not an instructor, and heaven knows I shudder at the thought of becoming a student, but there are other uses for one with my talents."

"Do tell," Scott said, a corner of his mouth quirking in a rare smile. "Combat exercises? Self-defense training?"

"All very important," Fantomex said, "and I could use the practice to further develop and hopefully expand my current abilities, but I was also thinking of more practical considerations. Someone needs to keep an eye on Weapon XIII, and I'd also like to be of assistance to Avery, should she require it in her training. I think you'll see I can be quite helpful to your cause, but I would ask something in return."

"Oh? And what would that be?"

Fantomex put his arms behind his head with a knowing smile. "Obviously, I'm not going to be able to function under the appalling conditions in this facility. Have you been in the kitchen lately?"

Cyclops looked down at his empty espresso cup and then back up at Fantomex. "What did you do?" he asked, the suspicion back in his voice.

"Just made a few updates for you," Fantomex said, presenting himself as the picture of innocence. "Come, I'll be happy to show you. Do you like charcuterie?"

Cyclops stared at him, and then deadpanned, "Who doesn't?"

Fantomex threw back his head and laughed. What a strange existence he had led. Thrilling, dangerous, painful, but never boring. He'd been torn apart but, miracle of miracles, somehow managed to put himself back together again, though he hadn't done it alone. Now he had a second chance, a second life to explore at his whim. Perhaps he was still a long way from knowing himself completely or discovering where this new life would take him. But he was ready to see what adventures the universe had in store for him next.

It was, on the whole, an auspicious beginning.

# ACKNOWLEDGMENTS

For those of you reading this in the distant future, this book was written during a time of... well, during a time. Without the support of all the following folks, it may very well not have been written at all.

To the folks at Marvel and Aconyte, in particular my wonderful editor Gwen, my heartfelt thanks. You all delivered good news in the year 2020, a feat I had deemed impossible. Talk about superpowers.

Agent Sara, gamer and lovely human being, thank you for sticking with me in a year where it was almost impossible to write, and yet somehow, here we are. Your emails kept me going.

To Elizabeth, Gary and Kelly, thank you for being there for me, and thank you for understanding when I couldn't be there. Grieving and pandemics are a lousy combination, but you made it a bit easier.

Susan, thank you for being you, and for being the book whisperer when I needed gentle things to read.

Finally, to Dad and Jeff for being my strength. And to my mom. This is the first one you won't get to see, and I'm never going to be okay with that, but without you, it would never have happened. I knew you would have been very irritated with me if I'd quit. So I didn't. Love you tons.

# ABOUT THE AUTHOR

JALEIGH JOHNSON is a *New York Times*-bestselling fantasy novelist living and writing in the wilds of the Midwest. She has also written several novels and short stories for the *Dungeons & Dragons Forgotten Realms* fiction lines. Johnson is an avid gamer and lifelong geek.

*jaleighjohnson.com*
*twitter.com/jaleighjohnson*

# MARVEL XAVIER'S INSTITUTE

*The next generation of the X-Men strive to master their mutant powers and defend the world from evil.*

# MARVEL HEROINES

*Showcasing Marvel's incredible
female Super Heroes in their own
action-packed adventures.*

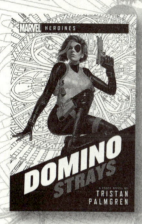

# WORLD EXPANDING FICTION

## *Do you have them all?*

**MARVEL CRISIS PROTOCOL**
- ☐ *Target: Kree* by Stuart Moore

**MARVEL HEROINES**
- ☐ *Domino: Strays* by Tristan Palmgren
- ☐ *Rogue: Untouched* by Alisa Kwitney
- ☐ *Elsa Bloodstone: Bequest* by Cath Lauria
- ☐ *Outlaw: Relentless* by Tristan Palmgren

**LEGENDS OF ASGARD**
- ☐ *The Head of Mimir* by Richard Lee Byers
- ☐ *The Sword of Surtur* by C L Werner
- ☐ *The Serpent and the Dead* by Anna Stephens
- ☐ *The Rebels of Vanaheim* by Richard Lee Byers *(coming soon)*

**MARVEL UNTOLD**
- ☐ *The Harrowing of Doom* by David Annandale
- ☐ *Dark Avengers: The Patriot List* by David Guymer *(coming soon)*
- ☐ *Witches Unleashed* by Carrie Harris *(coming soon)*

**XAVIER'S INSTITUTE**
- ☐ *Liberty & Justice for All* by Carrie Harris
- ☐ *First Team* by Robbie MacNiven
- ☑ *Triptych* by Jaleigh Johnson
- ☐ *School of X* edited by Gwendolyn Nix *(coming soon)*

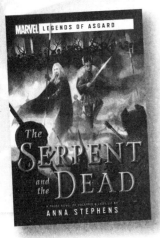